"It wou

to som

"I like that no one can see us," Lyndsay murmured. "We're in our own world out here, alone."

"I can't imagine not living near the ocean," John replied.

She drew in a breath. "There it is!"

A tiny, faint ray of light appeared on the eastern horizon. And while she held her breath, it grew larger and larger. She could see John clearly in the early-morning light. He had a wide smile on his face.

"Is it always this calm?" she whispered.

"Never." His voice was low. "This is my first time, at least."

She turned her chin and caught his gaze directly. For a moment they shared a look, and then with a low groan, he leaned into her.

"I can't fight it anymore..."

Dear Reader,

Welcome to a new Wallis Point, New Hampshire, story, set in the fictional seaside town first described in *The Long Way Home* and *The Secret Between Them*.

Lyndsay Fairfax is an undercover police officer sent to investigate a series of high-end thefts. Posing as an interior designer working in a congressman's beach home, she befriends a group of tradesmen and becomes part of their community in hopes of tracking information about the notorious burglary ring.

But along the way, Lyndsay falls in love with John Reilly, a returning marine veteran and protective leader who's taken responsibility for his family's restaurant and the welfare of his troubled younger brother.

Lyndsay must keep her cover and follow the evidence wherever it leads her, even if it points to a suspect that will surely bring her personal heartbreak.

Thanks for reading Lyndsay's story! I hope you enjoy the romance.

All the best,

Cathryn Parry

CATHRYN PARRY

—

The Undercover Affair

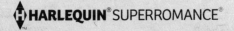

HARLEQUIN® SUPERROMANCE®

Recycling programs
for this product may
not exist in your area.

ISBN-13: 978-0-373-64051-5

The Undercover Affair

Copyright © 2017 by Cathryn Parry

This edition published by arrangement with Harlequin Books S.A.

For questions and comments about the quality of this book, please contact us at CustomerService@Harlequin.com.

Printed in U.S.A.

www.Harlequin.com

Cathryn Parry is the author of nine Harlequin Superromances. Her books have received such honors as the Booksellers' Best Award, the Cataromance Reviewers' Choice Award and several Readers' Choice Award nominations. She lives in Massachusetts with her husband and their seventeen-year-old cat, Otis. Please see her website at www.cathrynparry.com for information about upcoming releases or to sign up for her reader newsletter.

Books by Cathryn Parry

HARLEQUIN SUPERROMANCE

Something to Prove
The Long Way Home
Out of His League
The Sweetest Hours
Scotland for Christmas
Secret Garden
The Secret Between Them
The Good Mom

Other titles by this author available in ebook format.

For my dad, James Parry.
Thanks for always being there for us.

CHAPTER ONE

"OH-OH-SIX, M-S-T. A white box truck. That's the tag and vehicle description for the crew of movers. They gave their names as—"

A shadow fell across the decoy catalog where Lyndsay Fairfax had scribbled her morning's surveillance notes. Instinctively, she covered the jottings as she lifted her head.

Outside her car window, a man's gaze met hers—the bartender from the Seaside Bar and Grill, whose parking lot she was currently sitting in. Her "police brain" automatically noted the details: six feet tall, dressed in jeans and a long-sleeved T-shirt. He had brown hair with piercing gray-blue eyes.

She hadn't expected anyone to sneak up on her like that. There was no exit on this side of the parking lot, which meant he must have come from the house behind the restaurant.

He stared, his attention lingering on her face. She'd noticed him during the past week while she ate lunch at the Seaside with the group of home contractors from the wealthy cul-de-sac she'd infiltrated. But *he* wasn't the object of her investigation in Wallis Point, New Hampshire, and so she'd never endeavored to meet him. Her police task force hadn't mentioned investigating him or the Seaside Bar and Grill.

With her phone still pressed to her ear, Lyndsay gave him the sweet, friendly "Lyn Francis" smile that her undercover alter ego had been using all week while she passed as an interior designer for Mrs. Kitty MacLaine and her congressman husband.

Unlike the contractors in the small community that she'd been monitoring, this man didn't smile back at her. And something in his wary eyes made her pause.

His frown deepened as he moved past her vehicle.

Chewing her lip, she watched him, following his progress down the restaurant's small, gravel parking lot to a commercial van labeled Seacoast Beer Distributors idling in the far spot. The bartender stood outside the passenger door, hand on his hip, as he rapped on the window, then initiated what appeared to be a not-so-friendly conversation with a younger man, also on his mobile phone.

She blew out a breath. Of course—the bartender was preoccupied with the state of his establishment's beer lines.

"Lyn, are you there?" her partner's gravelly voice asked over the phone.

"I'm here," she said, relaxing into her seat again.

"What's going on?"

"A local passed by the car. He's gone now."

"Be careful. The most important thing is to keep your cover."

"Don't I know it." Pete, her partner during the past week, was a grizzled old-timer with years of experience under his belt, and though she was an experienced state police officer as well, this was her first time undercover. Pete seemed protective of her for it, and she didn't mind. She got to do the interesting work, gathering and relaying the information to him, while he sat on the other side of her phone calls.

She craved the work. She *needed* the work.

"Okay," she said, "moving on, the two guys who go with the white box truck are the McAuliffe brothers, James and Brian. James goes by Jimmie. Both are about five-ten. Midtwenties. Live locally. The truck has no identifying company name or logo, and I'm given to understand that they're freelancers who work for themselves by word of mouth."

"Got it." Pete's voice was a murmur, as if he was concentrating because he was typing the information.

"That's all for today. I hope this is helping the burglary investigation," she said wistfully, keeping her eye on the bartender, his back still to her. She was leaving this afternoon. She was going to miss the assignment, as well as her lunches at the Seaside with the contractor teams.

"Yeah, it's helping. So far we've been ruling people out as suspects. We'll find out more about the investigation tomorrow."

"Right." Tomorrow was the day the burglary task force was meeting at headquarters, up in Concord. She hoped to be part of phase two, because to be part of the team that brought down the ring of thieves preying on wealthy homes along the seacoast was what she most wanted.

The bartender glanced her way, and it wasn't a friendly look. He was suspicious of her still. And that could jeopardize things…

On a whim, she said, "Pete, could you please look up and tell me who lives at 118 Seaside Drive?" That was the home—connected to the Seaside Bar and Grill by a covered walkway—the bartender had come from.

"Affirmative. There's a Margaret Reilly, age sixty. And a Patrick Reilly, age nineteen."

Definitely not the bartender. He looked to be in his thirties. She thought she'd heard one of the contractors calling him John, but she wasn't positive.

"Lyn?"

"Please check if Margaret Reilly owns the Seaside," she said. There was a Margie who worked in the kitchen. Until now Lyndsay hadn't connected that Margie might live right next door.

"Hold on, let me check…affirmative, as well. What's going on?"

She wondered if John could be Margie's son. He would be the right age. "Pete, could you check if there's an address for a John Reilly in Wallis Point? Age thirty-something." It was just a whim, but she wanted to cover her bases.

"One minute." There was a short pause. "Affirmative again—22 Cove Road."

That was about two miles away, closer to the cul-de-sac where she worked. Lyndsay had memorized the Wallis Point street maps prior to arriving at her assignment.

She didn't know what, if anything, this information told her. Bartender John, possibly John Reilly, was still standing by the beer truck, and every few minutes he stared toward her. She needed to find out if he was, in fact, John Reilly, Margie's son.

"Lyn, is there something I should know?"

"Yes. Please add Margaret and Patrick Reilly to the list for background checks. It seems everyone in the area stops by this place at one time or another. Hold off on John Reilly for now, though." She would verify John's real name in a few minutes, but Pete could get started. "I know we initially didn't have the owners of the Seaside Bar and Grill on our surveillance list, but I think it's prudent to check them out."

"Will do."

She stretched her shoulders. "Okay, then. I've passed you information on everyone who has visited or is affiliated with the congressman's neighborhood during the past four days. Is there anything else you need from me before I wrap it up here and head back north tonight?"

"Yeah, we need one more thing. No, make that two."

"Great." She could multitask. And she liked assignments. "What do you have?"

"I need you to get into the Goldrick house this afternoon." That was the vacation home on the lot directly beside the MacLaines'. "You're specifically looking for any artwork on the walls. Paintings that look as if they might be worth something. We're not seeing anything on the insurance company reports, but we want to make sure."

Her heart sped up. Finally, police work that was more directly connected to the burglaries that Pete and other members of the task force were investigating. "No problem. Does this mean I'll be continuing with phase two of the task force?"

"One step at a time, Lyn."

"I was invited up to Concord for the meeting tomorrow," she said cheerfully.

Pete laughed. "Because I recommended you. You're doing great work so far."

He hadn't said what her future was to be, one way or the other. That was up to Commander Harris, she supposed.

She wasn't going to give them any reason not to let her continue.

"I'll head inside to lunch, and then get to it," she said. "What was the second objective? You said I have two."

"The second objective is the same as always. Keep your cover, Lyn."

"Why are you telling me this again?"

"Because I want to stress to you that keeping your cover is your first, last and major objective, always. Never forget it."

"Right," she said cheerfully again. "I'm an interior decorator currently contracted by Design-Sea. This week, I'm working on a proposal for Congressman MacLaine and his wife."

"You're so subtle," Pete said dryly.

She laughed because his sarcasm was unfounded. She *was* subtle. She felt like a duck in water doing this kind of work, and that was a great feeling.

Except where *he* was concerned. She darted a glance toward John, the bartender, as she hung up with Pete. Staring at her, yet again. She was giving herself a third agenda item for this lunch break, and that was to find out his full name and his particulars so Pete could run his background check.

Exiting from the car, she grabbed her purse, which carried her concealed Glock, then headed inside the Seaside Bar and Grill. The air smelled fresh and briny, and the wind blew through the opening of her jacket, making her shiver. She opened the door to the eatery, smelling something delicious, like freshly baked bread.

She checked her watch: 11:46. The kitchen was open but still a bit early for Andy Hannaman's crew, the group who were working on the Goldrick home. They didn't habitually leave the oceanfront cul-de-sac until noon, then it was a six-minute drive to their lunch spot.

Taking a seat in the back corner, Lyndsay strategically chose her favorite position where she had a view of the parking lot and road, plus a view to the entrance as well as the kitchen entry, with the long wooden bar beside it.

She waited. John would be inside soon, as well as Andy. Both her objectives could be achieved together. She could chat with the crews and organically, without suspicion, gain an invitation to look at the Goldrick renovation, as well as unobtrusively ask for John-the-bartender's particulars.

In the meantime, Millie, the waitress who stood only as high as Lyndsay's shoulders, came and took her sandwich order.

"I'd like the BLT, please." Another strategic decision, designed to initiate a conversation with Andy. Millie nodded at her, then scuttled off. The little waitress didn't speak much—she just did her job.

For the moment, Lyndsay was alone with her thoughts. Nothing to do but sit at the scarred table and gaze over the parking lot and street to the dunes beyond, with a sliver of dark blue ocean in the distance. The beach at Wallis Point reminded her of summer vacation from her youth. Also of romantic vacations from her marriage, but she didn't like to think those thoughts.

Millie brought her a glass of iced tea, which she set beside Lyndsay's department-issued mobile phone on the table. "Thank you, Millie."

She received a brief nod and a smile in reply. Followed by the retreat of quick paces from soft-soled sneakers.

Concentrate. Watch for Andy Hannaman's crew.

She checked her perimeter. Cocked an ear for the sound of a vehicle pulling into the gravel lot.

Instead, the door opened, and John the bartender walked inside, followed by the young man from the beer truck. The young man wore a uniform shirt with a logo, and his body language indicated that he was reluctant to follow John. The two men headed behind the bar, and she observed as John explained in a low but authoritative murmur what he needed the young man to fix. Evidently, there was a problem with the beer line.

Distracted from her purpose, she gave them her full attention. John's head was bent. He had a short haircut, like a lot of the police officers she worked with. But it wasn't just his looks that drew her notice. There was something to the way he moved. The subtle cock of his hip, the deliberate, staccato punch of his fingers tapping against his forearm as he concentrated. His mannerisms showed he was impatient. Alert. Coiled.

He turned, and for a split second, she caught him studying her, too. Smiling as if she was nothing more than a red-blooded woman checking out an interesting, red-blooded man, she gazed directly at him.

Her line of sight was broken by Millie, bringing out her bacon, lettuce and tomato sandwich. It smelled delicious, and Lyndsay's stomach rumbled, craving food, so she nonchalantly turned her attention to that and dug in.

She wasn't *really* drawn to John, she told herself. She'd been wary of romantic relationships with men ever since Jason had passed and she'd been widowed. Since then, she'd tried to live on, tried to press forward and be cheerful and find something meaningful to do.

Her solace had been to keep busy, with work, work-related training classes, sessions at the gun range. Anything not to be alone with her thoughts…

Then this opportunity had arisen—to work undercover, a chance at maybe later being promoted to a detective. Her dad had been so thrilled to hear about it. She'd thought maybe… maybe her life could be more fulfilled if this professional assignment worked out and she became a full-time detective. She would get to work on bigger cases, help more people than by being a police officer in a squad car. It would also be a job where she could actually wear street clothing and feel more like her long-ago, pre-widowhood self.

She glanced down to where her duty belt usually dug into her hips. Not today. Today she wore a dress she'd chosen because she liked it, with brown tights underneath and ankle boots, plus a short leather jacket that fit her undercover status.

She glanced at John.

Only to catch him staring at her again. Then, after that split second when they met gazes, he abruptly looked away. And he continued his conversation with the beer distributor guy.

John bent over, and for a moment she was treated to the sight of his clearly muscled torso that had been hidden by his oversize black T-shirt. He had...a nice body. She inhaled and crossed her legs beneath the wooden table. But it wasn't the appropriate time or place to be thinking of such things, not by a long shot.

She forced herself to look away from the bar and toward the door. Through two sets of plate glass windows she saw the small parking lot where her sporty, black, undercover car was by itself. In early April, the place was still briskly cool, too early for the summer season, and thus, not crowded with traffic and beachgoers on vacation.

The sound of tires on gravel crackled, and Lyndsay refocused. Right on time, Andy Hannaman and his crew had arrived in their large white work van with Hannaman General Contractor stenciled in red paint inside a white oval-shaped logo.

In the front seat was Andy's son, AJ, and in the back seat, AJ's friend Chet Evans. A black pickup truck followed the van into the lot. Moon

Buzzell, who was building a new tile shower under Andy's direction at the mansion next door to where Lyndsay was undercover, had shown up.

As Andy exited his van, he saw her through the window and waved. Cheerfully—because she had genuinely come to like him—she waved back. Andy was older than her, closer to her father's age than to her own, and she felt comfortable with him. It had helped even more that he'd taken her under his wing on their four-mansion cul-de-sac in the wealthy section of private beach. None of the residents were back yet; it seemed all of them had hired work out to local contractors in order to prepare for the upcoming summer season.

Andy strode inside, trailed by his son and two employees. Lyndsay wasn't worried about them—she'd spent four days now as part of their little community.

To Lyndsay's pleasure, the contractors and workers in the cul-de-sac had bought her cover story lock, stock and barrel. Indeed, she'd enjoyed these lunches and afternoon breaks with Andy's crew so much, she'd even *felt* like an interior designer, which wasn't so strange, considering that had been her original life's plan when she'd first left home, at eighteen. The police force had come later.

"Hey, Lyn." Andy greeted her with a smile.

Lyndsay nodded to Andy. "How's it going?"

"Great. I saw you taking off early for lunch," he remarked, sitting across from her at the table.

"Yeah, playing hooky," she admitted sheepishly.

He laughed, the lines around his eyes squinting as he did so. He was in his late fifties, she judged. Andy reminded her so much of her father, with his graying temples and crinkled blue eyes.

He peered at her plate. "So you took my advice—I told you to try the BLT. What do you think?"

"You're right, it's really good." It was easy to give him a genuine smile—she liked the sandwich. A movement caught her peripheral vision, and she chanced a glance at the bar. John was ducking into the door toward what was presumably the kitchen, and Millie was beside the register, taking a phone order.

Andy saw her glance away and turned around, noting what she'd been looking at. Then he turned back. He seemed like he was going to ask her something—possibly about John—so Lyndsay intercepted that thought. *Not the right time.*

"What are you going to have today?" she asked Andy. "Want me to read the menu for you?" He usually squinted as he strained to read the menu blackboard across the room. "There's a pastrami on rye. Salads, but I know you don't like salads, so—"

"Pastrami on rye." Andy nudged his son. "Will you order for me while I hit the can?"

Yes, the crew had grown ever more comfortable with her by the day, to the point where they were no longer worried by their language. Lyndsay hid a smile and focused on what was left of her sandwich. The bread and the vegetables were fresh, and the bacon had been cooked just right.

When she'd finished a bite, she turned to Moon Buzzell, nicknamed "Moon" because of his round face and somewhat spacey manner. Or so she'd been told by Andy. Moon had just returned from the soda case and was opening a bottle of blue sport drink.

"Hi, Lyn." He gave her a goofy look. "You came out early today."

"I did." She deliberately kept her gaze from the bar and focused only on him.

Moon's cheeks turned red. "Andy told me today is your last day."

"It is. I'm hoping I can come back and implement my proposal, but we'll have to wait and see if it gets accepted."

The door opened. Lyndsay made sure to smile and wave at the crew of guys—and one gal— who streamed inside before heading over to the soda case. *The Burke crew*, she privately called them. She'd already recorded information for all of them. It was a close-knit microcosm of men and women who serviced the wealthy beach homes. But she'd gotten to know their habits.

John was back behind the bar. Today one of them asked him for a draft beer. Instead of a draft, John opened a bottle of local brew for the gregarious painter without comment.

Lyndsay took a sip of her iced tea and pretended to pay full attention to Moon Buzzell as he recounted to her his opinion of the hockey game the night before. At the same time, she observed the McAuliffes.

They'd arrived alone, in their white box truck with the New Hampshire license plates whose numbers she'd already phoned in to Pete. The two men put in a to-go order and stayed apart from the others. Both scrolled their phone messages quietly as they waited.

"How is the shower stall coming?" she remembered to ask Moon after he'd finished a bite of his Italian submarine sandwich.

His face brightened. "Stop by and see it. I should be done tomorrow. Maybe you could put one into your design plans for Mrs. MacLaine?" he asked hopefully.

Bingo, here was her opening. *Job done.*

"If I have time," Lyndsay said offhandedly, as

if it wasn't important and she was really busy. Even though the design plans were just a front, she was doggedly spending a few hours each day calling up her foggy memory of how to wrestle with the design software installed on her task force-issued laptop. "What are you using for tile?"

"They wanted standard white subway tile." Moon scratched his head. "I think." He shrugged. "For sure the showerheads are something else. Special order, real high-end."

"I'd like to see that," she said. "Okay, you've piqued my curiosity. I'll stop by this afternoon. The MacLaines were looking for some high-end suggestions," Lyndsay lied.

Moon stopped chewing and swallowed. "Keep me in mind for the installation. I could use the business."

"Of course," she promised.

Andy returned from the bathroom. Over the rim of her glass, Lyndsay saw the McAuliffe brothers gathering up to leave. Millie was busy with another table, so it was John who passed the two brothers each a white plastic bag and rang up their orders, which they paid separately. One of the brothers took his phone, touched the screen, then pressed it to his ear.

At the same time that the McAuliffe brothers were on the move, Andy approached John at the bar, leaning casually in to speak with him. The two men seemed to know each other. John still kept that level, guarded expression while Andy talked with his hands and grinned.

Both men turned and looked at her. Andy brazenly, without guile, and John surreptitiously.

They're talking about me. It looked like Andy was going to bring John over to introduce him to her.

John's gaze remained on hers. And even though his look was stoic, almost fiercely shielded behind lips set in a solid line and facial muscles gilded bronze and hard, his eyes told a different story. They searched her, up and down.

To her legs beneath the short dress. The thin T-shirt she wore beneath the leather jacket, and the high ponytail that bared her neck and collarbones to him.

Oh, no. Had she overplayed her role? All she'd wanted to know was his name. And to keep her cover, but he certainly didn't look suspicious of her now.

He looked like he was *interested* in her. As a woman.

Swallowing, she glanced at her hands. She didn't want to feel attracted to anyone. Not on an undercover assignment. Not during her big career break.

She glanced up again, and he took another

long look at her, gazing directly into her eyes. She exhaled, not sure what to do. It wasn't an unpleasant feeling he gave her, on the contrary. But professionally, it could be dangerous.

Andy seemed to notice her torment. With growing realization, he stared from his friend to her. His friend noticed, too, giving Andy an irritated look, then turned back to the evident problem with his beer tap.

Quickly, Lyndsay turned to Moon and murmured, "Who is the guy behind the bar with Andy? What's his name?" The more advance intel she had, the better for her to play her part. She was giving up on subtly, but this was typically lost on Moon, anyway.

"Who, John Reilly?" Moon asked.

Bingo, that's all I need. "Yes, I guess that's his name," she murmured. "I haven't been introduced to him yet."

Moon shrugged, not looking too happy that her attention was on John Reilly instead of on him. "He's usually in the kitchen when it's busy."

Indeed, two more contractor vans had pulled in. It seemed that everyone at the beach was getting ready for summer season.

"So he's a bartender here?" Lyndsay murmured quickly. "Or is he an owner?"

"Owner." Moon sighed and took a guzzle of his sports drink. "It's a family business."

Ah. So Margie must, indeed, be his mother.

Andy ambled back to their table. Lyndsay swallowed but stared steadily at him.

"Would you like to meet my friend John?" Andy asked her.

Act natural. She'd told Andy three days earlier that she'd wanted to meet as many people as possible in the area. *I'm building my business from the ground up*, she'd told him. That was part of her cover.

"Sure," she replied in a neutral tone. "But I can see that your friend is busy now. Maybe another day."

But Andy didn't take the hint. He glanced at John, then sat at the table, placing his bag of chips and his pastrami on rye before him. "I've known John a long time," he remarked. "Coached him in youth hockey back before I got married and had kids. He left for the military when he grew up."

"Oh." Lyndsay lowered her gaze to the remaining crumbs on her plate. Her own husband had been Army Special Operations. A Ranger. But no one needed to know that.

"John came home a few years ago," Andy was saying. "But he came back different than he was before. He never used to be so quiet."

She nodded, not saying anything. Maybe this explained what was going on with her. She *couldn't* be personally interested in him. It was just that they had more in common than she'd realized.

"Well," Andy said, sighing, "you're leaving us tomorrow anyway, right? Unless Mrs. MacLaine accepts your design. And if she does and you come back, then maybe I'll introduce you to John."

"Sure." She smiled at Andy. "We'll do it then. And put in a good word for me, because he's been giving me funny looks all morning."

"I know he comes off as intimidating sometimes, but you don't need to be worried about him. He's a good guy, Lyn."

"I'm not worried," she said lightly, taking another sip from her iced tea. But her gut told her that maybe she should be. Across the room, John Reilly was staring at her, intently.

He hadn't stopped staring at her.

JOHN REILLY STOOD with arms crossed, watching through the break room window while Lyn Francis roared out of his parking lot in her little black Audi. He could feel his eyes narrow the longer he watched her. He didn't know what it was about her, but there had been something—something he couldn't put his finger on. On the surface she seemed to have been making a business call in his parking lot—some sort of catalog that she was reading numbers from—but there was more to it than that. Something that set off his inner alarm bells. The more he studied her, the more curious he felt about her presence.

He stuffed his hands in his pockets. It wasn't that she was attractive. She definitely was, but that wasn't why he'd been watching her in the first place. Not the only reason, anyway.

The door opened suddenly beside him, and Millie, his mother's best friend and their long-time waitress, moved inside as quiet as a ghost and began to wipe down the table. That was a reminder to John that he had other priorities to concentrate on. Lyn Francis wasn't his business. The Seaside Bar and Grill was.

Gritting his teeth, John nodded to Millie, then headed out behind the huge, carved wooden bar that was the pride and joy of their small beach-restaurant business. John's father had built the Seaside twenty-five years before. John had helped put up the shelves in the back, and he knew exactly, by feel, the spot where he had once secretly carved his initials. John was *part* of this place. He couldn't just walk away, much as he sometimes wished he could.

The lawyer's bill for his brother had come due today. John needed to meet with the bank and somehow scrape up the money to pay it. And on top of that, the screwup with the beer line not working wasn't helping matters at all. It was costing them, too.

John squatted beside the open closet that led to the big silver keg of domestic beer beneath the bar. "What do you think?" he said to the technician—Cody. "Can you get this line fixed by five o'clock?"

That was when the after-work crowd came in. And John couldn't keep selling bottled beer for the same price he charged for cheaper drafts, because John was such a good guy to his old friends. He was losing money on the deal.

Cody sat up and scratched his head. "Don't know," he mumbled. "I got a call in to my supervisor." He looked at John. "Actually, I need to leave for a while. I'll be back later, though."

"No," John said reflexively. If Cody left, he likely wouldn't be back today, and John wasn't going to let that happen.

Cody blinked. "I *have* to leave."

"Why?"

"I, um, need to get a part."

"Really?" John crossed his arms again. For not the first time today, he wished he was back in active service. That way, people might actually listen to him and follow his orders. "And what part is that, Cody?"

Cody gave him a stubborn look, but John stared him down.

Cody's cheeks turned red. "I need to replace my flashlight. The bulb isn't working, and I can't see."

John had a million flashlights on the premises. Without a word, he leaned over the bar, reached the top shelf, then chose among three working flashlights. The first was large, more of a weapon than a source of light, the second was medium with a bright glare, and the third was small with pinpoint accuracy—just right.

John turned the small flashlight on and put it into Cody's hand. "Go to it. If you need anything else, I'll be right here."

Cody made a small noise in his throat that sounded like something between a groan and a whine. John felt his teeth clenching. He knew he was probably feeling some prejudice against Cody because of his youth and poor work ethic—similar to John's younger brother's youth and poor work ethic, and Patrick wasn't exactly giving John an easy time of it, either. But these two young guys would have to grow up and learn to be responsible. He'd said that to his brother, and his brother had told him to get off his case.

John sighed and rubbed his hand over his eyes. He was dealing with Cody right now, not Patrick. "Look, Cody, you need to get this done by five o'clock, no excuses."

It irritated John to have to be a hard-ass in

order to get the job done. He had the skills to fix the beer line himself with much less time and emotion expended. But if he touched these beer lines, then he voided the contract with the distributor.

John played by the book. He was honest. He was direct.

He stared at Cody. "Are we clear?"

"Okay. Give me a few minutes." Cody's shaggy mop top and beard disappeared under the counter.

John planted his feet and crossed his arms, watching over the kid. He would stay here as long as it took.

Across the room, Andy Hannaman stood, stretched, and gathered his group's plates and empty bottles. John glanced for Millie, but she was probably in the kitchen with his mother. It was after one o'clock, past the lunch break and well before quitting time, so the place was nearly empty. He went around the bar and helped Andy clear the table of dirty plates and empty wrappers.

"Thanks," he told Andy. He appreciated that his old friend was there to help him.

"I don't see why you didn't want to say hi to her," Andy said.

"Who?" John asked, though he knew *who*. The cute blonde with her ponytail and big blue eyes was still on his mind. He had no idea why—it bugged him that he couldn't put his finger on the specific reason why—but she did something to him, and it wasn't *just* because she was hot. A lot of hot girls walked through these doors during summertime. This whole question of why he was getting uneasy vibes about her was driving him nuts.

Andy rolled his eyes at him. "Lyn's nice. She's a sweetheart, actually. I saw you two looking at each other earlier."

"You saw wrong," John growled.

"Moon said she was asking about you, too."

Now this just pissed him off. "Stop this line of thinking."

Andy squinted at him. "I don't get it. What's the big deal? I thought you'd be happy. You can't judge all women by—"

"All women?" John nearly exploded. His former marriage was old news, years-ago news, and what he did or didn't do with his dating life was no one's business but his.

"Don't get riled up," Andy said, holding up his hands. "I'm just trying to help you. She's a decent sort. An interior designer working for the MacLaines. Lyn's not a slouch."

"I never said she was a slouch." But that made him think. *The congressman?* That would imply that she worked for a high-end firm, and that she had serious skills. He turned to Andy. "Why is she so friendly with *us*?"

"What's wrong with us?" Andy looked genuinely flummoxed.

John sighed. Even if Andy didn't see it, the lady was suspicious. A woman like her, with her hot car and her good looks and her high-end interior design skills—at least, according to what Andy had just said—here, in this place? In this little dump of a bar in this sad, dead-end stretch of beach?

"You don't think she's *too* friendly?" he said. "Getting to know all you guys on the crews?"

"No. It's good for her business, and frankly, it's nice."

"You don't see any ulterior motives?"

"Like what?"

He didn't want to get into his reasons for watching everyone in the bar so closely. "She's *too* alert," John mused. "Too interested in us." She paid too much attention when most people didn't pay any attention at all—fiddling with their mobile phones all the time as they were.

She seemed to be hiding something—he thought of the way she'd covered up her notes when he'd come up behind her in the parking lot. He hadn't imagined it—she'd flashed him a surprised, guilty look before giving him that sweet smile that would turn any man's knees to jelly.

"I caught her," he muttered to himself. "I know I did."

It was almost as if she was *trained* to pay attention to everything going on around her, and his sneaking up on her had been a rare slipup.

Andy burst into laughter. "You've been spending too much time behind the bar, my friend. You need to get out of this place and mingle more."

Sure, *he* could laugh, John thought. Andy didn't have a younger brother in trouble with the law. But not even Andy knew the extent of the trouble—John hoped nobody did. As much as possible, John didn't want the information to get out.

Andy just shook his head sadly at him. "You've really grown paranoid. I'm worried about you."

John doubted that. And the more he thought about the idea of her being so alert, like some sort of secret investigator, the more it made sense that's what she was. *That's* why he'd been so drawn to her—his subconscious had been alerting him to the danger she posed. Making him notice things about her that he normally wouldn't study in a person.

She's had situational-awareness training, the same as I have. He would bet the Seaside on that fact.

And if he ever saw Lyn Francis again—or whatever her name was—then he was going to confront her about it.

Thoroughly.

CHAPTER TWO

Meeting of the Seacoast Burglary Task Force
Concord, New Hampshire

LYNDSAY TIGHTENED HER duty belt across her hips. Regulation gun, nightstick, flashlight, handcuffs and key were all in place. After a week of undercover work in her chosen street clothes, the duty belt felt tight and uncomfortable. But she was still an officer—not yet a detective—and so she was required to wear her uniform for the meeting with the other members of her task force.

With one last look in the mirror, she smoothed her hair bun and straightened her collar. Leaving the ladies' room, she headed upstairs to the conference room in the massive, granite-faced headquarters building.

She was outside in the corridor when her mobile phone vibrated. She glanced at the screen and saw that it was her father's number. Since she had a few minutes before the meeting officially started, she moved to a window in an alcove off the main corridor and took the call.

Outside, the lazy river wound along the heart of the state capital. Not wanting to be overheard taking a personal call in a professional setting, she kept her voice low.

"Hi, Dad."

"Lyndsay! I wasn't sure if I'd be leaving you a voice mail. You're off the undercover assignment now, I see."

"Yes. I'm about to head into a meeting. What's up?"

"Oh, I'm just calling to check on you. Wanted to make sure everything went well."

"It did." Lyndsay watched a police car turn the corner of the building, down on the street several floors below. She knew her dad wanted to hear details about her assignment, but she couldn't say anything just yet. "I met my objective for the week, so I can say that I'm pleased."

"You were successful, I assume."

She smiled to herself—her dad always expected the best of her. She could forgive him for the pressure of the expectations—she knew he loved her, and she knew how he loved the job.

"Well, I'm not sure if my small part will help catch the bad guys, but I'll get a better idea shortly." Honestly, she wasn't sure about the big picture, but that was because she'd been on a need-to-know basis. Today, she hoped to be moved beyond that.

"I'm proud of you for seeking out the assignment," Dad said. "It's a tremendous opportunity you've snagged."

"I'm not sure what happens now," she admitted. Her father was her best confidante, and she'd missed not talking to him during the past week. A police chief himself, recently retired, he felt nostalgic for the job. And, he enjoyed living vicariously through her. It drew them closer, and she didn't mind that. In fact, she liked it. "Dad, honestly, now that I've got a taste of it, I'm not keen to go back to patrol."

"Enjoyed being an undercover detective, did you?" The pride in his voice was unmistakable.

"Yes, I did like it. Very much." She thought briefly of the freedom and the camaraderie she'd felt at the beach. It *had* been fun. Even being checked out by a handsome bar owner was something she'd decided she could handle. Especially after she had called Pete yesterday afternoon and he'd relayed that so far, John Reilly's background wasn't raising any red flags. In fact, he had an honorary discharge from the Marine Corps. She should be able to relate to him when and if the time came.

"…You need to go in there and *tell* them you want the promotion to detective," her father was saying. "You need to step forward and ask for the increased responsibility. Obviously, they needed a woman with your skills for the short-term task force. Who would have known that year in interior design school would come in handy for you? But the point is, you can't let them discard you now. There's a bigger picture, and you need to insert yourself—"

"I know, Dad." He was getting too passionate. Among the drawbacks of having a father who had also been in law enforcement for his entire career was that he sometimes got *too* involved.

"So what's your game plan?" he demanded.

Going with the flow, that was her plan. Working with what came up, as it came up, had always gotten her through life's difficulties. "I'll handle it, Dad. I'll be okay."

He sighed aloud. "Aw, I'm just so proud of you." His voice lowered. "I never had the opportunity to do what you're doing. I always regretted that."

"I know," she said softly. Her dad had been the big fish in a small law-enforcement pond—a small town in the mountains, the chief of police on a tiny force. Now he was driving her mom a bit nuts being underfoot all the time. "I'll come and visit you both soon, but I have to go now, okay?"

"Remember to ask for the job, Lyndsay."

She smiled in spite of herself. "Ten-four, Dad. And say hi to Mom for me."

At two minutes to the hour, she found her conference room. It seemed that she was the last person they were waiting for, and as she sat, she lifted her chin higher and glanced surreptitiously around.

She was the only woman at the meeting, and she assumed that meant she was the only woman on the task force. Around the table she recognized Commander Harris, the imposing and serious man in charge of the task force as well as the superior who'd initially selected and interviewed her for the assignment.

Pete—her backup partner—caught her gaze and smiled broadly. Beside Pete were two other men that Lyndsay didn't recognize. Commander Harris introduced them as Wesley and Simon. Wesley was a young, nerdy-looking camera technician. Simon was middle-aged and fierce, with a thick growth of scruffy beard and a tattoo showing on his neck above the collar of his dress shirt. He looked as if he'd be more at home on a drug enforcement or organized crime undercover task force. Lyndsay knew that a burglary task force was tame compared to operations that the state police were known for. Frankly, she was glad for this one. She'd spent her time at the gun range and at the gym for martial arts class, and she was confident of her skills. But she'd rather not be undercover with violent people if she could help it.

"Pete has taken the information you gathered from your surveillance, Officer Fairfax," Commander Harris was saying, "and he was able to ascertain that none of the principals were the likely perpetrators of the burglaries."

Lyndsay nodded. That was good news—she'd been hoping that none of her new friends were involved in anything illegal. She had suspected that was the case, but that Pete had confirmed it made her breathe easier.

"Furthermore, I'm told that nothing out of the ordinary occurred to break your cover. Is that the case, Officer Fairfax?" Commander Harris asked her.

"No, nothing out of the ordinary happened," she confirmed. Frankly, the assignment had been easier than she'd thought. She hadn't even had to lie much, really, because it was true she'd been trained as an interior designer. Sort of, if one year of design school counted.

"You did good work," Commander Harris said. Pete gave her a quick smile. Wesley blinked, but truthfully, he looked greener than she did. Simon didn't change his expression—he still looked bored by the whole thing.

Licking her lips, she shifted in her seat, wondering if she should break in and ask questions. She was aching for a broader view of the case.

"Last night we had another burglary ten miles up the coast," Commander Harris said, his tone grim. "Our fifth burglary since February. Same MO. Paintings and jewelry stolen, and a safe cracked and emptied."

"Any signs of forced entry?" Pete asked.

"None. The homeowner had a surveillance system, but nothing registered as out of the ordinary. The alarm never triggered. And there was no evidence of forced windows or doors."

Simon sat up taller in his seat. "Sounds like an inside job."

"We're considering that possibility," Commander Harris replied. "I'd like you to check it out, Simon. The theft has been kept from the police blotter. There's no media attention. These paintings were uninsured, so there will be no outside interference."

Simon nodded. "I'm on it."

Lyndsay shifted in her seat. Obviously, paintings were an important part of the common thread. She thought of Pete's request. The Goldricks had indeed displayed one valuable oil painting—a modern landscape, which she'd dutifully noted to Pete. She hadn't told him yet, but within the MacLaine home there were two huge oil paintings over the congressman's fireplace, but she didn't know if the paintings were important or valuable. They were both female nudes, of the same model. To Lyndsay's mind, the congressman's private possessions weren't her business, and she'd known better than to offer her opinion. But, if all the thefts had been of paintings... Maybe she should say something.

I want to be a detective, she thought. *Good detectives always get to the facts.* She cleared her throat. "Do all of the burglaries to date involve stolen paintings?" she asked. "Sir," she remembered to add.

Commander Harris glanced at her. "Yes. Cut from their frames."

"Like a museum heist," she blurted.

"A lot easier than that," Simon muttered. "These homes aren't the fortresses that museums are."

"And the safes," Wesley added. The team was really solidifying now. "Don't forget the haul from the safes."

"How much is that estimated to be?" she asked politely.

"From what we're being told, tens of thousands in cash," Commander Harris replied.

"Don't know if I believe that." Simon leaned back cynically and clasped his hands behind his neck. "Has to be a lot more. What business are these new vics in?"

Lyndsay turned to Commander Harris because she was curious about the answer, too. He seemed to be hesitating. All she knew about the MacLaines was that Paul MacLaine, recently retired as congressman, now worked part-time as a political lobbyist. Technically, he was a *former* congressman, but nobody around Wallis Point referred to him thus. Paul was quite wealthy. He hadn't started out that way, but he had made money during the past decade by investing wisely. That was the scoop Andy had told her.

"All five burglaries are from private homes on the seacoast. No one was home during the burglaries, although three of the homes have live-in staff who weren't on the premises at the time."

The MacLaines didn't have live-in staff. During her four days alone in the house, she'd seen and heard nothing suspicious. When she'd left the house yesterday, the two paintings were intact over the fireplace, and the wall safe behind the smaller of the two paintings was undisturbed.

"Line of business of the owners?" Simon pressed.

"Private businesspeople, as were the owners of the other four homes," Commander Harris replied. "Nothing nefarious involved that we can see."

"Or they wouldn't have come to us for help," Wesley pointed out.

"How did the task force start?" Lyndsay asked. Simon rolled his eyes at her question. She swallowed, but glanced to Commander Harris. "If you don't mind my asking, sir, I'm unaware of the reasons for the formation and what our broader scope is."

"You may ask all you want, Officer. You've played an important part thus far—and you will be playing a key part in the future."

"Excellent." She sat back in her chair.

"Pete, why don't you fill in Officer Fairfax— Lyndsay—as to the history of our task force. Wesley, as well."

"The first burglary occurred five weeks ago," Pete said, leaning forward, his fingers interlaced. "I was a detective on the first case. When the second burglary occurred a week later, I noticed the similarities. About the time of the third similar burglary, Congressman MacLaine notified the governor." Here, he glanced to Commander Harris.

Commander Harris took up the narrative. "The congressman was concerned that a more unified, centralized and elevated effort be formed, across agencies, to apprehend the burglars. So as of a week ago, we have a task force. The expense is not inconsiderable, and each of you will have clear, focused duties, which will continue for no longer than two weeks. At that point, the governor expects an arrest or arrests."

She nodded. "What has everyone been doing so far?"

"Lyndsay—" Officer Harris addressed the others "—has been undercover as interior designer Lyn Francis. She has a complete online persona as Lyn Francis, thanks to Wesley." Here, Wesley smiled at her. "Lyn Francis is the only person on our task force with an undercover alias, and we will get to her mission in a few moments' time."

She couldn't wait to hear it.

"Pete," Commander Harris continued, "has been investigating the background of area contractors as flagged by Lyndsay. We have reason to believe that locals are involved, and Lyndsay's efforts here are crucial. Pete is also serving—and will continue to serve—as backup for Lyndsay. Simon has been following up on crime scene investigations, as well as investigating insurance company reports, alarm system company personnel, and staff at burgled homes. Wesley is with us part-time. He will be installing cameras at the congressman's home, but we'll get to that later, as well." He turned to Wesley and nodded.

It seemed to be a signal, because Wesley tapped at the keyboard of a laptop before him.

On a wall screen, a photograph of Congressman MacLaine appeared.

"This is Congressman MacLaine," he said unnecessarily. The congressman's familiar long face and full head of thick, brown hair, was a common fixture in the local media. Lyndsay hadn't actually met him or his wife yet. She also hadn't dared to poke about *too* much in their possessions in any of the twelve rooms of their oversize beach cottage.

"Lyndsay," Commander Harris said, "the congressman has specifically requested that you stay in his cottage, beginning Monday, for the next two weeks while he and his wife are away on a cruise vacation. There is a guest room that looks over the street, and you may set up in there."

Her mouth was open. She hadn't expected this order, at all.

"Wesley will be there on Sunday evening," Commander Harris continued, "to place a network of hidden cameras in the MacLaine home, which will give a complete picture of the surrounding grounds as well as the rest of the street and the three mansions facing them. While he is there, your job will be to cover and assist him."

She blinked. "Do you expect the congressman's home to be targeted? Has there been a tip?"

"Not at this time. The congressman has requested the cameras. If his home is to be targeted, he wants evidence. He's funding this part of the effort, though that is not to be made public knowledge."

She nodded. "Of course." But still it niggled at her. What was she supposed to *do* there? "With all due respect, sir, what will I be investigating?"

He gave her a censorious look, so she folded her hands and waited. Sometimes it was difficult to follow the dictates of the chain of command.

"Officer Fairfax, your primary mission is to maintain your cover. Do not break it for any reason. I repeat, for any reason. Not even the local authorities have been made aware of your presence, or of the existence of our task force. If you are so much as stopped for a traffic ticket, you will give them your cover name. If necessary, you will allow yourself to be arrested and even locked up."

She gaped at him.

But Simon was nodding. "Been there, done that," he muttered.

She glanced at Pete. He was shrugging.

"This isn't a game, Officer Fairfax." Commander Harris gazed sternly at her. "You're to keep your eyes and ears open. You will remain at the MacLaines' home, and your backup officer will maintain contact with you by phone.

Additionally, you two will conduct a short daily meeting at a nearby rendezvous point."

Pete leaned over and murmured to her. "There's a convenience store nearby, just a walk out the back slider and down the beach. I'll fill you in later."

"But what police work will I conduct?" she asked Commander Harris. She'd already gathered the names of the local contractors. She couldn't imagine what else he needed her to do, just sitting idly at the congressman's home all day, watching and waiting for a break-in that might never come.

"Your daily investigative duties will be up to your backup officer," Commander Harris said. "Rest assured, your undercover presence is extremely valuable, and we have more than enough work to keep you occupied, if you will listen for one moment." He sent her another censorious look, so she pinched her lips together and waited.

Commander Harris nodded to Wesley. The computer technician pressed a button for the next slide. A picture that looked like a driver's license photo flashed on the screen—a female who looked to be Lyndsay's age. She had shoulder-length, dark red hair, and a direct, fiery gaze. "This is Kitty MacLaine."

Interested, Lyndsay straightened her spine. She hadn't seen a photo of the congressman's wife before. Information about the congress-man's private life was woefully scant on the in-ternet. She knew; she'd searched for it.

Kitty looked quite a bit younger than the con-gressman, but Lyndsay knew better than to make a comment.

"Kitty is not aware of the task force. She's not aware, Lyndsay, that you are an undercover police officer. But she is aware of you as Lyn Francis."

"Oh," Lyndsay murmured.

"On Monday morning at nine, your assign-ment is to meet with Kitty MacLaine in her home and review your design plans with her."

"What?!" Lyndsay nearly exploded. Her *de-sign plans*? She hadn't expected that any of her computer renderings would be seriously con-sidered by anyone. She swallowed, a vain at-tempt at tamping down her panic. "But I'm not a professional designer, sir. Surely, she will see through that."

"You have to trust us," Commander Harris said, his tone sharp. "As you know, you've been given an internet cover as a designer working under Karen Talbott, owner of the DesignSea company. What you didn't know was that Ms. Talbott's seacoast home was the first one bur-gled, and she's been eager to assist us. She's also a friend to the congressman, and it was his influence that got her onboard with us."

"So...I'm to meet with Ms. Talbott first?"

"I recommend it, yes," he said calmly. "Although Ms. Talbott is pleased with your ideas and feels you have talent."

Someone snickered—Simon, it sounded like. Lyndsay knew her face was red, but she didn't give him the satisfaction of turning to look at him. She focused on Commander Harris. "I don't know anything substantial about Kitty, or her desires and needs," she protested.

Commander Harris looked blankly at her. As did Pete.

"For example, is she the congressman's first wife? How long have they been married? I understand they don't have children, but—"

"Is that relevant?"

"Certainly. I know from—" from Andy Hannaman, but it wasn't relevant to mention *his* name "—from a longtime local that the congressman's beach home has been owned by him for almost twenty years, but that during the past five years or so, he was rarely there. Then suddenly this past autumn, after he retired, he started visiting more often."

"And?"

"And, An—the local," she corrected herself, "said that he was with a wife he'd never seen before."

The commander sighed.

"Also, does he have any children by any former relationships? I wasn't able to tell from his internet profiles, but I assume not."

"No, the congressman has no children," said Commander Harris wearily.

"I know you assume this is all peripheral to the task force," she said to the room at large, "but I really should be clear with these details."

"Karen Talbott," he said in a no-nonsense voice, "will fill you in with what you need to know from the design standpoint."

"And then I'm to review the design plan with Kitty MacLaine on Monday? What exactly are her expectations?"

From the short silence, Lyndsay wondered if Commander Harris had fully thought this out. She waited.

The room was quiet. Everyone was staring at her, it seemed, waiting for *her* to say something.

Finally, Pete leaned forward. Maybe he felt responsible for giving her a good recommendation. "I'm sure that Kitty is expecting her interior to be redesigned," he said gently.

"But that is *not* police work."

"We have approved contractors we'll send to

assist you. And you'll get a budget, courtesy of the congressman, to implement the design."

It dawned on her that they assumed that the one year of design school she'd had under her belt, years before she'd joined the force, was enough to fulfill this crazy cover story. She shook her head, exasperated.

"We've invested in you," Commander Harris chided her. "The task force needs you to continue the cover for two more weeks."

She resisted the urge to throw up her hands in defeat.

But was it defeat, really? She would be doing investigative police work, as well. That was the most important thing. There was always the hope that she could catch the criminals in the act and make a collar. The potential upsides were too good to pass up.

Besides, she really couldn't refuse them now.

"Fine," she said. "I'll do it. I'll call Karen Talbott this afternoon and set up a meeting."

"Just keep your cover," Commander Harris repeated. "Whatever you do, it is imperative that you not compromise your cover."

JOHN UNLOCKED THE front door of his family's restaurant, then flipped the window sign to Open. Outside, the sun was rising, although clouds were gathering on the horizon. Across the street, he saw the vacant public parking lot and behind that, sand dunes. In the far distance, across the blue-gray sea, were fishing vessels and the season's early lobster boats, chugging out to check the baited traps.

He drew a hand through his hair. Another summer coming. Every morning was the same. The years and seasons were all starting to run together. He felt like he was spinning his wheels here, but he didn't know what else to do.

From the corner of his eye, he heard his brother cough softly. Patrick slouched on a bar stool, electronic device in hand, absorbed as he played a video game. The soft glow of the screen in the early morning gloom lit up his pimply face and scraggly hair.

John could never get too mad at Patrick. His brother was young. He'd been at home when all the bad stuff in their family had gone down.

"You want to help me start the coffee?" John asked. "Andy's crew will be coming soon."

Patrick pretended that he didn't hear him. Or maybe he wasn't pretending, because he was wearing earbuds. He reached down to scratch his lower leg, which made his pants ride up. The ankle bracelet, placed there by the county court system, showed clearly.

John stalked over and pulled his brother's jeans back into place. "People will be coming in," he said tersely, once his brother had removed his earbud to glare at John. "You need to help us in the kitchen."

Without a word, Patrick sullenly got up from his chair. The game went into his back pocket. Patrick shambled into the kitchen. When he was gone, John leaned over, head in hands. Sometimes he had no idea what to do with his brother beyond getting him through his next court date without incident. *June 5*. *Just get through to June 5*. The goal was to get Patrick released from court-ordered house arrest without prison time. Since he'd been through a rehab session successfully, the lawyer had told them that Patrick's release was a strong likelihood, as long as John could help Patrick keep to the conditions set forth by the court.

If John wasn't successful…

His mother poked her head from the kitchen. "I'm thinking of making clam chowder today."

"Sounds good, Mom," he said wearily. "I'll write it up as a lunch special."

She nodded and disappeared. She seemed okay this morning, and that was good.

When John had first returned home, she'd been upset about his dad and his brother—understandably—and he'd had to calm her on nearly a daily basis, it seemed. Only lately did she seem like herself again. She was humming an upbeat tune in the kitchen, and he was glad for it.

The rumble of a truck engine sounded outside. A quick glance told him that Andy's crew had arrived for breakfast—his mother's special muffins and their morning coffee fill-up. His mom made everything from scratch; even the coffee was from freshly ground beans. Andy was a longtime customer, and he knew their routines. He knew about what had happened to John's brother Justin, of course, and John's dad, but John wasn't sure how much Andy knew about Patrick's recent legal problems. From what John could tell, Andy wasn't aware of the arrest and conviction, and John's promise to the court to watch his brother. John hoped Andy didn't know, anyway.

Feeling wary—always wary—he met Andy at the door. Wordlessly, still sleepy, Andy handed over the large insulated coffee carafe, followed by the empty plastic cooler that John filled with lemonade for them each working morning.

"Gonna be a nice day, even with those clouds," Andy remarked.

"Yeah. Summer's coming." But no sooner had John let the words out, then a familiar black Audi pulled off the coast road and into their little lot. The hot blonde driving made her habitual, tight, three-point turn, then backed her two-seater into an equally tight space between Andy's van and the restaurant's front door.

John closed his eyes briefly and groaned silently.

"Look who's back," Andy said cheerfully. "The congressman must've liked Lyn's designs." He winked at John. "Go. Talk to her. Give her a chance."

While Andy headed inside the restaurant, whistling loudly, John folded his arms, kept silent, and watched. Andy was wrong about her, he felt it. Something was definitely off—something suspicious—and if she was an investigator of some sort, then that was trouble his family didn't need.

He stepped outside the restaurant and approached her car. Planted his feet.

Lyn Francis—or whatever her name was— had hopped out of the Audi.

John caught a quick glimpse of the sleek leather interior before she shut the door. The shelf where the back seat would have been was stuffed with fabric samples and paint-chip wheels. Could be part of a cover story. He felt his nails dig into his palms. When she finished locking the door and turned, noticing him standing there, she smiled. But her gaze lingered on his face, and her smile died.

Yeah, he was irritated—mainly that he needed

to even do this in the first place, that his brother's criminal behavior had put him in this position. He was aware that his mood likely showed all over his face. He'd been told he had a look, a scowl that he used on enemies as if shooting at them in a firefight, and yes, he was pretty sure he was giving her that exact look now.

She swallowed, as if surprised that he was angry with her. But he gave her credit; she didn't wilt under his scrutiny. Instead, she lifted up her rib cage, stiffening her back as she stared *him* down.

His gaze dropped. A bump showed at her waist, beneath her shirt. A gun. She was carrying a concealed sidearm—he was positive of that.

"Did you wake up on the wrong side of the bed today?" Lyn gave him a saucy smile, oblivious to his thoughts.

He didn't trust her. After what Patrick had put him through, John didn't trust anybody on their word, not without his own verification.

He planted his feet wider and kept his gaze directly on her eyes. Pretty, soft blue eyes. But even pretty girls with soft blue eyes could be deceitful.

"You're a cop," John said roughly. "Aren't you?"

CHAPTER THREE

IN THE SPLIT second when Lyndsay had first seen John standing before her with the sun behind him, outlining his erect stance and muscular arms, something within her had lifted. It may have been crazy of her, but she'd been genuinely interested in seeing him again.

What a mistake that was. Because now her systems were screaming in alarm. She was doing everything she could to face him as an actress would. A very good actress.

"You're a cop," he repeated.

Her vision swam, and the earth seemed to move beneath her feet, even hearing the accusation for the second time. But she managed to school her face into something resembling disbelief.

Talk him out of it! her mind screamed at her. *Deflect him!*

Keeping as steady as she could, she leaned against the hood of her car, splaying her palms flat on the metal, still warm from her drive.

It wouldn't be hard to act flabbergasted over

what he'd just said, because honestly, he'd thrown her off balance from the moment he'd peered into her car window that day in the parking lot.

"Why would you *possibly* think I'm a cop?" she asked, trying to sound incredulous.

And while he scowled at her, she gazed into his gray-blue eyes. The pupils were enlarged, making his eyes seem dark and hard.

She crossed her arms, shivering. She'd worn a thin sweater under her short woolen pea coat, but it wasn't warming her.

"You're not denying it." He crossed his arms, too.

"Because you're joking, right?"

"I never joke. You're a cop."

"I'm *not* a cop," she spit, suddenly angry. She wasn't going to let anyone stop her from doing her job. It felt *good* to be angry about that. "How can you say something so weird to me? You haven't spoken to me before, not once, not even a 'hello' greeting, and I've been coming to your restaurant for almost a week now."

He exhaled, and his breath made a small puff in the cool air. Briefly he glanced away. But then he was back, glaring at her again. "I've been watching you."

"Yes, so I've noticed."

"*Because* I have situational-awareness training. I was in the military. And you appear to have that training, too."

"I haven't had military training," she said as calmly as she could.

"Cop training, then." He cocked his head. "It shows."

"I don't know what you mean." She met his gaze.

"It means that as much as you act friendly and chatty to everyone here, you're *always* aware. You're always looking around." He pointed at her. "Last Thursday you couldn't even talk on the phone without constantly looking around the parking lot."

"So? Isn't that painting it with a broad brush?" She jumped on his mistake. "Is everyone who is aware while they're speaking on the phone— which, by the way, is a good thing—a cop?"

He snorted, not backing off. "I've watched you for days. Every time you're here, you sit in the corner in the same seat, exactly the same seat that I would sit in," he pointed out, completely changing the subject. "You sit in the power seat. The seat where you can come out with guns blazing if you have to."

"Guns *blazing*?"

"You know exactly what I mean," he said quietly.

She knew her mouth was hanging open. She'd

already known he'd been in the Marines, but who *was* this guy?

Ironically, every ounce of her law enforcement training was telling her to keep the upper hand in the situation. *She* needed to be in charge.

But now, all she could seem to do was gape and stare at him, as if she was outside her own body looking in. Her hot, shocked body.

"But the real clue is the sidearm at your waist." He nodded toward it. "You're wearing a concealed holster, aren't you? There's an imprint of a small handgun. Right here."

He reached to point at the outline of her Glock, and this time her training did kick in. Deftly, she reached out and blocked him before he could touch her pistol.

Her hand clasped his, inches from her weapon.

They both stared at each other, breathing hard. Her adrenaline was pumping. He was a danger. To her, to her mission.

She didn't let go of his hand.

He blinked at her, at the surprise he must have felt, because he stared in confusion.

Stop this, she told herself. *Let him go.*

She dropped his hand, knowing she'd just outed herself by her actions. The fact that she'd grabbed his hand aggressively, as a police officer would, rather than just swatting his hand away, didn't look good.

He opened and closed his fingers, shaking them. "Okay," he said finally, speaking quietly again, "forget the handgun. I'm open-minded about that, and it's best not mentioned anyway. But you can't deny to me that you've had military-type training."

No, she could not. Particularly after the way she'd just crushed his fingers.

She needed to tell him *something*. Something logical and true, while still concealing the whole story.

"My father was a police officer." She hadn't wanted to tell anyone this, but she was fast seeing it was her only way out. "Maybe that makes me different from other women you're used to, but my dad didn't have sons. He had me, his only daughter."

John nodded slowly. "Okay."

"He taught me self-defense maneuvers. And to observe my surroundings. And to sit in corners of rooms in order to better check for danger. But I *am* an interior designer, not a cop."

He seemed to be assimilating the information. "Did your father *want* you to be a cop?"

"No." She couldn't help smiling. When she'd been young, her dad had thought her hopeless that way. She'd been a girly-girl, drawn to all things feminine. She participated in Girl Scouts.

Cheerleading. Heck, she really had signed up to go to interior design school.

"So, the way he was, it just rubbed off on you," John stated.

She nodded slightly, wondering what was happening. The conversation was turning into a mix of half-truths and half-lies. None of it comfortable. "I...should really just grab a coffee and then get back to work."

"Yeah. Me, too." But he wasn't taking his eyes from her.

This...wasn't good. Yes, he'd seemed to buy her story, but in convincing him, she'd exposed herself, too. And he hadn't said a thing about himself.

"Why were you watching me, anyway?" she asked. "Do you watch everybody to see if they're police officers? Do police officers worry you or something?"

He looked sharply at her.

"What is it?" she pushed him, tilting her head to see his expression better. "You're allowed to question me, but I can't question you?"

"I'm a Marine veteran," he said forcefully.

She knew that, but he didn't know that she knew that. She gazed steadily at him. "So you're no longer active duty? Are you a reservist? Or are you transitioned out?"

"I'm out."

"Were you honorably discharged?"

He scowled at her. "For several years now."

"How many years?"

He thought for a moment. "Four."

He would have been active duty while Jason was still alive.

"Were you in theater?" she asked.

His jaw worked. "Iraq and Afghanistan."

So had Jason.

The thought made her reel. What if they'd known each other? It wasn't beyond the realm of possibility.

She felt...even more off balance than she'd been. She'd prepared as best she could for this assignment, but being faced with the possibility that someone here had known her late husband hadn't been part of that. Without thinking, she leaned back against her car, felt the door handle on her backside.

"Are you okay?" he asked. Her reaction would make anyone suspicious. To keep him off the trail, she had to throw him another kernel of truth, however painful for her.

"My late husband was in Army Special Operations. I can't really talk about it, but he..." She shook her head. A raindrop spattered down on her face. It had gotten dark outside. It looked like it was going to rain harder.

"Can we get in the car and talk for a few minutes?" he asked.

"I'd rather not. I'm fine."

"It's raining, Lyn." His look had changed to one of concern. She realized that it had worked, that he believed her, that she'd deflected him from accusing her of being a police officer. He'd even called her by her undercover name.

It had taken the truth to do that. And now he wanted to *really* talk. Just great.

She shook her head, then turned and fumbled with her door handle, opening it and rushing inside. The rain seemed to pour from the sky, hitting the windshield, running down it in quickly gathering streams.

She heard her passenger door open, and she glanced over, startled. John was getting in, too. He sat on the leather seat and ran his hand through rain-spattered hair. He still wore his short, military-style haircut. She should have realized this about her initial attraction to him.

"When did it happen?" he asked her. "How?"

He had such a direct way about him. She'd sworn she wouldn't go there. But she was cornered, and it was easier to tell him the truth, or something with a kernel of truth. That seemed to be working.

"Six years now," she murmured. "Jason died

in a training accident." She clamped her lips shut. Too much information. Too much of it true.

All of it was true.

He was gazing at her with such tenderness. She'd never have guessed him capable.

Don't say you're sorry. Please don't say you're sorry. Everyone says they're sorry...

"You've made a big sacrifice," he said.

Something about his tone made her pause. "Are *you* married?" she asked.

He gave a short shake of his head. In response to her unasked question, he explained, "Divorced."

"Oh."

"I'm fine."

"Ditto," she murmured.

But she rubbed her hand over her eyes. He just put her *so* off balance. She glanced away from his wry smile and the T-shirt that fit his wide chest in such a nice way. "Well, the rain has slowed now. I've got to get to my job site. Please...don't tell Andy what I said, all right? I don't want people to gossip or feel sorry for me or anything like that."

He made a cross sign over his heart, then pressed it to his lips.

He had such nice lips.

Without a word, he turned away and opened the door. The rain had petered to a misty drizzle. Without saying goodbye, he got out of her car and walked into his bar.

Lyndsay turned on the engine, threw the shifter into Drive and headed for her meeting at the MacLaine home, her morning coffee put off.

As she careered down the coast road, she blew out a breath. Had she just screwed up? Or had she done the right thing?

All of this was new to her. She couldn't get her mind wrapped around it. Yes, it was true there was something about him—she respected his forthrightness and the fact that he noticed things about people. But John noticing too much about her put the operation at risk. She needed to be extra careful where he was concerned.

CHAPTER FOUR

Congressman MacLaine's Beach Cottage
Wallis Point Beach, NH

FORTY MINUTES LATER, Lyndsay's weapon was secured inside her glove box. She sat inside her car, engine idling, in the driveway of the MacLaine cottage, waiting for Kitty MacLaine to show up for their morning appointment. Kitty was twenty minutes late.

Though the rain had stopped, the sky was nevertheless gray and overcast. The wind was brisk, and the clouds moved quickly—a volatile weather pattern.

When she'd arrived here, she'd still felt volatile. Her mind kept wandering over her encounter with John. To save her cover, she'd had to confess so much truth to him. She couldn't help thinking about Jason, too. She'd had no idea what she was getting herself into when she'd first been drawn to him. It had been at a party during her first year of college—a lifetime ago, it seemed. She'd been sheltered and naïve, out in the world on her own for the first time. She'd fallen head over heels in love and had done an impulsive thing—she had married the soldier in her hometown that summer. Her parents had supported her decision—eventually—but it hadn't been easy at first, because then she'd moved across the country with her new husband. She hadn't even finished her college degree until years later when she was a young widow not knowing what else to do with her life.

Well, she knew what to do now. And that's what she needed to focus on. Her professional assignment.

She pulled out her phone and dialed Pete.

"Lyn?" His voice was scratchy, but he was alert, even at this early hour. That was a good sign.

"Hi, Pete. I need to tell you something. I met with John Reilly and—"

"Oh, hey, I was just going to call you about them."

She paused. "What's happened?"

"I've got information about the background checks."

"Go ahead. I'm listening."

"Margaret—Margie Reilly is a widow. As you know, she's co-owner of the Seaside and lives next door to the business."

"Right."

"Patrick Reilly is the interesting case. We're pretty sure there is a juvenile criminal record, which is closed. Probably related to drugs, because a stint in drug rehab does come up on the adult record."

She remained silent. Drug use among area teens was a terrible problem.

"What's interesting is that Patrick is currently on home detention, wearing a court-ordered ankle bracelet."

She sat up, shocked. Maybe this explained why John was on edge. Why he so carefully watched anyone who came into the family's establishment.

"What's the charge?"

"An assortment, all boiling down to possession of drugs."

"Is he pre- or post-judgment?"

"He pled guilty, but his status is presentencing. The hearing is scheduled for June 5. The John Reilly you reported, the Marine veteran brother? Well, he's on record as being a court-appointed sponsor. He's signed a statement promising to supervise his brother as he's allowed out of the family home to work in the business. Otherwise, Patrick can't leave the two properties. There's a notation about him working in the kitchen."

Which would explain why, as a patron, she'd never seen him.

Then it occurred to her. "Should I investigate Patrick as potentially being involved with the burglaries?"

"Simon already did that. The bracelet tracking indicates he's never been past the boundaries of the family home or restaurant. Evidently, the brother watches him like a hawk. He also has a court-appointed counselor who drops by to give drug tests unannounced. Patrick has never tested positive."

"I understand." Yes, this explained John's protective behavior. "Tell me, Pete, is there anything I should do in relation to Patrick?"

"No. In general, keep your eyes and ears open, but don't attract undue suspicion."

"Right." She glanced up as the rumble of an engine sounded, then snapped to attention. From her position facing the street, she saw Andy's van head up the hill. Raising her hand, she waved, wondering if he knew the story about John's brother. Probably. Andy knew everybody in town, it seemed.

He waved back. His son, AJ, sat in the front seat; their helper, Moon, followed in his pickup, the sides dirty. Both vehicles turned into the driveway next door.

"Okay, Pete, I need to go."

"Has Kitty arrived?"

"No, she's late. I hope she's still coming to meet me."

"Want me to check for you?"

"Not yet. I'll call Karen if there's a problem."

"Keep me posted."

She watched Andy's team hop out of their vehicles. They were late for work, too. Maybe they had stopped at a building supply store, or maybe they were freshly come from the Seaside Bar and Grill, perhaps even quizzing John about just what she and he had been discussing inside her car.

Enough. Her future course was clear: no more lunches spent at John's establishment. Not for the foreseeable future, not until the morning's incident had passed from memory.

"I'll see you tomorrow morning at our meeting point," she said to Pete. They'd agreed on the market down the beach.

"Good luck with the congressman's wife."

"Not a problem." She hung up.

Frowning, she kept her gaze forward, scanning the street, waiting for Kitty MacLaine's vehicle. Lyndsay hadn't mentioned the encounter with John to Pete because John's concern made sense to her now. If she saw him again, she could handle him. Still, it really would be better to avoid the Seaside for a few days. Let

John cool down. Let him think that he'd upset her, talking about Jason.

Her immediate mission was clear: convince Kitty that Lyndsay was a capable interior designer. In no way should people suspect otherwise.

I have to live here, she thought. *Two weeks, while the MacLaines are on their transatlantic cruise.*

Fourteen more days and nights—mornings and lunch breaks and evenings—working in the house beside Andy's crew. They were going to wonder why she didn't head to the Seaside with them for lunch. She needed an excuse. Maybe Kitty could give her one—if she showed up.

Her mobile phone trilled. *Pete again.* Connecting to the line, she said, "Yes, Pete."

"I'm down the street from you, headed up the coast to meet with an insurance company. Thought you might like to know that the congressman's wife just zoomed past. She almost hit me—the woman is a menace. My guess is that she'll be at the house in no time."

"Thank you." She really was thankful that Pete was alert and looking out for her.

"No problem. Remember, Lyn, keep your cover." The phone clicked off.

As he'd warned her, up the street roared what had to be Kitty MacLaine, driving a cherry-red

Mercedes SUV. Kitty exceeded the speed limit by at least fifteen miles per hour—Lyndsay would've been hard-pressed not to issue her a ticket, had she been in uniform.

Kitty parked her vehicle in front of Lyndsay's and hopped out with a saucy wave. Lyndsay felt the smile on her lips and waved back. Given the petite woman's attitude, she surely would've talked Lyndsay into a warning instead of a ticket.

Kitty reminded her of a firecracker. Flaming red hair, a petite, straight-up-and-down boyish build and a manner of walking that fit about three quick steps into what Lyndsay usually took as one long stride.

With a blazing smile on her face, Kitty met her at her driver's door. Lyndsay gathered her oversize purse from the seat beside her and stepped outside. The salty air felt sharp and fresh to her nostrils.

"Lyn Francis? Are you Lyn?" Kitty asked in a loud, clear voice. The words were fast and crisp and seemed to run on in sentences that made Lyndsay strain to keep up. "'Cuz I am so excited to get started today. I'm honored to have you here. I've been a huge fan of DesignSea, your firm, and I can't believe that Paul commissioned you as a surprise for my birthday!"

"Oh, happy birthday, Mrs. MacLaine," Lyndsay said, feigning innocence. In Lyndsay's presence, Karen had conducted a phone call with Kitty's husband on Saturday. The congressman had filled them in as to what he wanted to do for his wife.

"Call me Kitty. And I already checked you out online on the DesignSea website. What a beautiful portfolio you have."

"Thank you, Kitty." Lyndsay tried not to gulp. When Commander Harris had said that Wesley had made her a plausible background story, he hadn't been kidding.

Lyndsay followed along as Kitty wove her way past a picket gate, down a pathway edged by beautiful beach landscaping with rambling beach roses, not yet budded, and clumps of local grasses planted artfully in between white pebbles.

"I can't wait to see the finished home," Kitty said. "I've been staying with my sister in Maine while Paul finished up work in DC. Well, let me get out my keys." Kitty fumbled with a jangly, oversize key ring. Picking out the appropriate key, she unlocked the front door, then squinted at the panel that housed their home-alarm system.

All of the micro-cameras that Wesley had installed last night were well hidden. Lyndsay knew—but Kitty didn't—that they covered every angle of the exterior of the home. In fact,

Wesley might be watching them both entering the home now, for all Lyndsay knew.

"Just a moment while I let us in. But you already know about the security…" Kitty keyed the numerical code into the panel with one finger. Lyndsay stayed respectfully back until Kitty waved her way inside.

The foyer never failed to take Lyndsay's breath away. It was the bank of windows straight ahead that gave the most beautiful, calming view of the beach and sky that Lyndsay had seen from any home, ever. She would love waking up to those windows in the early morning, watching the majestic white seagulls fly through the air. The cloud formations over the wavy blue-gray ocean at dawn. The expanse of soothing beach sand.

"Sit down, let me take your coat," Kitty urged. Lyndsay complied, and sat on the beige leather couch in the downstairs living room.

"Your purse is so beautiful," Kitty cooed.

"Thank you," Lyndsay said. It was made of the softest almond-color Italian suede, and she hadn't been able to resist it. "It was a splurge, but I have a weakness for pretty things." She stroked the soft suede. It was nice to feel like a woman sometimes. These past years, she hadn't seemed to receive that pleasure enough.

"May I?" Kitty asked.

"Of course," Lyndsay replied, and the congressman's wife stroked her hand over the suede.

She looked at Lyndsay and smiled. "I love your plans for the upstairs sitting area."

Lyndsay felt the flush of pleasure spread in her chest. That had actually been her idea, not Karen's, though Karen had warned Lyndsay that the final detail approvals were to be all Kitty's, of course.

"I know that Paul helped by showing you ideas of my tastes," Kitty said, "but honestly, I never would've thought of that style of flooring. And enlarging the closets is a wonderful idea."

Lyndsay's heart seemed to slow. "Closets?" she asked. There had been nothing of the sort in the design plans.

Kitty stared at her directly, as if waiting for Lyndsay to contradict her.

"Let's talk about the back terrace," Lyndsay suggested. "I understand that's where we're starting."

Kitty's hand stilled on Lyndsay's purse. "No, I don't think so."

A crew was already lined up to pour concrete and to bring in plants. There was to be an undercover officer working alongside the legitimate laborers. The task force had set this up.

"Perhaps we should review the plan as discussed with your husband," Lyndsay said.

Kitty's face darkened. "No. I'm happy with the back patio as it is. I like the outdoor hot tub. Instead, I'd prefer that the master bedroom suite and the upstairs living area be updated. You and I will keep it as our surprise for Paul."

If she were a real designer, rather than a police officer, Lyndsay would be terribly concerned. But her job, above all, was to keep Kitty happy, and therefore unsuspicious. Her only real concern with the design plans she and Karen had decided upon was to keep her police-employee laborers busy with a cover story. She needed to fit them in to Kitty's plans somehow.

"Very well," Lyndsay said calmly. They would skip the concrete pouring, but keep the plants. They were on order, with a police planter set to install them. Also, the hot tub would stay.

"Tell me about the master suite, Kitty. It's been locked, and Congressman MacLaine asked that I not enter."

Kitty waved her hand. "Probably because his safe is in there."

"His safe?" Her heart beat faster. No one had said a word about a second safe. Had the congressman even mentioned this to her commander?

"Should I be worried? About the liability," she explained.

Kitty shook her head. "That's not a consideration."

"Okay." Lyndsay kept her voice cheerful. "It sounds like we'll be going against what your husband ordered, then."

"This is my project for my birthday. And I've wanted it for a long time."

"How long have you lived here?" Lyndsay asked conversationally. In the academy, she'd been taught that when a person got upset, that it was best to keep him or her calm.

"We haven't lived here much since we were married. I never liked that he lived here with somebody else. It reminds me too much of...not *me*." Kitty's jaw moved.

Ah. So here was the point of tension.

"And this is your first renovation on the house?" Lyndsay asked gently.

A short nod. There was an internal anger to her that Lyndsay could sense. A resentment against her husband, perhaps.

Lyndsay directed a bright smile at her. She could calm a person in a bad mood. It was one of her strengths. Besides, she felt compassion for Kitty, moving into a house that her husband had shared with another woman.

Kitty wasn't exactly acting in concert with

him. Beneath the smiling surface, she seemed unhappy. Maybe she usually hid it behind a manic, enthusiastic persona. That march of busy-busy-busy. Lyndsay recognized that particular coping mechanism, as well. Being lonely, she did it herself sometimes.

Lyndsay stood. "I'd love for you to walk me through the house, Kitty. When your husband hired my firm, we spoke about your tastes over the phone, and he filled out some questionnaires for us, but obviously, it's preferable to hear about your wishes directly from you. I'd love to see what you feel about everything. Hear what you have to say."

Kitty's mouth pursed in thoughtfulness. "What exactly did Paul say to you about my tastes?"

"You like blues and greens, ocean colors. You want a clean, contemporary design that uses natural materials. Much like what DesignSea specializes in," she said hastily.

Kitty nodded. "He *did* do a great job choosing the design firm," she admitted.

Excellent. Lyndsay silently praised Commander Harris for that decision.

"Why don't we head upstairs?" Honestly, Lyndsay was dying to get into the master bedroom suite and investigate that safe. The team needed to be informed.

"First, let me tell you what I want done with *this* room," Kitty said. "Right now it's just a big empty space with a couch and two chairs. I want to keep the pictures of me—" she pointed to the two nudes over the fireplace, and Lyndsay recognized Kitty right away "—but not on white walls. And we'll need to replace the cracked tile floor. I'd prefer nice vinyl flooring—not wood—since we are at the beach. I really want to see a nice, inviting space with color and modern floors and furniture."

"Of course. I'll make sure that this room is painted and decorated to give it a beachy feel."

"Yes, like what you did in your design. I want you to fix up the whole house like that."

"We only have two weeks," she gently reminded Kitty. "And I have to do *something* with the outside terrace because I already ordered the plants and the crew, but I'll tell you what, I'll leave the hot tub and anything else that you want me to keep. And for now, besides the living room, we'll choose one other room to transform, exactly as you'd like it. But just one. Which would you like?"

She prayed Kitty didn't choose the kitchen, because then she would have to refuse her. But if she'd said that upfront, then Kitty might have chosen it. Kitty seemed to have a perverse streak in her, and Lyndsay, while she felt compassion for her obvious unhappiness, had no desire to tap it.

"All right. Let's go upstairs." Kitty set her chin. She stood, walk-marched over to the curving staircase to the second floor and motioned Lyndsay to follow.

Lyndsay knew the floor plan well, having already worked here for four days. Honestly, what needed the most work was the guest bedroom suite, the rooms where Lyndsay would sleep, which were a wreck, with peeling paint and old, stained carpeting.

Of course Kitty did not choose the guest bedroom suite. Lyndsay followed her down the hallway toward the master bedroom.

Lyndsay paused. Curiosity made her stay quiet.

Kitty tried the handle, but the door didn't open.

"It's locked," Lyndsay said. "I was asked not to enter."

"Well, I want it updated. I hate our furniture, I hate our window treatments, I hate the paint color." Kitty pulled out her key ring again, and flipped through the keys. Dramatically, she opened the door and stepped inside, waving Lyndsay after her. "Isn't it ugly?" she asked Lyndsay.

A king-size bed. Two nondescript dressers—his and hers. Two windows with messy old blinds, drawn. That same white paint that was in every other room. Builders' grade.

Wordlessly, Lyndsay entered the small hall that led to the door into the master bath. Also in the hallway were two walk-in closets.

The safe must be inside one of them. She would check that out later. Turning, she saw a small alcove built into the corner of the room. Here were two more original paintings. Watercolors, smaller than the oil paintings of Kitty downstairs. She peered closer. There was a woman in both paintings, but she didn't look like Kitty. She sat on the beach in front of this cottage, frolicking with two golden retrievers.

"I want this entire master bedroom area updated," Kitty was saying, "including new furniture and bedding. And of course I want the master bathroom remodeled by the time I return from my trip. The open sitting room at the top of the stairs, too. So in summary, I'd like the downstairs living room painted and both main floors, up and down, need to have flooring installed. Of course, that is in addition to the master bedroom and bathroom update."

"Kitty…" Lyndsay warned. It was inconceivable that she could manage all that in two weeks, plus act as an undercover detective.

Defiant, Kitty moved to stand beside her. "I know you have our credit card on file. I know you have a generous limit and more than enough time to implement these small changes for me."

I can't do all the flooring, or the master bathroom tiling, Lyndsay was about to say. But Kitty was gazing at the two watercolor paintings with a strange look on her face.

Lyndsay stilled, watching her.

"It wouldn't be a bad thing if *these* went missing," Kitty spit.

"What do you mean?" Lyndsay asked, her heart beating faster.

Kitty turned and gave her a cryptic smile, then lowered her lashes. "I'm sure they're insured."

Whoa. The cop in her was straining on the leash, eager to interrogate Kitty.

"Who are they?" Lyndsay asked instead, casually. "The woman and the dogs, I mean."

Kitty snorted. "The less said about that, the better."

What did this mean? Lyndsay bit her cheek. Had anyone on the task force interviewed or considered Mrs. MacLaine? Lyndsay would bet not.

"Your husband is an art collector?" Lyndsay pressed. She leaned closer to the paintings. The signature was an illegible scribble. "Who's the artist?"

Kitty laughed. "It's not important. The important thing is that I'm trusting you with the key to this room. But as a reminder, only you are to enter inside. Absolutely no other people can."

"No movers? Or tradespeople? I can't change the furniture or paint the walls in that case."

"Well, then you must be with them at all times, no exceptions. My husband prefers this door be locked. No one should be left in here alone."

"Understood." Lyndsay nodded. She was most excited about the knowledge of the two previously unknown watercolors, and about Kitty's strange reaction to them. Lyndsay realized she was leaving a whole lot of questions on the table, but she didn't want to make Kitty suspicious, and there were other avenues she could take to find answers. The investigator within her was chomping at the bit, in fact.

Still, with all this reno work to supervise, it was going to be a very busy two weeks. Good thing she *liked* to keep busy. "I'll do what I can."

"Thank you," Kitty said. "I'll be excited to come home and see what beautiful things you've done for me." She gave Lyndsay a heartfelt, happy smile.

And Lyndsay couldn't argue with that. She liked to see people happy. Who didn't?

She needed to get the information she'd learned about the paintings to the task force. She would discuss it with Pete during their meeting.

On the plus side, all this work gave her the perfect excuse to skip a few lunches at the Seaside with Andy and his crew.

"You're a hard driver, Kitty. But thank you for trusting me with your home. You have a good trip, and I'll have the big reveal ready when you return."

KITTY'S RED SUV wasn't gone from the driveway thirty minutes when the front doorbell rang. Putting down the laptop where she had been looking for anything related to the watercolor paintings—and coming up empty—Lyndsay reluctantly headed to her guest room, where she had a commanding view of the street.

Andy's van was parked in her driveway. AJ sat in the front passenger seat. Moon in the rear. The engine was idling.

Sighing, Lyndsay headed downstairs and pulled open the door before Andy had a chance to ring the doorbell again.

He met her with a grin. "You're still here. That's a good sign, right?"

Unable to hide her own smile, she grinned, too. It had made her quite happy to have some detective work to attend to.

Andy hooked a thumb over his shoulder. "We're heading to the Seaside. Wanna join?"

Where she would come face-to-face with John Reilly again? Not on his life.

"Wish I could, Andy," she said cheerfully, "but I'm swamped. Mrs. MacLaine loaded me with work. Would you mind bringing me back a sandwich?"

"Okay. You want an Italian sub?"

"Um, yes, please." She really wasn't hungry, but she might be in an hour or so. "Hold on, let me get my wallet." She held up a finger and dashed to the kitchen before Andy could protest. In two seconds, she was back again. "Here's a twenty. I forgot to pick up supplies, so if you could throw a few bottles of water into the bag, I'd be grateful."

Andy took the bill and plopped it into his shirt pocket. Peering at her, he asked, "Is everything okay with you and John? I saw you guys talking this morning. It looked kind of heated."

She forced a smile. "Everything is okay. Really."

"Okay. If you say so." Andy tipped his hat. She remained at the door until Andy hopped back inside his vehicle, then backed the van into the street. From the back seat, Moon gave her a wave.

Smiling to herself, she waved back. But it wasn't until she'd closed the door that she felt truly relieved.

She could only wait and see what John would do now, then deal with it as best she could. Hopefully the background alias that the task force had built for her would be enough to cover her.

It had fooled Kitty. Pray that it fooled John, too.

CHAPTER FIVE

JOHN SAT AT his usual table in the restaurant—the same seat that Lyndsay had favored—and stared at his laptop screen.

Lyn Francis checked out. He'd found her social media profiles and her professional portfolio, though Jason Francis was too popular a name to verify. But in his gut, John doubted that she'd lied about him.

He leaned back and closed the laptop. Frankly, he was acting as if he was obsessed with her. Two days she'd missed coming in to his restaurant, and he was taking it personally. All this stuff with Patrick was making him not trust people. When Lyn had spoken of her family, it had seemed real to him. For that alone, John was inclined to give her the benefit of the doubt.

The door opened, and John glanced up to see Andy and his crew filing in. John waited to see if she was with them, but, no. Yet again, no Lyn.

Feeling antsy, he tucked the laptop under his arm and headed toward the kitchen. At the doorway, he came face-to-face with his brother, staring dully at him.

How long had Patrick been watching? John shot him a look. His brother leaned over and scratched his ankle.

John could tell Patrick to get in the kitchen and help with the phone orders or with unloading the dishwasher, but he suddenly felt tired.

He circled around Patrick without comment and headed into the kitchen. His mother wore an apron and disposable food-prep gloves. Paper slips were tacked on the ledge over the table where she worked assembling sandwiches for a telephone order.

They weren't high-tech at the Seaside. The main reason John had come back, and then stayed on, had been to keep the books, handle the computer work and do the heavy-lifting maintenance tasks. At night, he also handled the bar. It wasn't a small job to manage the place. His mother ran the kitchen operations and the daily menu, but John took care of almost everything else.

While John stood there, the waitress came in with a slip she'd taken from another telephone order and lined that up with the others.

John put the laptop away in the small office, locked the door behind him, then came out to stand with his mother. Distracted by his presence, she frowned. Once she'd had a great laugh, but he rarely heard it anymore. Her Italian mom—a grandmother John remembered with affection, a petite round woman with an infectious laugh, too—had taught her most of the recipes she enjoyed making for the Seaside, and he watched her for a moment as she took a length of freshly made bread, picked up a serrated knife and sliced it in half, as if she were performing a sacred ritual.

Then she measured out a spoon of Italian oil and herbs—her mother's homemade special. She spread it on the bread and added thinly sliced portions of salami, ham, mortadella. The same way she'd taught John to make his own sandwiches from the time he was young.

She smiled slightly as she did it—indeed, it seemed to be her only pleasure. He didn't have the heart to suggest that they talk about selling the place. It had been her dream that Patrick one day take it over, and according to her, that was what Patrick wanted, as well. John felt dubious about that, but said nothing.

"Where's your brother?" she asked, her voice barely audible over the music that was playing over the kitchen radio.

"I think he went back to the house," John said. The small Cape-style home was connected to the rear of the Seaside by a covered walkway his father had constructed when John was young because his father had disliked cold weather.

John had intended to look at the dripping faucet near the dishwasher, but instead he put on a pair of food-prep gloves and picked up one of the pink paper slips. He and his mother worked companionably, constructing sandwiches, side by side. Not saying a word, which was the way that John liked it.

His mother finished the order she'd been working on, then bagged it. She glanced at John. "Your brother's light was on all night in his room again."

"What was he doing?"

"Reading, I suppose."

"That explains why he's tired all day."

"Will you talk to him?"

John talked to him, but it never seemed to do much good. He felt himself gritting his teeth. "Sure."

"He's not like you, John. I worry about him. He's just so sensitive." Her knuckles were white from her grip on the paper bag.

John wasn't going to mention that, sensitive or not, Patrick should be in the kitchen helping her. His mother wasn't blind. She knew that. She also knew that John always put his family first. Always.

"I don't know what else I can do for him," he said, surprised at his own resentment of Patrick.

"I wonder if we could talk with the court about him getting more services for counseling?"

John had been working within the system as best as he could. Frankly, it was exhausting. "Sure, Mom."

"And why don't we call and talk with his lawyer?"

"Because I talked with his lawyer last week." Each time they spoke it cost the business more money—money they didn't have. "He said there's nothing more we can do until the sentencing hearing."

His mother bowed her head. An oldies station played on the radio, which John knew reminded her of times when his dad was alive.

John felt a slow burn. He'd been a teen once, the same as Patrick, but he hadn't hung out with peers who'd done drugs. After Patrick had first been caught and arrested, the courts had begun testing him. He'd convinced John that he was clean.

But then, once they'd stopped the random testing, Patrick had started using again. This time, he got caught because of the way he'd been financing his drug buys. By petty theft. He'd been caught red-handed fencing gold jewelry from a neighbor. And of course, he failed the subsequent court-ordered drug test.

John had felt duped, angry.

Maybe that was part of the reason he'd been so hard on Lyn Francis. Because he'd been fooled by his own brother, maybe he was sensitive about being taken advantage of again.

He heard crying noises. His mom had sat down on her stool, her head in her hands.

Pain, helpless pain seemed to fill him.

"Mom, I hired the best criminal defense lawyer I could find." John stood beside his mother and rubbed her back, which was shaking from the force of her crying, warm and damp from her emotion. "He's going to do everything to keep Patrick from being locked up. He says there's a good chance he'll just get probation. Once we get past that, we can do more."

His mom lifted her head. Red-rimmed, tearful blue eyes met his gaze. Struggling to smile at him, she clasped his hand. "I'm sorry I'm so emotional. I've been trying to hide it from you, but it's just the date. I always feel this way on the anniversary."

For a moment, John was puzzled. And then with a sickening realization, he followed her gaze to the counter and to the daily calendar, set to today's date.

It was the anniversary of Justin's death. The

middle Reilly brother. John felt as though he'd been punched in the gut.

"Four years," she said tearfully.

"I forgot." He had. In all the drama, John had forgotten.

He put his hand on her shoulder. "How about if we take a break this afternoon? I'll call Millie's sister and see if she's available to fill in—"

"No." Wiping her eyes and braving a smile, his mom shook her head. "Please, I'd rather work."

He understood. His mom found her solace in this business she'd built with John's late father.

"I'm going to take a walk on the beach," he said quietly. "Will you be okay while I'm gone?"

"Yes. You go do that. Remember Justin." She gave him a shaky smile.

Numbly, he nodded. His feet seemed to move on their own. Almost without seeing, he pushed through the bar, past Andy and all the rest of the crews, across the street and over the dunes to the stretch of beach beyond. He felt like he needed to breathe. To get out of that room, out of that restaurant and away from those memories.

A forlorn gray sky was overhead, spitting rain on his unprotected head. Drops beaded on his bare arms, prickling his skin with cold, but that didn't matter; his own discomfort would never matter. He stared at the angry waves—

high and rhythmic in their crashing, their never-ceasing crashing—storming on the shoreline as he watched.

He should have been home that day. He should have been with Justin, watching out for him as he'd always watched out for him. Instead, John had joined the Marines because he'd wanted to get out and start his own life.

His mother's tearful eyes always reminded him of that without saying it aloud. Patrick's sullen rebellion expressed it. Maybe if John had been home, then things would have turned out differently.

Before John had left, Patrick was a little kid who had idolized him. When John had returned, for Justin's funeral, then again a few short months later, for their father's funeral—Patrick no longer looked at him the same way.

John bowed his head, faced into the wind, fisting his hands against the rawness. He dug his sneakers into the sand, the approximate spot where his brother's lifeless body had been found. He'd drowned. No one had known exactly what had happened, which was the hard part. The toxicology report had been inconclusive. The death had been ruled accidental, even though his brother had grown up on the water and was a fantastic swimmer. The whys and the hows of the drowning were a mystery to this day.

An anguished sigh came out of him. But he didn't cry. John never cried. Even though all he could see was his brother's face. Justin had been more than his brother—he'd been John's best friend. His very best friend in the world.

Hey, John. The only one who'd written him letters that actually made him laugh.

John owed it to him to be here. His brother had loved this place. Had never understood why John had been so restless and wanted to leave Wallis Point. Had wanted more than to work at a family sandwich shop and beach bar.

Justin had been the family surfer. Beach bum. Charmer.

John turned and glanced at the restaurant. He wondered if Lyn would come by today. He wouldn't mind sitting in her car with her again, even if just to watch the rain. To feel the warmth from her breath that fogged the cold glass.

TWO MORNINGS LATER, Lyn still hadn't come to the Seaside. John felt itchy, but was starting to feel resigned to her decision.

The door opened, and Andy strolled in with his oversize coffee carafe.

"Lousy day outside," Andy said, sliding the carafe across the counter. It made a sound like nails on a chalkboard.

John grimaced.

"You got up on the wrong side of the bed," Andy remarked.

Hadn't Lyn said that to John, too, on that last morning he'd seen her? But John said nothing to Andy. Took the carafe to the kitchen to rinse it before he filled it up again.

He'd fixed the sink last night. The faucet was no longer dripping like a sieve.

"How are you, Patrick?" he heard Andy say behind him.

"Good," Patrick answered. But Andy wasn't supposed to be here in the employee area.

"What are you doing here?" John asked Andy, feeling tired and grumpy.

"I could ask you the same thing." Andy leaned over and stared him in the face. "What did you say to Lyn Francis?"

John bit down on his tongue. He was tempted to ask about Lyn, but with Andy, it was better to act as if she'd never affected him at all. "What do you mean?" he asked noncommittally.

"I saw you talking with her in her car that day." Andy pointed at him. "Ever since then, she doesn't leave the MacLaine house. She's even having her groceries delivered. Did you know that?"

John felt his neck tense. "How is that my fault?"

"That's what I'm asking you."

John couldn't help going over that morning,

yet again, in his head. He stared at the stream of water pounding into the carafe. Man, had he been an ass, accusing her of something that maybe seemed true to him only because he was sensitive to being duped, then forcing her to talk about her late husband. He'd probably hurt her. Maybe that's why she hadn't come.

Suddenly having to blink, he shut his eyes.

Andy, for once, stayed quiet. When John finally looked at him, Andy was arms-crossed, studying John.

"You were rude to her, weren't you?" Andy said.

"I'm not going to talk about this with you," John replied quietly.

"No. Of course you aren't. You could be a stubborn pain in the ass when you were a kid playing hockey, but I thought you'd outgrown it. I guess you proved me wrong."

John shut off the water. "Do you want to make your own coffee?"

"If you act this way with everyone, you'll chase off all your customers."

John opened his fists, then closed them. What did Andy want, for him to admit that he'd been wrong? That in his paranoia over watching out for his family, he'd seen a potential bogeyman that hadn't turned out to be there?

Because if she really was a cop, then she

would still be here watching them. The fact that she wasn't here was evidence enough for him.

"Is she okay out in the cul-de-sac?" he asked Andy. They both knew there weren't too many neighbors living on the peninsula this time of year. "Is Lyn alone at night?"

Andy pressed his lips together in that caricature of sage owl that John remembered from his high-school days. He took a coffee cup from the overhead rack and filled it from the family's communal pot, then sat on a stool before the prep table.

"I'm worried about her, too," Andy confided. "She's up on ladders by herself. I saw her through the windows, pulling down paintings from the walls. A stupid stunt—I wouldn't even do it, but she's obviously got something to prove or she wouldn't be doing it, either."

John had been accused of doing stupid stuff out of pride. He completely understood. "She wants to do a good job for the congressman. How often do you check on her?"

"During the day? Every few hours. But she sleeps there, too. And Cynthia and I don't live in the neighborhood, so it's inconvenient for me to stop over after hours. You live close—*you* should check on her."

John itched to hop in his pickup truck and head out to the cul-de-sac. But even if Lyn let him in the house, then what? It wasn't as if he could strike up a friendship with her.

"John, for cripes' sake, what is your problem?" Andy demanded. "Are you okay?"

"Peachy."

"I'm serious. It seems like, lately, all you are is suspicious of people. Come on."

John whirled to face him. "Did you ever think that I might be taking a break from relationships in general?"

"Oh, yeah. I forgot that you were divorced. Three years ago," he said sarcastically. "And it's not as if it lasted very long."

"Right. Go back to forgetting about it."

Andy stood. "I wasn't asking you to marry Lyn."

John laughed sharply. The idea was so ludicrous, he couldn't even speak. Him, getting married again?

"Think about it," Andy urged. "Bring her out some food or something, some night."

They both knew that wasn't going to happen. John nodded stiffly. "Sure."

"Right." Andy nodded.

It would happen when pigs flew.

IN THE DUSK of early evening, Lyndsay stared at the men standing on her doorstep, not able to believe her own eyes. Or hear her own ears.

"You did *what*?" she asked Andy.

Moon stood beside him, arms crossed, mouth in a tight line. Andy's son stood beside him, also looking concerned, shifting from side to side.

"I know someone," Andy said stubbornly. "Don't ask me how, but I had him run that contractor's license plate for me."

"But…you have no legal reason to do that," Lyndsay sputtered. Then she remembered the background she was supposed to be hiding. "Do you?" she tacked on.

Andy scowled at her. "It doesn't concern you that your tiling contractor's vehicle is registered at an address that doesn't exist? I knew he looked shady. I knew it and I proved it. I did you a favor, Lyn."

She was trying not to panic, she really was. Here, she thought she'd done a wise thing, as far as Kitty's goals and expectations went, by having the task force switch out the patio-concrete-pouring contractors and substitute them for a tiling contractor—in reality an undercover detective, driving an undercover vehicle. But Andy wasn't supposed to know about any of this.

"He works for my firm all the time," she protested. "He seemed fine to me."

Andy set his chin stubbornly. "First, that's not a professional vehicle he's using. It screams fly-by-night or scammer. I don't think you should use him again. Not until we're sure he's legit."

"But he did a good job," she repeated stubbornly. "He's fine."

"What did he do?" Moon asked. "I heard pounding."

Was nothing private in this cul-de-sac? It had seemed so friendly when she was in information-gathering mode. Now their friendliness had turned into nosiness and was biting her in the butt.

"He removed the tile in the master bathroom," she explained. It had been slow going, and he wasn't finished yet. Her contractor had, in reality, been mainly there to check out the oil paintings of Kitty in the living room—Lyndsay had even prepared by taking them down for him to inspect them—as well as the watercolors of the mystery woman in the master bedroom.

That was the contractor's real strength—art appraisal. That he had a beard like a caveman and questionable hygiene had been inconsequential to her.

"I can do that for you," Moon said. "I'm a master at tiling. Why don't you have your agency hire me?"

"You already have a job," Andy pointed out.

"Yeah, but you could spare me," Moon countered. "Lyn can't."

"Look." Lyndsay held up her hands. "I appreciate you guys looking out for me, I really do, but I'm capable of working with my own firm's contractors."

The men exchanged glances. "I'm just helping you out," Andy said.

Yeah, by running a vehicle's license plates. Good grief. What was Andy doing, going to a friend in some official agency on the sly?

"How about if I talk to him for you," Andy said. "Check out his credentials."

She knew he was a genuinely good person who wanted to help. Andy was the type who kept his eye on his kids, his kids' friends, his neighbors. He surely volunteered to help when coaches were needed, or an adult for counsel. She had no doubt about Andy's good intentions.

"Sorry, Andy, honestly, I'm going to have to ask you to back off. I appreciate that you're trying to help, but I'm fine." She rubbed her back—it was killing her. She was going to bed late every night, exhausted.

And it was lonely. So achingly empty in this big house, quiet but for the television and the stereo system.

"You don't look fine," Andy remarked. "You look stressed out."

"I have a lot of work to do, that's true. But I'm safe. Don't doubt that. There's an alarm system in the house which connects to a private security firm."

"But if you fell off that ladder—"

"—then I have a phone I can use." She patted her pocket. "Right here. On my person. Always."

"At least come to dinner with us, Lyn," he pleaded.

"I'm sorry," she said firmly. "This job is important to me, and I'm behind on my tasks as it is."

Andy held up his hands. "You have my phone number if you need it." He glanced to his son. AJ lived at home with him, too.

"Yes, I do," she agreed gently. She mustered a real smile for him. It was kind of them to offer their company for dinner, and if she wasn't undercover, then that wouldn't have bothered her in the least. She would have felt included. One of the team. Not so lonely.

But as it was…

"I really do have to go, guys. I'll see you all in the morning for coffee."

Holding up his hands again, Andy reluctantly let her close the door on him.

No. No, no, no, she thought.

Through the side window, she watched them head down the walkway and climb into their van and pickup respectively, then wheel out of the MacLaines' driveway.

When she was sure they were gone, she slumped to the floor. They were running their own background checks of sorts! What else could go wrong?

She was on the verge of hyperventilating. Luckily, it was time for her nightly meeting with Pete. She needed to let the team know that license plates were being run and to make sure that her support team backed up her cover by dotting their i's and crossing their t's.

Gathering her Glock, she armed herself, then she put on her raincoat and tossed her wallet into her pocket. Locking the doors and setting the home alarm behind her, she headed around back, then down the beach.

It was nearing dark outside. She'd brought her flashlight, and she used it to light her way. Every night she made this trek to her prearranged meeting spot with Pete.

The walk was easy. The evening wasn't as cold, and what little wind there was came from the sea. She walked on the packed sand of low tide. The smell of fresh salt air calmed her nerves. No one else was on the beach.

She turned in to the back door of a mid-size convenience store, grabbed a red plastic basket and headed to the far aisle, away from the register. At this time of night, and this early in the season, the store was nearly deserted. She spent a few moments choosing some fruit in the sparse produce section, then glanced up to find Pete.

Simon—he of the tattooed neck and twisted sense of humor—stood in the back of the market near the refrigerated section. Curious, she joined him, the handle of the shopping basket drooping from her arm, and a few apples and a banana rolling around inside the basket.

She leaned over and studied a selection of packaged hamburger. "Where's Pete?"

"Busy."

"All right," she muttered to Simon, dropping her voice low because there was no coded way to say this, "then please pass on this message. Tell Gary to be careful. The neighborhood contractors are suspicious because his work van is unmarked and unprofessional-looking. So much so that they ran his plate."

Simon's eyebrows lifted, but that reaction was quickly replaced with his usual bland expression.

She sighed—Simon was anything but reassuring—and put the hamburger in her basket. This market didn't carry the grass-fed version she liked, either, but it would have to do.

"Don't worry," he said, chewing his gum. "I'll look into it."

"If there is a problem, we will need to arrange to send somebody else to lay tile. Immediately."

He shrugged. "I'll pass it on."

Why was she getting a feeling that this wasn't a priority to him? She rested her basket on the floor. The true priority was the investigation, not the renovation, of course. "Please do it." She came to her original point. "Did Gary find out anything about those tiles I showed him?" The task force had decided to use the covers as their code. So the *tiles* were really the paintings.

Simon looked at her blankly.

"Come on, Simon. The tiles are essential to this job. Where are we at right now?"

A woman wheeled her cart slowly past them. They waited until she passed. Despite how frustrated Lyndsay felt, she needed to remember to speak in code so that anyone who overheard this conversation wouldn't suspect what they were talking about.

"Do you have a picture of the tiles he was working on with you?" he asked in a low voice.

"You know I do," she whispered. She pulled out her phone and showed it to him.

"Good. Give it to me and take this new one."

"What? Why?"

"In case this was hacked." He pocketed her phone, then passed her another.

She stared at it in disappointment. It looked exactly the same, but it wouldn't have her contacts or her photos. "Is that a real problem here?"

The thought of her phone being hacked took the risks of this investigation to another level.

"Possibly. Only talk to Pete when you see him—he'll be off-line otherwise."

"What about if I'm in the middle of a situation and need a hand?" The task force had given her an emergency number to call.

"You have a number. But don't overuse it."

"Okay, now you're making me nervous," she said in a laughing tone. "What's going on?"

Simon gazed at her full-on. She had to blink at the intensity of his dark brown eyes. Coupled with his neck tattoos, she felt—

Oh, no, she suddenly realized. "There's been another *event*, hasn't there?" she guessed. Another break-in spelled trouble.

Simon gave her a terse nod. Glancing to the left, he waited until a couple was out of sight. Then he passed her something small, wrapped in a cloth case. "There was an unexpected guest who ended up taking a trip down the stairs. The party organizers—" this was the task force's agreed-upon name for the perpetrators "—didn't stick around, so we're even more eager to catch up with them."

"What is this?" she whispered, slipping the package into her pouch.

"A special alarm. Plug it into an outlet beside

your bed. If there's a power outage, it will alert you. You're not a heavy sleeper, are you?"

"With this job, of course not."

He nodded, understanding what she meant. Law enforcement jobs were shift work. Oftentimes, it was tough to get to sleep afterward. Lyndsay always felt wired at the end of a shift.

"If the power goes out unexpectedly, get outside to call us immediately. Don't try to fix the electricity yourself."

"Are power outages common to all these events? Is that something the organizers plan for?" she asked. It was possible that cutting the power to the houses could allow the thieves to bypass the security systems.

"We're not sure yet, but it's a possibility."

"You know, I had the television on the local station all day to keep me company." Newscast after newscast, recycling the same stories. A wayward raccoon, an early season hurricane down in the Caribbean, a multi-car crash that had sent several to the hospital. "I heard nothing about this."

"Private parties don't get broadcast."

Of course. The task force had been keeping reports of the most recent burglaries out of the media.

"Did they get the same party favors this time?" she asked.

"Oh, look at that." Simon made an elaborate show of checking his watch. "It's time to leave." His expression was deathly serious.

"I'm on the planning committee, Simon. I need to do my part."

"You *are* doing your part. It's essential the venue gets redecorated in time. At some point, we'll need you to do more. In the meantime, do whatever it is an interior designer does."

Yet another reminder to maintain her cover. "Tell me about those tiles Gary examined, at least."

"Sorry, gotta go. Just keep at the redecorating and if the organizers show up unexpectedly, do what we discussed." Follow protocol.

"If there's an unexpected meeting, then I'll start the agenda." She would make the arrest. "I know. You don't need to remind me."

"Make sure you call us right away."

"I heard you," she snapped.

Simon gave her a death stare. "I mean it, Lyn. Forget about those fancy tiles and focus on getting the venue ready. And call me if there's a power outage."

No power outage came.

Another long, uneventful day of Lyndsay working to keep her cover, this time accepting deliveries for pallets of upscale vinyl flooring and making phone calls to furniture showrooms to inquire about specifications and availability. Gary never showed up. Neither did any other contractor. And she was too tired to worry about that, or about what the locals might do next to inadvertently threaten her cover. And what about John—was he part of Andy's scheme? Had she somehow shown more evidence to convince John that she really *was* a cop? What if he was the one who'd suggested that Andy get the license plate run? And what if they both decided to have *her* plate investigated, too?

Just dwelling on the possibilities was enough to unnerve her. Thank goodness internet shopping was a great distraction. Lyndsay used her iPad to order the throw rugs, pillows and accessories needed to make the house a spectacular redo for Kitty.

The flooring installation was still her main problem, and time was running out. Gary had left the tiles and grout for the master bathroom on-site, but she'd never tiled before and had no idea how to do it.

In desperation, she watched YouTube videos. Didn't help a lot. Inside the bathroom, she poked at a piece of half-pulled-up tile, thinking that maybe she could at least remove the rest of the floor herself, to help the situation somewhat, when all of a sudden, a burst of water shot into the air.

Gasping, she wiped at her wet face. Cold water seemed to be flooding everywhere. Had she broken a water main, or something? Whatever they were called? She knew nothing about plumbing.

And the water didn't stop coming—it just gushed and gushed. Her feet sloshed inside her sneakers. "No, no, no! Stop!" she shouted, but no one was there to hear her. All she could do was stand and gape, her hands in her hair.

Her heart pounded, her pulse raced. *Everything* was being ruined.

The carpet in the hallway. The legs of the furniture. The ceilings downstairs—was it possible the plaster could fall?

Shut off the water! a voice inside her screamed.

But how? She tried to call up any knowledge of plumbing she could think of…

There was a valve under the sink. She fumbled with it, tightening it, but this didn't stop the shooting stream of water coming from the floor. Neither did the valve behind the toilet.

Maybe there was something downstairs in the utility closet. Or near the street.

She had no idea. And she couldn't call the emergency line, because this wasn't a burglary situation. She couldn't even call Karen, because it would take too long for her to get here.

Lyndsay didn't know what else to do but run across the street to get Andy's help. She didn't stop to find her coat, and her gun was upstairs in the guest bedroom, unsecured in her holster and sitting on the bed, but she ran outside into the sunlight anyway, a sob escaping from her throat.

Stop crying, she told herself. *Pull yourself together!*

She ran into the Goldrick cottage. Andy was leaning against a counter, drinking a cup of coffee. The entire living room had been gutted since the last time she'd been here. Moon and AJ were on their knees hammering hardwood flooring together. She vaguely registered that it had a gray wash, trendy but beautiful.

She'd been spending much too long looking at flooring catalogs—she was officially going crazy!

"Andy, can you come next door, please? Hurry, it's an emergency!"

Andy's face perked up. Emergencies were his forte, thank goodness.

Without waiting for him to follow, she ran back to the MacLaine cottage, her wet sneakers slapping on the pavement, her breathing loud.

She was going to have a heart attack if this kept up.

When she got inside the MacLaine home again, the hissing sound of the water flowing from the pipes seemed even louder than before. "Do you hear that?" she asked Andy, her voice sounding hysterical.

Andy stood inside the foyer and cocked an ear. "Why didn't you turn off the water, Lyn?"

"Because I don't know how!"

The hissing sound was crazy. And worse, a great big, wet stain had formed on the ceiling overhead. Her stomach sank. "This looks horrible!"

"Yep, it's pretty bad," Andy agreed.

She gaped at him. How could this be? She wasn't used to screwing up. She liked to do things right. To be a model police officer, a good daughter, a fun and understanding wife...

And there was water *everywhere*. It leaked from places she hadn't expected. Obviously, she'd hit a hidden pipe. It was messy and unexpected and she was afraid, so afraid that her cover was going to be blown, that the task force would be affected, that the burglars weren't going to be caught. And, yes, even that the MacLaines were going to find out and think less of her for it.

"Where is the utility closet?" Andy asked,

calm in all the excitement. But of course he was, this wasn't his job on the line.

"There!" She ran ahead, opened the door and flicked on the light. "Down those steps."

The steps creaking under his weight, he disappeared for a moment. She heard the grating sound of metal on metal, and just like that, the hissing stopped.

Lyndsay exhaled in relief. The silence was wonderful.

Andy came back and shut the door behind him. "Let's go take a look at the damage."

Nodding numbly, unable to swallow, she followed him upstairs.

It was an absolute disaster. The whole floor—carpets, tile, everything—was covered in water. Feeling shocked, she could only stare at the disaster she was responsible for.

"You'll need to move into a hotel," Andy said, matter-of-fact.

"No! I can't leave the house. It's out of the question." Not for more than fifteen minutes, in fact, or else she was supposed to notify Pete.

Andy rubbed at his chin. "We'll have to find you someone to fix the pipes, then."

A plumber? On a Friday evening? "I…don't know anyone." She gazed at him. "Do you?"

Andy thought for a moment.

"Yes," he said. "I know someone." He glanced at her. "Do you have a problem with John Reilly?"

John Reilly. Who'd accused her of being a cop.

"Why would *he* be able to help?" she asked nervously.

"He was a plumber's apprentice."

She blinked, her mind feeling scrambled. "I thought John co-owned the restaurant."

"He does." Andy casually rocked on the balls of his feet as he studied her reaction. "He also has an uncle who's a licensed plumber. Frank, I think his name is. John worked with him when he was young, before he joined the Marines, enough hours to qualify as an apprentice. I'm sure Frank can stop by next week to check on John's work, if that's important to you."

Why hadn't this come up in Pete's background check? She would have to have a word with Pete when she saw him.

"Um, does John have liability insurance?" she remembered to ask. Karen had mentioned something about that. No one was supposed to work on any aspect of the MacLaines' renovation project without it.

Andy rolled his eyes at her. "He's not going to sue anybody, Lyn." He shrugged. "He's your best option. Give me the go-ahead and I'll call him. Otherwise…" He held up his hands and shrugged.

She doubted John would come, even if Andy asked him. "I don't know," she said.

"Trust me on this, Lyn."

Did she have a choice? She wasn't about to call the emergency number because of broken plumbing, so it looked like she was stuck with Andy's suggestion.

She sighed. "Okay. Please ask John to come. And thank you, Andy."

But before John arrived, she needed to secure her Glock. The last thing she wanted was for him to be staring at her holster again, reminded of all his suspicions.

CHAPTER SIX

JOHN WAS READY to pick up Patrick's video game and throw it against the wall. He was at his wits' end. What to do with a brother who was so uncommunicative, so ungrateful, and so in need of someone to give him a swift kick in the butt?

John had been closer to Justin—closer in age, closer in temperament. Patrick was so much younger. He was the baby and a momma's boy. It frustrated John. How foolish, how needy had the kid been to get in trouble with drugs to begin with?

John confided in no one, of course. Talking about it with other people wasn't a good idea, in his opinion. Like everything else John did, he knew the best thing was to put his head down and press ahead.

Since he'd been home, he'd tried many different ways of connecting with Patrick. Work had failed. He had to nag his brother to get him to do anything around the restaurant. Conversation? Patrick wasn't interested. Honestly, play-off hockey on TV was John's last shot for the night.

John picked up the remote and tuned the channel to the pregame. Boston versus Montreal.

He sat beside his brother on the couch and nudged him. John had taken the night off, and he'd let Patrick off, too. Millie and her sister were covering for them.

Patrick glanced up from his electronic device and sighed.

There was a knock on the doorjamb. Before John could react, Andy came lumbering through, yakking on his phone and waving at him.

"You have to stop doing that," John said to Andy. "This is private space. It isn't part of the restaurant."

Patrick watched Andy with interest. *Great.*

Andy shut off his phone and tucked it in his front pocket. "John," he announced, "There's something I need your help with. You need to come with me *right now.*"

"Sorry, I'm off duty." John shot a quick smile to Patrick. "My brother and I are about to watch the game."

Andy's brow furrowed. "It started yet?"

"In a few minutes," Patrick said.

John blinked. Those were the first words his brother had said in over an hour.

"Hmm." Andy leaned closer to the TV, which was showing a beer commercial. Then he shook his head. "John, this is serious. Lyn is in trouble."

John's heart slowed. Patrick stared at him as if to ask, *Who's Lyn?*

He shouldn't listen to Andy. He shouldn't let himself care. He had more important things.

"What kind of trouble?" John asked.

"She was trying to remove some floor tile herself, and she broke a water pipe. She didn't know how to turn off the water. The place flooded."

"She needs a plumber, huh?"

"I told her about you."

This would give him the opportunity to see her again. He glanced at his brother.

"*I'll* stay with Patrick," Andy said. "I want to see this game."

"You do?" Patrick asked.

"Sure," Andy replied. "I love the sport. I coached your older brothers."

"You coached Justin?" Patrick asked.

"I did. He was a left wing."

The interaction would be good for Patrick. John wasn't sure about the ankle bracelet, though. He was nervous leaving Patrick in Andy's company.

"I'll head over to her place later." John didn't feel like he could take the chance of leaving Patrick right now.

But Andy was already sitting on the stuffed chair opposite Patrick, jabbering about the opposing team—which players were rumored to be injured and who was expected to have a big game tonight. Patrick was lapping up the attention. John had never seen a kid more in need of a father figure.

Patrick glanced over at John. "You don't have to stay."

"He'll talk your ear off."

"I don't care," Patrick mumbled. "Let him watch with me if he wants. You go."

John expelled a breath. If he didn't go, it would look suspicious.

"John, can I talk with you a second?" Andy gestured him to the hallway. John followed.

"Look," Andy said, spreading his hands, "I didn't want to say anything, because I know you have your hands full. But I know your brother is on house arrest."

Oh, great. If Andy knew, that meant a whole lot of people knew. John let out a long breath.

"It's okay, John. I don't think any less of Patrick or you for it."

"It's not me I'm worried about."

"Patrick? Why? You've got to let him live his own life."

John stuffed his hand in his pockets, not answering.

"So will you go help Lyn, please?"

Andy has probably told her about Patrick,

too. Or if he hadn't yet, it was only a matter of time until he did.

"How is she doing?" was all he could think to ask.

"I think the stress of being alone out there is getting to her. She's only here for a couple of weeks, and she's far from being done."

She needed help. That made it easier for him. Part of him did want to see her. Find out why she hadn't been to the Seaside, at least.

Andy clasped his arm. "I called AJ to meet you there with some equipment. Go. Talk to her. Forget about us."

LYNDSAY DROPPED THE last of the dry towels she'd found in Kitty's linen closet on to the puddle on the floor, and ran downstairs to answer the doorbell.

John stood on the welcome mat with his fists in his jacket pocket and a wary cast to his expression. He stared at her like the intense alpha male that he was.

Well, hello to you, too, she thought.

"Hi," she said out loud, crossing her arms. "Thank you for coming."

He gave her a slow nod. Those gray-blue eyes hooked on hers and held.

She inhaled, stepping back. Best to keep this

all business. "Right. The plumbing problem is upstairs," she said in a crisp tone.

He nodded. "Okay."

This didn't feel comfortable. She wasn't sure if he still thought she was a cop or not. Rubbing her arms, she decided it was probably best to be honest about everything she possibly could with him.

That limited her conversation mostly to the state of her emotions. "Um, I'm glad you're here, John, because I'm really over my head here." She lifted her arms in feigned helplessness. "I'm honestly overwhelmed, and I don't know what to do."

He seemed to relax a bit. "Yeah, I know what that's like."

"You do?" She gave him what she hoped was a winning smile. "I, um, haven't been outside much these past few days. I'm even having my groceries delivered. It's my first big, solo assignment with this firm, so I'm trying to do a good job."

He nodded. He could've mentioned that his restaurant delivered meals, but he didn't. She was thankful for that.

He glanced at the ceiling above the foyer. The water stain was clearly showing. He gazed at her. "You'd rather not tell your client until the leak and the damage are fixed, I assume?"

She nodded, relieved that they were both speaking more freely. "Yes. I'm trying to…make them happy and give them everything they asked for. This damage isn't going to reflect well on me, I'm afraid."

"Don't you have any contractors helping you out?"

"Ah… I did, but Andy had his license plate run and then he told me he wasn't comfortable with him being in the neighborhood." She decided not to mention that she would have continued to use Gary anyway, had she been in a normal situation. But she was in anything but a normal situation.

John squinted at her. "This contractor was from out of the area, I assume?"

"Yes. He was from a company that my firm uses."

John gave another wry smile. "Andy is sort of the unofficial ruler-of-the-roost around here."

"I noticed." She sighed again, for John's benefit.

"We're just going to have to work with the situation." John was careful to gaze into her eyes. With a start, she remembered she was in jeans, wet at the knees, a paint-spattered baseball shirt and a ponytail that was in all likelihood ratty and tangled, seeing that wisps were constantly getting in her eyes. But John didn't look down

at her wet knees, or her—she'd just realized—
wet, white T-shirt. She was glad about that, too.

He glanced behind her, up the stairs. "Why
don't you show me the problem?"

"Well, okay. It's in the second floor master
bathroom. Before he left, my contractor was removing the old tile, and when he was smashing
it, I think he may have damaged a pipe. It didn't
rupture until after he left, of course, and as you
can see, I've had a huge mess to clean up. Andy
turned off the water, thankfully, but I'll need to
get that pipe repaired."

"That's not all you'll need," he muttered,
glancing at the ceiling stain.

"How so?"

He looked her in the eyes again. "First, show
me the pipe."

"Okay." She'd secured any evidence of her real
job behind the locked door of her guest room.
Thankfully, that part of the house had escaped
damage. "Come right this way."

She headed up the front staircase, and he
followed. On the way up, she self-consciously
grabbed her long, gray, woolen sweater from the
rail where she'd tossed it during the confusion.
She put her arms through the sleeves, drew the
front edges tight, then tied the fabric belt around
her waist. That covered up her wet T-shirt.

When they came to the threshold of the master

bathroom, she paused. John seemed to be noting the squishy hallway carpet as he lifted his foot up and down. Then he glanced at her sweater. "Andy turned off the heat, I assume?"

"I guess so." Was he implying that it was cold in here? Even though it was April, it was cool outside, and she'd been running the heat at night.

"It's a forced-hot-water heating system," he explained. "You won't have heat tonight until the pipe is repaired and the water is turned back on."

She hadn't realized that. "I'm really glad you came, then."

"Not a problem. Let's take a look at it."

She followed as John went inside the bathroom, his sneakers sloshing over the flooded, broken tile. Taking off his coat, he draped it over the edge of the old-fashioned soaking tub, then took a small penlight from his back pocket. As he crouched down, his shirt rode up, and she couldn't help staring at the skin it exposed above his waistband. A sexy, muscular lower back.

Scooping her damp hair away from her eyes, she bent over him. It was tight inside this small alcove section of the bathroom, and she felt aware of the closeness and the heat of his body as he worked.

Abruptly, he clicked off the flashlight and straightened. Caught off guard, she didn't move away in time. They bumped shoulders.

"Oh," she murmured. Her cheeks flamed. "Sorry about that. I'm just anxious, I guess."

He raised one eyebrow at her. "No need to apologize."

Downstairs, the door creaked open, loud enough that Lyndsay jumped.

"Lyn?" It was AJ Hannaman's voice. "Are you here?"

"Yes!" she called. "I'll be right down."

Without glancing at John, she headed downstairs to the foyer. From the footfall on the stairs behind her, she knew John followed. Just inside the front door, Andy's gangly son smiled sheepishly when he saw them both. "My dad sent me over with this." AJ hefted what looked to be a very heavy toolbox.

"Great," John said.

They all trooped back up the stairs.

To his credit, John looked at nothing on either side of him. He didn't gawk or appear to judge. Not at the towels she'd spread, or at the MacLaines' personal possessions. He just headed back inside the partially demolished bathroom.

Her sneakers still damp, she stepped carefully over the spongy mess and joined him again. He squatted on the floor as he sifted through the contents of the toolbox.

"Do you think you can fix it?" she asked, unable to keep the hope from her voice.

He straightened, palms on his knees. He turned slightly. AJ was right there, behind her.

"I need you to go buy a part," John said calmly to AJ.

John jotted down a part name on a notepad he'd fished from the toolbox. What was it about John that all who encountered him obeyed him?

John noticed her nervous expression. "It's not the end of the world, Lyn. I'll fix it. No one will be the wiser. You'll be fine."

"Just look at the mess." She twisted her hands.

"We're lucky the electricity is working—that way I can set up the fans. We'll need to turn up the carpets and dry the floor beneath as best we can. Hopefully that will keep mold from forming. We can probably salvage the carpet this way." He glanced at AJ. "Do you have any fans in your dad's van?"

"Yeah," AJ answered. "Three of them."

"Excellent. Let's go bring them in now."

"Okay," AJ said.

They left, then she watched as John and AJ lugged in three of the largest industrial-size fans she'd ever seen. John picked two of them up like they weighed nothing, then trudged up the stairs.

"Thank you," she said honestly as he headed into the bathroom again.

Coming from inside the bathroom, she heard the rattle of a doorknob.

Oh, no. Was he trying to access the MacLaines' forbidden bedroom? She ran inside just in time to catch him trying to force open the door.

"We can't go in there," she said. "That's off-limits."

His bent head lifted to her, and she was struck mute by his remarkable light blue-gray eyes. Like gunmetal.

"We have to," he said pragmatically. "If there's carpet and it's wet, it will mold."

She nodded uneasily. "There's carpet," she reported.

"Then we'll need to roll it back, along with the padding beneath it. Hopefully, the damage isn't too bad. Best-case scenario, we dry it out, then put it back. With a cleaning, it will be okay."

"And…worst-case scenario?" she asked nervously.

He gave her a wide grin. "You'll need to write somebody a big check to replace it."

She gulped. It was true the MacLaines had been generous with their budget, but she and the team would be accountable if there was a problem.

Quickly, she made her decision. "Turn around," she told John. "Keep your eyes closed."

He raised his eyebrows at her. Oh, she could have kicked herself. She sounded exactly like the highway cop she was.

But she gave him a saucy smile, so he complied.

Lifting his chin to the ceiling, as if letting her know that he was in charge and this yielding to her whims was only temporary, he crossed his arms. With a grudging twist of his lips, he shut his eyes.

As quickly as she could, she groped for the hidden spot where Kitty had shown her the brass key, then gripping it in sweaty fingers, she plunged the key in the lock and turned...

The door must have been swollen stuck, because it didn't budge. Great, she would need to have this fixed, too. She put a shoulder into it, cringing when she only seemed to give herself a bruise.

Behind her she heard a grunt, and felt John's body heat, his slight snort of expressed breath. "Move aside," he ordered softly.

She was learning not to argue, just sigh and step aside. It was easier this way.

With one firm push John had the door open.

Inside, it didn't look bad. In fact, it looked the same as when Kitty had shown it to her. Lyndsay took a tentative step inside.

Squish.

Immediately she groaned. The carpet was a sopping sponge.

And the bed...that huge, mammoth, monstrosity of a bed with its frame—and legs—made entirely of wood…

The water couldn't be good for it.

"I'm lucky that Kitty asked me to replace the furniture. I already ordered her a new bedroom set. This might not be such a bad thing if the old one is ruined." But she was worried about the clothes closets. Holding her breath, she peeked inside. Both were designed such that shelves kept everything up off the floor. Only a pair of rubber flip-flops were on Kitty's floor, not put away. How lucky she was that Kitty was neat.

She poked her head back from the closet, and saw that John was stepping carefully around the room. "Not all the carpet is wet," he reported. "Just the side near the bathroom."

"Is that good news?"

"It is."

She blew out a breath in relief. She needed to keep this carpet.

"However," John said, "we still need to clear out the furniture on this side so we can pull up the rug to dry it. Help me move this bed." He stripped off the bedding and pillows, set it on a couch on the other side of the room, and was in the process of dragging the mattress upright.

Feeling herself blushing, she rushed over to help him. Grabbing the mattress by the handles, she used all her strength to lift her end and walk forward with tiny, awkward steps as he led the way to a drier place in the den.

She suspected that he bore the heavier burden, but she wasn't about to protest.

"Okay. Steady," he told her. She lowered her end, then stepped out of the way, watching him.

The muscles beneath his T-shirt strained as he lowered the mattress into place. A slight sheen of sweat glistened on his brow, but he shot her a wry smile.

She didn't know what to say. She felt strangely tongue-tied. *Aware*, that was the word. Aware of his strength. His maleness. Her own vulnerability.

But she wasn't lonely. In fact, she felt rather... pleased with his company. He hadn't acted suspicious of her, asking questions and probing. Could it be that he was accepting her at face value?

She faked giving him a sheepish look. She didn't feel sheepish, not at all. "Besides the box spring, there are two more overstuffed chairs and a bedside table."

"Let's get to it, then."

She nodded, and walked ahead of him. "Um, please remember not to mention to anyone that you were in the MacLaines' bedroom."

He paused beside the first chair. With a secret

smile to her, he crossed his heart with his hand. "What bedroom?" he said, winking.

She exhaled. "Thank you, John. I mean it."

He bent and picked up the chair himself, in one swoop. "You'll owe me, though."

She blinked. Her heart raced harder. "How so?"

With a chuckle that made a low rumble in his throat, he strode out the door with the chair. As he passed her, over his shoulder he called, "You'll have to eat dinner with me. As payment for my time."

She relaxed. Was that all? "Okay. I have groceries, so I can make us something."

He came back into the room. Shaking his head, he said, "No. Out to dinner."

"Oh, no," she said firmly, brooking no nonsense. "Forget it. I'm much too busy. This is going to make me lose two days as it is, and I can't afford—"

"You can't take the time out for an hour to have a meal at a decent place?"

She shook her head. She didn't want to go down this road and argue with him about this, because the truth was, she couldn't just leave without arranging it with the team. Going to lunch at the Seaside had been part of her duty earlier, but now, staying close to this beach house and keeping her cover were her duty.

She sat in the chair and realized she was worrying her lip.

"What is it?" He leaned on the arm of the couch opposite her.

She decided to just come out with it and be as blunt with him as he was with her. "Honestly, John, it's just that you were so suspicious of me earlier. I've…been thinking about that." She swallowed.

"Yeah. About that." He stared at his hands.

Her heart was pumping crazily. She had to be very careful how she behaved here. *Wait. See what he has to say.*

He finally looked into her eyes. "I'm afraid I owe you an apology."

She released her breath slowly.

"I'm sorry I confronted you the way that I did." His brow creased, as if weighing a decision. "I did it because I'm under a lot of pressure. The court made me responsible for employing my younger brother, and I've been…protective of him. It makes me extra suspicious of strangers. When I saw you in our parking lot that day, reading what looked like numbers into your phone, my antennae went up. I thought maybe you were an investigator or a cop checking up on my brother."

"Well, I'm not," she said softly.

"Has Andy said anything to you about me, or my family?"

She hesitated. "He told me you were in the Marines. That you'd come back quieter than you used to be before you left."

He gave her a hurt look. "It's true I was in combat, but I'm not suffering from PTSD, if that's what you're thinking. I'm quiet only because I hadn't expected to be working in the family restaurant. My brother has drug problems, you see, and he's been through rehab twice. I'm hoping this time it sticks. He...has a court date June 5, and I need to get him through that without incident."

She reached out and touched his hand. "It sounds like you need a break."

He laughed softly. "Yeah."

Impulsively, she made a decision. John had made a big leap in coming clean with her. To a point, she could trust him. "Yes. I would love to have dinner with you." But she still couldn't leave the house. "Why don't we order something in and eat here?"

He smiled at her. "Sure. Let's do that. We'll make it easy." He fished out his phone from the back pocket of his jeans and pressed at the screen. Someone on the other end appeared to pick up right away, because John said, "Hi. This is John. Can you send Jeff over with a Margherita pizza and a large salad? I'm in Congressman MacLaine's cul-de-sac…" He gazed at Lyndsay. *"What's the house number here?"* he mouthed.

"Um…" She drew a blank.

"…Ah," he said into the phone, "I don't have the house number, but my truck is parked out front. On the beach side of the street, second house in." There was a pause. "Yeah, I know. Get to it when you can."

He discontinued the call. "Sorry we don't have much in the way of dessert. I wish we did."

"You have a sweet tooth?" she asked.

"Yeah, anything chocolate." He laughed self-consciously.

Just knowing that small detail about him seemed so intimate. She liked it. "I make killer chocolate-chip cookies. If I had the ingredients on hand, I'd make a batch for you."

He smiled. "That would be great."

"I owe you a big thank-you for coming to help me out."

"No problem." He stood. "The order will take a while—Jeff, our nighttime delivery guy, says it's busy. So how about we finish up with the furniture, then we'll lift up the carpet?"

She nodded, and he picked up the small table in the alcove. Flexing, he stretched his arms over his head.

And stopped.

He put the table down. His head slowly tilted.

She went over to stand beside him. John was staring at the two watercolor paintings with a strange look on his face.

"What's the matter?" she asked him. It seemed personal to him the way he gazed at the paintings.

He slid a sideways glance at her. "Nothing. They seem familiar, is all."

Her heart beat faster. "How?"

He shrugged. "I don't know. They depict this stretch of beach. Take a look at the jetty in the background."

She peered closer. He was right. "Do you know the artist?"

He gazed at the watercolors. "No, they're not signed that I can see." With a quick shake of his head, he bent to pick up the table again. "Are you going to help me?" he said with a smile. "Or move out of the way?"

She grasped two legs of the table. It was probably nothing, but he had given her a clue about the paintings. Maybe it was even safe to assume that Congressman MacLaine's first wife was the subject. Too bad she couldn't call him herself to ask…

Backing out of the bedroom with mincing steps while he walked forward, muscles nicely flexed, was making her throat dry. John really was an attractive man. *But I'm here for the investigation,* she chided herself. Tomorrow she would venture out to the beach and check exactly what the paintings showed. Perhaps there were locals she could question...

Her reverie was interrupted by AJ, returning with the plumbing part John had wanted, and John made quick work of fixing the leak. AJ stayed to help, because he said he was interested in plumbing. Lyndsay hovered near, but spent most of her time wringing out wet towels and sopping up water.

After John finished and tested the water and heating systems, AJ went home. It was just the two of them. Just as they finished setting up the last of the fans, the doorbell rang and their hot pizza was delivered. It smelled mouthwatering.

She put out two place settings on the kitchen island, using Kitty's seashell-themed ceramic plates and aqua-blue glasses.

John washed his hands, then sat at the stool opposite her. He waited while she helped herself to a slice.

The crust was crispy; the sauce and cheese sparse but delicious.

"We have a wood-fired pizza oven in the kitchen," John said. "But it can get busy, especially on Friday nights. I apologize that we had to wait so long."

"I didn't know you have a pizza oven." She wiped her mouth with a napkin.

"Yeah, a good part of our afternoon and evening business is take-out pizza. Lunchtime is mostly sandwiches."

"Which makes me curious." She set down her slice. "How is it that a Marine veteran—who now co-owns a restaurant—also has the skills to be a plumber?"

John took a long swig of cola before answering. "You really want to know?" he murmured.

She already knew the answer to her question—sort of—from Andy, but she wanted to hear the details from John's lips.

"I wouldn't have asked if I didn't want to know."

He made a small laugh with a slight exhalation, as if her answer amused him.

She *was* feeling more comfortable with him. Some of her caution was even wearing off, enough to want to know more about *him*. She was interested in him.

"I went to Wallis Point Vocational High School and trained in plumbing," he said.

"Oh. That was before you joined the Marines?"

He nodded. "I worked for my uncle during summers and for a few years before I joined up."

"Did you like plumbing?" she asked. "Honestly, you seem pretty good at it to me."

"It's been a handy skill to have, especially as a small business owner, and I still help my uncle every now and then when he needs an extra hand."

She believed him. "Did you ever think of *starting* a plumbing business?" she asked him.

He smiled at her, his eyes crinkling. "Funny you say that. A long time ago, my brother and I had a plan to go into business together. Reilly Brothers Plumbing." His smile faded. "But then my father made us an offer to go into partnership on the restaurant. I didn't want to. My brother did. I joined the Marine Corps and..." He shrugged. "I liked it."

"But now you're co-owner of the Seaside."

"Yep, I came back after my father passed away, and it's for the best for everyone." Abruptly he stood and found his jacket. "Sorry, I really should get back and check on the business now. Fridays are busy nights. And then there's my brother." He shrugged. "You should be all set with your water, and with the rugs. Just keep the fans on until morning. I'll stop by and check on it all after the morning rush."

She wiped her hands and stood, too. Obviously, he was as busy as she was.

"Okay," she said. "Thanks for everything. I mean it, John."

He gave her a mock salute. "Anytime."

Then he was out the front door, carrying the toolbox to his truck and carefully placing it in the back.

She watched him, hands in her pockets as the truck lights faded around the corner. He'd helped her so much tonight, and she really did feel less lonely. It just made her achy that he was so mysterious. And wary. And yet, so responsible.

JOHN STRODE INTO his mother's family room in time to see both his brother and Andy pumping their fists into the air.

Andy stood when he saw John. "Boston won a nail-biter, four to three."

"A real close game," his brother said, his eyes shining.

John shoved his hands deeper into his pockets. It was good his brother was happy. Andy was a decent guy for doing this for him. Nosy, but decent.

John walked Andy out to his truck, alone. The evening rush had tapered off, but there were still a number of cars in the darkened lot. John checked to be sure no one could overhear before he spoke.

"Lyn's water is working and turned back on," he told Andy in a low voice. "The wet carpets are drying out. I'll check on them tomorrow morning."

Even in the faint light of the streetlamps overhead, John could see that Andy was smiling. "Good. I don't know what it is about Lyn, but I worry about her like a daughter." He eyed John. "And you two Reilly boys were like sons."

"Yeah, well. What do you think of the third Reilly brother, Patrick?"

Andy cleared his throat. "Margie is friends with Cynthia. She's been sharing some of her concerns."

His mother went to church with Andy's wife, Cynthia. Of course. John closed his eyes. He'd never thought his mother would be the one to let the news out. "Do a lot of people know?" John asked.

"No. It's not a shame to you, John—don't think of it that way. It happens to people. Yeah, it's true that Patrick is going to have a hard row to hoe, and that some people will hold it against him, but you don't have to feel responsible. You can live your own life, you know."

John was trying. But it wasn't as simple as Andy made it out to be.

"I told Lyn about him," he said.

"That's great!"

"Because I assumed that if you hadn't already told her, then you would be telling her soon." He gave Andy a hard look.

Andy had the grace not to protest.

"Look," John said. "My priority is getting Patrick safely through his court date. That means I can't have people coming in here looking to talk to him about his problem, or gawking at him, or what have you. Especially if he's going to run the Seaside someday. And I promised the court I'd watch him. I promised my mother I would protect him and get him through this. She's terrified of him going to prison, with good reason. I'd appreciate it if you would support me with this."

"John, you always know I support you."

"I know." John clapped Andy on the back. "Just do me one more favor. Don't say anything else about me to Lyn. Okay? Not one word. Anything else that she knows about me has to come from me in my time, as I trust her more. Can you honor that?"

Andy gave him a sly smile. "About time you did some courting."

John didn't know about that. It was true he was intrigued by her. And he really didn't know all that much about her beyond the fact that she was a work-focused interior decorator and widow of a Special Ops soldier.

If he decided to get to know her better—big *if*—he would make his own assessments.

He waited until Andy had driven off, then turned and went into the house. The light in the television room was off; his mother had gone to bed, and Patrick appeared to be inside his bedroom. The door was closed, but a sliver of light shone underneath.

John knocked on the door. "Patrick? Can I talk to you?"

The reply was muffled; John couldn't tell what he'd said, so he opened the door and went inside. Patrick was lying on his bed, wearing headphones. When he saw John, he sat up.

John leaned on the edge of the doorjamb. The room was a mess, but he wasn't going to say anything about it. It was hard enough on him and Patrick as it was.

"I'm sorry I've been rough on you. I'm just trying to get us both through the court date. I'm thinking that after that's over, we'll work more about transitioning you to running things around here."

Patrick blinked. "Okay," he mumbled.

"How was it with Andy? Would you like him to come back and visit you?"

"Yeah. He's a good guy."

John nodded. "I've been keeping our friends away not to hurt you, but because I thought I was protecting you. How about if I go easier with that?"

"Yeah. That would be good."

Not a great conversationalist, his brother, but John shared that trait, so he couldn't complain.

"Okay, then." He stood awkwardly. "Want me to turn off the light?" He turned for the switch. There was a picture on the wall beside it.

"No. Leave it on," Patrick said.

But John was staring at the picture. It was a watercolor painting of a beach scene and someone surfing in the distance. He'd noticed it before, of course, but he'd never really *noticed* it. And, now, when he looked closely, he saw that a signature on the painting was legible: "From Justin to Patrick."

A lump formed in John's throat. Justin's death was like a ghost that hovered over everyone in his family. Patrick missed him as much as John and their mom did.

John touched the corner of the frame. He hadn't known that Justin had taken up painting watercolors. It was an amateur effort, but pretty good.

Justin and Patrick had surely grown closer while John had been away in the Marines. Dumb of John, but it had never occurred to him before.

"Good night, Patrick," he said softly, and closed the door behind him.

On the way to his truck, it occurred to him that this was where he'd recognized the watercolor paintings that Lyn had shown him earlier. He'd known the style had seemed familiar, but he hadn't been able to place where he'd seen it until now.

It was probably nothing. Justin had always had a lot of friends.

CHAPTER SEVEN

LYNDSAY SPENT A fitful night. Dozing off, she had an erotic dream, and the man in the dream wasn't her husband. It's was John's face she was seeing. John's smile. John's eyes. John's touch.

She woke in the early dawn hours, shaken. How was it that she was so taken by a wary but kind bar owner/Marine veteran she'd only recently met?

She needed to shake off her confusion, because later this morning—after the rush, he'd said—he was coming over to check on the plumbing work and the drying carpets, and she'd better get herself straight before he arrived.

Outside her windows, the weather looked sunny, with puffy, white clouds. She'd been cooped up too long with little outdoor exercise, and she needed to walk and stretch her legs. She assumed that John wouldn't arrive until after nine o'clock, so she tossed on her jogging clothes and sneakers.

Before she went downstairs, she checked on last night's problems.

The water damage was still depressingly evident. Turned up carpets. Stained walls. A stack of tile that needed to be laid.

There was no way she alone could fix what needed to be fixed. She could never coordinate or finish what she'd promised Kitty in time. The place was a disaster.

She'd never felt so overwhelmed. Her eyes filled with tears. Blinking, she wiped her eyes on her sleeves.

As she stumbled downstairs, she happened to pass the alarm panel in the hallway. *There are cameras here*, she remembered. Wesley had installed cameras that recorded everything happening on the outside of the house.

She stopped, feeling even worse. Why hadn't she thought of them last night during all the excitement? Surely, someone in the task force monitored them. They would have seen her running outside yesterday, in tears. They would have seen Andy arriving to help. Then John, then AJ. They would already know that she'd faced an emergency last night.

And yet, no one had contacted her. No one had sent a signal. No one was really concerned about her at all.

She'd been deserted by her real team. These few weeks, she'd been truly alone, and she hadn't realized how much until now.

Shaking, she took out her phone. If she continued on the path she was on, then the MacLaines would return, angry with the home destruction she'd wrought. The men on the task force might solve the case without her. She would go back to her old life worse off than she'd been before.

She keyed in the emergency number that Pete had given her. Until now, she'd prided herself for not using it. No more. She needed the okay from Commander Harris to hire some properly vetted local contractors if he would not provide a department-vetted crew. She understood they were busy investigating the Seacoast crime scenes and following leads, but she needed the task force to step up and do their part for the MacLaine stakeout, too.

She walked out the back, through the patio doors and about a hundred yards onto the beach. She sat directly on the soft, cool sand to wait for Pete to arrive.

Two seagulls saw her approach, and they swooped in to stalk beside her. *No, I don't have any food for you*, she silently told them. The gulls paraded around, orange beaks in the air, then deserted her, too. She put her head between her knees. Maybe she just needed a good cry. She couldn't remember the last time in her life she had sat and indulged in a good cry.

"Lyn?"

A familiar, deep voice. She jerked her head up, blinking and wiping as fast as she could to blot away the telltale tears.

John stood there, an early-morning jogger in shorts and a gray sweatshirt. She hadn't even heard him approach—pathetic of her.

"What happened?" he asked gently, crouching beside her on the sand.

She made a small laugh. "Nothing. I'm just feeling sorry for myself, is all."

Straightening, he held out his hand, and she used it to hoist herself up.

"Thank you." She held his hand for a few seconds longer than she should have. He had a warm, strong, capable hand, and she really needed that right now.

Shoot, she thought. *The emergency call to my backup team.* She needed to undo the call she'd just made.

"Can you hold on a second?" she asked John, fishing in her pocket for her phone. "I need to finish a text message to my employer."

He nodded, walking a few paces away to give her privacy.

He wasn't leaving, though, she noticed. At least *somebody* wasn't deserting her. He cared enough to stand by.

With trembling fingers, she typed out the retraction code that let her backup team know all was well. *No need for you to come.*

She stuffed her phone in her pocket and rejoined John.

The sun hung just over the waves to the east. The Wallis Point sunrise was spectacular, and for a moment she stood still to appreciate the red-and-orange rays. "It's beautiful here," she remarked.

"Yeah. I try to get out on the beach every day."

"I should try harder, too." She walked companionably alongside him, headed toward the jetty in the near distance. She'd never actually gone in this direction. "I think I've been alone inside that house for too long. I love my job, but…it's really getting to me."

"How so?" he asked, turning to look her in the eyes.

She felt herself blushing under his close attention. "Just that I'm doing too much of it alone. I don't mean to complain, but I need to hire more tradespeople, and my firm isn't helping much at the moment."

He nodded. "I was going to mention that." He glanced at her again. "Do you have a budget?"

If she got approval from Commander Harris, she did. "Yes."

"Then I suggest talking to Andy about it. Moon really does have tiling skills—he could finish the bathroom floor quickly." John unconsciously moved faster as he problem-solved for her aloud, and since his gait was longer than hers, she had to walk quickly to keep up. "And AJ paints walls and ceilings," he continued. "I know they're contracted at the moment, but I'm sure they could squeeze you in. Andy thinks the world of you."

She couldn't help smiling at that. "Andy reminds me of my father." She missed not having him to bounce ideas off.

John smiled at her, too. "Yeah. I know what you mean about that." Then he frowned. "Sorry I had to leave you so abruptly last night."

"I understand," she said, slowing down as he slowed, too. "You're in charge of the restaurant and your brother. I just appreciate you helped me out of a bad jam. I don't know what I would have done."

"You'd have managed," he said softly. A few joggers were on the beach with them—she noticed him watching them.

"Did I interrupt your run?" she asked.

"No." He wiped his face with his long-sleeved sweatshirt. "I was just about finished anyway, and I need the cooldown." He glanced at her. "Honestly, I was coming over to check on you.

You must have read my mind, being outside as you were."

She laughed. "I'd originally had it in mind to walk this way anyway." She pointed toward the jetty, which was in the opposite direction of the boardwalk where she usually met her team. She'd meant to check where the paintings had been made, but now wasn't the right time. It would seem too forced. "Anyway, I was going to walk for fifteen minutes or so. Just to clear my head."

"It's possible to walk out on the jetty rocks," he said. "Past that, you can see a cove known for its fishing." He glanced back at her. "But I don't mind heading back and checking on the carpets now, if that will make you feel better."

"You won't get in trouble, missing the early shift?"

"I own the Seaside. How can I get in trouble?"

"True." She smiled. "In that case, then, let's keep walking."

"I was hoping you'd say that." He gave her a smile that showed a dimple. She felt like sighing.

"Do you run every morning here?" she asked him as they continued heading toward the jetty. He looked fit, not in a runner way but more of a soldier way. "I mean, I lived on post for a while, and I remember all the physical training after morning formation."

"That was a long time ago." He turned for a moment and watched a group of young men and women in wet suits, swimming after a boat. "Lifeguards," he pointed out. "They're prepping for hiring tryouts now."

Nice. But she didn't particularly care to talk about anyone other than him. "How long have you lived in Wallis Point?" she asked as she kept to her path just above the shoreline.

"Most of my life." He kept pace a half step ahead of her.

"Were you born here?"

"Mmm-hmm," he answered.

She took that as a yes. He shaded his face with his hand. Between his body turning away, the dark sunglasses and his noncommittal attitude, she understood something. "You don't really want to talk about yourself, do you?"

He grinned at her. "Nope. I'm not interesting. But you are."

"Am I?"

"Yes. Where did you grow up?"

"Very well. If you really want to know about me," she mentioned pleasantly, picking up a stick and using it to trace along the sand beside her. This was an easy question to answer. She had an entire false backstory mapped out. "Well, I've lived all over." Partly true, but not completely. "I'm an only child." She skipped the cop-dad part—he already knew that. "I went to college for interior design, then I got married."

She stopped chattering long enough to notice that John had a distracted look on his face. Of course, he probably didn't want to talk about her late husband. He'd been married once, too.

Yeah, she didn't want to talk about old loves herself, come to think of it.

"You have a local accent," he noted.

"I didn't know there was such a thing as a local accent."

He chuckled. "Everybody has an accent of some type, whether they realize it or not." He looked at her, as if wanting her to give a name of a hometown. She didn't want to get too specific like that. But his eyes watched her so closely.

A little boy was up early, flying a kite with his granddad. As she gazed up at him, she saw the kite begin to swoop down.

He turned around and saw it, too. With a look of concern and a warming, he pulled her close to him, out of the way.

"Sorry!" she heard the granddad call vaguely as he got the kite under control again.

John's arms were around her. His hand was on her head, as if protecting her from the sky.

She didn't need to be protected. The kite

hadn't come that close, and even if it had, the damage would have been slight.

Breathing slowly, she was instead vividly aware of how it felt to be within his arms. Easy. Pleasurable.

"Sorry," he murmured, stepping back.

"No, don't be," she found herself chattering. "You saved me from a potentially nasty head wound."

He smiled as if joking with her. "You know I wasn't trying to cop a feel or anything."

Not that it would be unwelcome, she bit back.

"Are you the type to cop a feel?" she asked lightly instead.

He barked out a laugh. "Yeah. Right." Then he glanced toward the house. "I should take a look at the carpet so I can get to the restaurant."

"Thank you, John. Come on."

"Sure." Now the sun was at their back, no longer in their eyes because of the curve of the beach.

"I spent part of my childhood upstate in the mountains," she said softly. "I don't know why, but I always felt lonely without siblings." It was absolutely the truth, and not what she'd planned on divulging. Mostly, she told him because she wanted him to know what was real about her. Crazy as that seemed.

He glanced at her for a long time, longer than

was natural as they walked to the MacLaines' patio. It seemed to her as if she'd surprised him, or as if he didn't quite know what to make of her. Either way, he held himself back somewhat. As if there were some things he kept to himself. Like her. They were both burdened with obstacles because of their circumstances, it seemed.

They passed by the outdoor hot tub, and he remained silent as if thinking over everything they'd said. On the surface, the quiet was congenial and friendly—underneath, she wasn't certain what was going on. She just knew that she felt good to be with him.

She unlocked, then opened the slider.

He stepped inside the homey kitchen. She was glad that one room, at least, hadn't been torn apart.

"Lyn," he murmured in that gruff, sexy voice of his, "if you ever need help with anything, you're welcome to come and get me."

"Okay," she said softly. She would gladly do that. Smiling at him, she led him through the kitchen toward the staircase. "I'll stop by the Seaside and avoid Andy the middleman," she joked lightly.

But John paused by the window near the front door, a crease on his forehead. "Actually, I meant to say that I live over there." Pointing, he indicated the house across the street. "Behind the blue house, two cottages are tucked into a cove beside the town dock. The smaller house, the gray one, is mine. Do you see it? Just head over there if you have any more problems you need help with. You're always welcome."

"Oh," she said softly. She stood beside him, gazing at the tiny speck of the corner of his house in the distance. She was grateful for the offer. For the concern. For the human connection, however slight. For suddenly not feeling so lonely anymore. "Thank you, John." Silly her, she had a lump in her throat.

He nodded. He seemed protective of her, and proud of it, too.

Which made her smile to herself. If only he knew, she didn't need his protection. Not at all. She just wanted his company.

Too bad she was leaving in a week. Successful in her mission or not, she still had to leave this pleasant little community when her job was finished.

JOHN GAZED AT yesterday's handiwork with satisfaction. In the daylight, the bathroom plumbing he'd fixed looked fine. He'd expected nothing less. No, it was the water-soaked carpeting and under-padding that he'd been most worried about.

Luckily, though, it had all dried out. If Lyn

chose not to tell the MacLaines what had happened, then they wouldn't see it, in his opinion. She would come out of the broken-pipes drama okay.

"I have a carpet-cleaning machine at the Seaside." He straightened, stretching his arms. "How about if I bring it by tomorrow? Any carpets that you choose to keep will look like new."

"Thank you," she said, straightening along with him. "Kitty wants the carpets in the main rooms replaced, but I need to keep the carpet in the bedroom, so I appreciate the offer, John."

"No problem." He liked being helpful with her. In his own life, Patrick wasn't real grateful for what John did for him, and honestly, his mom was so fragile he didn't expect much as a matter of course.

He blew out a breath. He didn't want to think about them right now. "In the meantime, Lyn, let's get this bedroom carpet stapled into place. I'd like to fix the swollen doors, too. My tools are at the house. I can get them and be back in ten minutes."

"Okay. If you don't mind." She gazed at him with her windblown hair and rosy cheeks, and part of him was a goner.

Mind? It was getting easy to be in her presence. He didn't regret taking the time to talk to her more. His suspicions were getting replaced by the beginnings of friendship. It made his burden with his family seem easier, somehow.

"Hang tight," he said. "I'll be right back."

On the jog to his house, he couldn't get her out of his head—this sweet mystery woman with the face like an angel, yet a cop father who'd taught her to carry a sidearm. No sidearm today, though. Not last night, either. He'd thought briefly of asking her about it, but he was deliberately not probing too much. The sight of her curled up on the beach crying had torn at his heart. Things here obviously weren't easy for her.

There had been that one moment with the kite mishap when she'd curled against his chest as if not wanting to leave.

At the end of the day, she was lonely. Maybe he was, too. In any event, he trusted her story. And the fact that she was leaving had made her a safe person to confide in.

At his house, he dug around in his toolbox to make sure he had what he needed. Then he hopped into his truck and drove to the cottage.

She met him at the door. Upstairs in that weirdly locked master bedroom, he fixed the doors, then showed her how to work with him to get the rugs straight so they could staple the ends again.

No one would be the wiser. The MacLaines

would never know she'd accidentally flooded the place.

The whole operation took about an hour.

"I don't know how to thank you," she said, rubbing her arms as she knelt in the bedroom, still empty of furniture. "Yet again, you've saved my butt."

While he'd been gone she'd changed her clothes, and now she wore jeans and a soft, fluffy sweater. When she'd leaned forward beside him, working, the loose edges had moved, showing him a sliver of skin on her back. He'd felt himself wanting to touch it. To move his hand up her back beneath the white sweater.

She sat back on her heels. "You know, it's a funny thing about those two watercolors," she said, pointing to the nook in front of them. "I wonder if you can tell me what you think of them."

Still distracted by her show of skin, he reluctantly glanced up to see what she was talking about.

Oh, the paintings.

"I'm trying to figure out whether to keep them in the design plan or not," she mused. "I checked the internet for the artist's name, but I didn't see anything. What do you think?"

That it was best not to bring Justin into it. John hadn't talked about him to her. He wasn't sure he was ready to. "I think maybe it's an amateur's work," he said carefully.

She tapped her chin. "I hadn't considered that. Then again, I'm not an art specialist. I wonder if anyone around here is."

"Not that I know of," he murmured. Where had Justin learned to paint? John wasn't even sure. It wasn't something he'd done when John was at home. "There are art colonies, especially in summer," he remembered.

"Yes, that's a good point." She was about to say something else about it, but he was saved by his phone ringing.

He glanced at the screen. It was his mother calling. "I have to get back to the Seaside," he said reluctantly to Lyn.

"Of course." She stood, looking at him as if not sure what to say.

He stood and set the table back in place, beneath Justin's paintings. "Shall I send you my bill?" he deadpanned.

"Um, yes, that's fine. I'm certainly willing to—"

He scowled at her. "End that talk. I was just joking with you, Lyn."

"Oh, right." Her cheeks turned pink, then she laughed.

Maybe she was confused by what exactly was going on, but he wasn't. Bottom line—he liked this woman. He was attracted to her. And by the way he'd been catching her looking at him, especially when they'd been on the beach together, he knew she was interested, too.

AFTER JOHN LEFT, Lyndsay let out a long breath. She couldn't deny that spending time with him had turned her mood completely around. She actually felt like smiling, which was a miracle after her disastrous early morning.

Standing in front of the watercolor paintings in Kitty's bedroom, Lyndsay contemplated them once more. The subject was a thin woman wearing a long skirt, her face obscured. She frolicked with two matching golden retriever dogs. A seascape was the backdrop, with a hint of the jetty showing in the background.

The paintings were pretty enough. If Lyndsay owned them, she might display them, too. John's point about them being produced at an artist colony made sense. Once more, she got the feeling that John knew more than he was saying, but then again, that was classic John.

He kept most things tight to the vest, although every once in a while he surprised her by showing his true feelings and what he'd been hiding. And he did so more frequently, as they got closer.

Yes, her job was to get closer to members of

the community and to keep her eyes and ears open. But how close was she supposed to get?

She shook herself. *Enough.* Time to get Pete on the phone so she could get back to work.

Now that John was gone, she armed herself and went outside on the back terrace. She was in the midst of dialing the emergency number to reach Pete when she saw a dark shadow creeping up behind her.

Adrenaline shot through her veins in an instant. Springing into action, she grabbed her Glock from her concealed holster and dove behind Kitty's hot tub.

"Lyn?" a voice whispered.

It was Pete, dressed in a generic brown uniform. Her heart still pounding, she lowered the Glock and stepped from her hiding spot.

"*What* are you doing?" she asked him, suddenly angry. "You nearly scared me to death."

"I got your signal earlier, and I needed to check for myself that you weren't in any danger." Pete lowered his hand away from his belt, where she knew he kept his concealed holster. Obviously, he was on edge, too. "Things are heating up, and we've been busy behind the scenes. There's a lot more going on with the case than you're aware of."

"Well, make me aware, and I'll make you aware about what's going on here."

"Okay," he said cautiously. "You first."

She pointed to a camera, above and behind them, aimed in the general direction of the hot tub. "Is anyone even monitoring these cameras? They're positioned all around the outside of the house, but does anyone even check on them?"

"No." Pete spoke in a low voice. "We don't have the staff right now. Wesley is busy fitting cameras in another house up the coast, and Simon and I are busy chasing down leads."

"Then why did we bother with this camera charade?" she seethed.

"Because if something happens and we need to check the recording on the saved hard drive, then we can. Furthermore, we'll have evidence for the prosecution."

"Okay, but if we're so shorthanded, then pull me off this renovation project and let me do some investigating."

"That would be tantamount to breaking your cover. No, Lyn. Based on the patterns of the break-ins, it's only a matter of time before this cul-de-sac is targeted. We need you here. I know how hard it is. I know it's boring work sometimes."

"*Boring* isn't the word I would use," she said sarcastically.

Pete sighed. "Did something happen that we need to know about?"

She put her hands on her hips. "Last night I suffered a water-leak blowout upstairs. I hired a local plumber to fix it, but the damage is significant. Worse, I'm even further behind on these renovations. I'll need the go-ahead to hire other local guys to repair the damage and complete the tile installation. I have Kitty's permission to use her credit card at my discretion, but I'm just letting you know from an operations standpoint so you don't flip out if you happen to catch one of the tradespeople coming and going on the cameras."

Pete's forehead creased. "Have we already vetted these tradespeople?"

"Yes, all of them. And by the way, you missed that John Reilly is a plumber's apprentice."

He shrugged. "Is that relevant?" He held up his hand. "Never mind. Hire whomever you need. Any other problems?"

She blinked, momentarily surprised that he'd agreed so easily. Pete was certainly different from Simon.

"Yes, there is something else," she continued, staying on the offensive. "I want to know what the follow-up is from Gary, the art expert you sent here last week. What did he say about the origin of Kitty's paintings?"

Pete planted his feet and gave her a look. She got the feeling he was going to launch into a speech, and he didn't disappoint. "Lyn, you don't need to worry about that aspect of the investigation because we—"

"Is my intel important to you or not? I'm keeping my eyes and ears open, as Commander Harris directed. And after Gary left, I learned further information from one of the locals, but I couldn't forward that information to anyone. Simon told me to stop communicating with you at all except in the case of a dire emergency. And sorry, it may not be dire to you, but to me, a waterlogged second floor with no working plumbing or heat *is*."

Pete winced. He held up his hands. "Okay. I get it. Don't blame Simon or me, though. We've been ordered to keep electronic communication to a minimum. We're pretty sure that hacking is involved, but we're not sure what technology the burglary ring has, and as such, we don't want to take chances."

"A burglary *ring*? Are we sure about this? How so?"

Pete sighed. "Sometimes we have to keep you in the dark, Lyn," he said softly. "That's why undercover work isn't for everyone."

"Don't patronize me. You and I both know that I'm the one on the front lines, and as such, I need to know what I'm dealing with."

He frowned at her, but she stared back. She'd

countered him well with her gun handling; he had seen that. No way could he claim otherwise.

"We have footprints from three different men," he said quietly.

Her heart pounded. How she wished she could be part of the fieldwork beyond this cul-de-sac.

"Any matches?" she pressed. "Any leads?"

Pete's lips pressed harder. "None."

So she was still a sitting duck out here.

"Have there been any more break-ins?" she asked.

"Since you met with Simon? No. But the thinking is that we've had the moonlight and clear atmospheric conditions. Now we've got some overcast weather and dark nights coming up, so we're expecting that to change."

Food for thought. She would have to be careful.

"Well," she said, "I'd like to share my leads about the paintings with the task force. Maybe that will help." She motioned Pete to the door. "I want to show you the paintings in question and talk about a theory I have."

Nodding, he followed her inside to the large downstairs living room. Kitty MacLaine, in all her tastefully nude glory, gazed at them from above the fireplace.

"I looked up the artist that the congressman commissioned for these on the internet," she said. "He's New York–based, he's famous, and the subject, of course, is my client, so these paintings are of interest. There are two smaller watercolors upstairs."

Without a word, he followed her upstairs, waiting outside Kitty's bedroom as Lyndsay withdrew the key to the MacLaines' private rooms.

She paused outside the door to the master bedroom suite. "Kitty asked that I not let anyone inside. Her husband has a second safe that he didn't mention to us inside one of the closets."

"Interesting," Pete mused.

"That's what I thought." She opened the door—easily and soundlessly now that John had fixed them—then pocketed the key. She led him to the alcove where they were displayed.

Pete stared at them. "Take a look at this." He pulled out his phone and scanned through some photos before holding out the screen for her to get a better view of one.

It was a similar watercolor, but with a different subject on the beach and no pets. "It's the same artist," she said.

"We're not sure."

"Sure we are. Look at the expression on the two women's faces." She pointed between his phone and her paintings on the wall. "It's the same."

He squinted closer. Made a small noise in his throat. "I hadn't noticed."

She had. She was detail-oriented.

"Where did you get this image?" she asked Pete. "Did you find it online?"

"No. There's nothing at all online—believe me, we checked with our image-matching software. We also checked with the top auction houses we work with. They had no idea what this painting is."

She got a feeling again. A hunch. She gestured to the photo on his phone. "Was this watercolor stolen from another seacoast home?"

He nodded grimly. "It was, along with a bunch of others. We weren't focused on this one right away, not until your tip, because other, more valuable paintings were stolen. We brought photos of the pictures here that Gary had taken to the owners of the burgled homes. In three out of five homes, they told us that these paintings were similar to what was taken from them. Two of them hadn't even realized their painting was missing—it wasn't on their radar to check, precisely because they aren't valuable."

She couldn't help smiling. *She* had done this. She was breaking open the case, she could feel it. Just to make sure and be careful, though, she asked the question: "Are there any other artists in common with all these break-ins?"

"So far? No."

"It still might be a coincidence. Maybe the thieves are just taking whatever art they can find in addition to the contents of the safes. Maybe they're art connoisseurs—who knows? But to follow this lead, we need to talk with the owners of the other paintings to find out where they got them and who painted them."

"We did that. In one case, the painting came with the house when the owner bought it furnished. It used to be a rental, and no one knew how it came to be on the wall. In the second case, the owner thinks his late wife bought it at a local crafts fair, but he's not sure. The third owner doesn't have a clue. He inherited the home from an aunt. He had only one image he could find of it, quite by chance. What I have on my phone is blown up from a bigger picture he gave me, of a room in his house during some sort of party. Wesley cropped it down to this single image of the painting."

"Has anyone talked with Congressman Mac-Laine about his two paintings?"

"Not yet. We can't reach him for another forty-eight hours."

"Can't you or I contact him through a satellite phone or something?" Cruise ships weren't completely inaccessible.

"We could, Lyn, but it's not important enough of a question to disturb him."

"Oh, the VIP gave his orders, did he?"

"His wife did. Evidently, she's adamant that she have his undivided attention." He glanced fiercely at her. "That's need-to-know, and it's to go no further."

"Of course." Without thinking, she made a lips-are-sealed sign with her fingers before her mouth. Just like John had.

Wow.

"Well," she said, moving right along, "I have a tip. One of the locals mentioned that there are summer artist colonies on the seacoast. My thought is that the talented amateurs sell their paintings for cash."

"Could be worth checking out. What's the name of the artist colony?"

"I plan to search the internet this afternoon."

"Sounds good. I'll set up a call with you and Commander Harris for Monday," Pete said. "Prepare to make a case to him for contacting Congressman MacLaine and then seeing where you can run with this."

"Thank you." She hadn't expected this from him, at all, and she appreciated it.

Pete glanced at his watch. "Meet me at the rendezvous tomorrow night at eight."

"I thought you were busy," she remarked. "That's why I got Simon last time."

"I'm still your backup, Lyn. And I do have compassion for your situation."

"Do you?" Without thinking, she glanced toward John's house. She wouldn't mind his help with her internet search.

"Tonight," she said impulsively to Pete, "could you please relieve me for dinner?"

He sighed. "Tonight?"

"I need to get out, just for an hour or two."

"Yeah. Okay." He scratched his head. "What I'll do is I'll access your cameras remotely from the hard drive and monitor the place in real time."

"You can do that?" she asked, surprised.

He looked guilty. "We have the web location and user ID and password, so, yes, we can."

Amazing. If she had known this, she would have requested it more often. "Great. I'll call you tonight when I'm ready to leave." She paused for a moment. "Do you like homemade chocolate-chip cookies?"

Pete grinned. "Love them."

"Then you shall be rewarded."

He smiled at her. With another glance at his watch, he stepped outside the room. "I'm off. Remember to keep your cover."

"Yeah, you, too." Since he'd taken the precaution of dressing in a bland uniform similar to the way a cable repairman dressed, if he was seen then she had a story for nosy Andy.

She let him out downstairs again, by the kitchen exit, and she stood before the back doors, arms crossed, as she watched him walk past the hot tub and over the sand dunes.

That had gone well.

And now she had an honest excuse to see John again.

FOR THE REST of the day, every time Lyndsay passed the upstairs windows, she gazed out at the gray cottage that John had pointed out as his. *Just head over there. You're always welcome.*

A sense of joy filled her, all the sweeter after her morning of anxiety. She loved the possibility of combining two things that gave her pleasure— talking with John, and forwarding her police investigation.

Humming, she decided to research artist colonies first. She found several that looked interesting, but they were upstate in the lakes region and nearer the mountains, which was ironically her home turf. She planned to ask John for help with the seacoast region, but only if they could speak organically about it. She didn't want to raise his suspicions.

Later in the afternoon, she phoned the small

market down the beach and ordered groceries to be delivered. Chocolate, butter, eggs, flour, sugar, baking powder and vanilla flavoring—she set to work mixing cookie batter using her mom's recipe. After the batch finished baking, she set it on a wire rack on the counter to cool, then turned off the oven.

She took a quick shower, put on some lip gloss and mascara, then threw on a thin pullover and a fresh pair of jeans and some sneakers. It felt naked being without her Glock, but she slipped her driver's license and some cash in a wallet and tucked that into her pocket, along with her mobile phone. When John's vehicle arrived in his driveway, home from work, she would call Pete, then head over. If she walked all the way around using the streets, it was a twenty-minute walk. Hiking a direct route across the street and through the grass path—the way John had jogged this morning—would take five easy minutes to reach John's front door.

She kept a periodic watch for him, but it wasn't until eight o'clock that John's truck drove into the driveway. She saw him turn off the engine and the headlights, then get out. Once inside, his house lights went on.

Her heart beating in anticipation, she forced herself to wait five more minutes before she called Pete.

She scooped her cookies on to a pretty plate and wrapped it with a sheet of plastic wrap. At the last minute, she decided to bring her Glock along. Because…well, it was part of her job.

She really didn't know what would happen, or who she would cross.

CHAPTER EIGHT

JOHN CAME HOME after a long afternoon and evening of staffing the bar, minding the till, watching the door. Saturday nights were always crowded. He wanted nothing more than to take a hot shower and chill out, away from the public.

Inside the bathroom upstairs, he peeled off his clothes and stepped under the steaming spray. The water pounding on his back, he leaned his hands against the tiled wall and zoned out for a few minutes. He was wound up from dealing with everyone else's issues. Backing up his employees. Herding and keeping an eye on his family. They were all good people, just…maddening sometimes. He got the feeling they'd all been in too close contact this past year. After Patrick was settled, John needed a long vacation to think.

Ding. The motion-detector alarm he'd installed for his driveway went off. Could be anything—a critter, probably. Still, he turned off the shower and groped for a towel.

Ding-dong.

That was his doorbell. His pulse kicked into

gear. Since it was nighttime and no one had called ahead, he doubted it was good news. Who was in trouble—Patrick? His mother?

He grabbed his jeans from the floor and tugged them on. The T-shirt he didn't bother with—it smelled like wood smoke and pizza, anyway. If this was an emergency and he had to leave the house, then he kept a hooded sweatshirt on the hook by the door. Boots were down there, too. And his wallet was still in his back pocket.

On the way past his bedroom, he caught a glimpse of Toby's gray-and-brown-striped tail. The cat hid himself under the bed. Good. It was the best place for him.

John took the stairs two at a time. The porch light had come on—he could see it through the side window, but whoever was on the other side wasn't in view. As he'd been trained to do in the Marines, he stopped beside the door.

He peered cautiously, until he caught a reflection.

Lyn Francis.

Every muscle in his body instantly relaxed. It should have told him something that his first reaction to seeing her was pleasure. And to think he'd once suspected her of being someone other than who she was. Seemed strange to think of her as a cop now. He'd caught her crying today—cops didn't cry. They were hard-asses, like Marines. They didn't worry about water leaks, and they didn't take long walks on the beach and lean against a guy's chest, lingering too long.

They also didn't show up at his house on a Saturday night holding a plate of what looked to be homemade cookies.

Smiling to himself, he opened the door. "Have you come to feed me?"

"Um, yes." Her eyes were huge as she stared at his bare chest.

He'd forgotten about that. He still had water droplets on him from the shower. Even his pants stuck to his wet skin.

He grabbed the sweatshirt, put it on and zipped it up so she would feel more comfortable. "Please, come in." He held the door wider as she stepped tentatively past him.

"I'm sorry," she said, her lashes dipping. "I should've given you advance notice. I obviously wasn't thinking clearly."

"That's okay. I have a motion detector. I knew someone, or something, was outside the house before the doorbell even rang."

She laughed. "Why am I not surprised?" she teased. Then she held her plate forward. "A small token of my gratitude for last night and this morning."

"Nice." He closed his eyes and breathed in the scent of the chocolate-chip cookie. "You brought the one thing we don't have on the menu." He gave her a smile. Her eyes were so hesitant and blue. And she'd remembered what he'd said about liking desserts—he appreciated that. "Want to have some with me?"

"Okay." She glanced around. His housekeeper had been by this morning—the place looked pretty good. It was clean, and the air smelled like lemon. She smiled shyly at him as they went into the kitchen. She set the plate on his kitchen table, then took off her jacket to hang it over a chair.

"I took your advice," she said, folding her hands and dipping her head. "Since I'm stuck here this weekend, I indulged in my love of baking. It's been a long time, but..." She nudged forward the plate. "Care to taste my efforts?"

"Thought you'd never ask." He reached under the cellophane and snagged the biggest one, right on top. He took a big bite. Bittersweet chocolate and crumbly cookie, crisp the way he liked it. Grinning, his mouth full, he waved her to take a seat.

She pulled out a chair, but Toby, that curious rascal, stealthily came out of nowhere and curled his tail around her ankle. "Oh!" she said, jumping in surprise. "You have a cat."

He reached over and hauled up the old miscreant so she could sit down peacefully. Holding him one-handed under his arm like a football, he pulled out a chair and sat, too, settling the creature on his lap. "Lyn, this is Toby. Toby, meet Lyn."

All smiles, she reached over to pet the tabby cat. "He's a handsome fellow, isn't he?" She scratched Toby behind his ear, the way that he liked it.

"He turned sixteen in March, or so I'm told."

"Wow, that's great. Was he a rescue?"

"No, he's—" *Justin's*, he was about to say. Strange, but it was the second time in one day that he'd been prompted to tell her about the third Reilly brother. Swallowing, he absentmindedly ruffled Toby's fur. Maybe it was a sign.

"John? Did I say something wrong?"

"No." He smiled to reassure her. "Toby belonged to Justin, my brother. The middle of the three Reilly brothers," he clarified. "I'm the oldest, Patrick is the youngest. When Justin—" He took a deep breath. "After he passed away and I came home, I took over Toby's care."

"I'm so sorry. I know that's a really weak sentiment, but I really am sorry, John."

He nodded. He believed her. "I know, Lyn."

"So…you've had Toby a long time. And you're taking good care of him." She stroked the cat on the striped fur between his green eyes.

"Yeah. We get along pretty good."

"How did Justin pass? If you don't mind my asking."

He didn't mind—not as much as he'd thought, anyway, and that was strange for him. Lyn wasn't like anyone he'd ever known. When her clear eyes assessed him, it was with gentle understanding. Maybe because they'd both been through loss.

He picked up a cookie, but he didn't eat it. He just sat with it in his hand, poking the crumbly edge. "He passed away four years ago in a drowning accident," he said quietly.

"Is that why you came back to Wallis Point?" She tilted her head and said, "And now you're taking care of everybody in your family, even Toby."

"I don't really think of it that way," he protested.

"But it's true."

"When Justin died, it was traumatic and sudden for my family. My parents and Patrick were in shock. Then my dad died of a heart attack a few months later, and my mom was…" He let his voice trail off. "It was bad, Lyn. And I couldn't be here right away because I was overseas." There had been so much guilt about how little he'd been able to do, about how his mom had been forced to make all the arrangements herself. He remembered that feeling, eating up the pit of his stomach.

"And so now you're the responsible one, taking care of everybody because you're the oldest and you feel like that's your job."

He took a bite out of the cookie. "Yeah, maybe that is the gist of it."

"Is that what you want?"

He smiled at her, this perceptive interior designer who'd dropped into his life and made him think about what he was missing. "No. But it's the way that I'm wired."

"Patrick," she said sadly. "You're really trying to help him, aren't you?"

"He's said he wants to take over running the restaurant. I was really praying that I could train him. That he'd avoid prison and adapt to this vocation that would make him happy again. He was just a kid when I left home."

"But…he's not doing well, is he?"

John shook his head. "No."

"And until Patrick's okay, you feel like you're in limbo?" She looked so pained for him that he wanted to do something about it.

"You know, Lyn, I didn't tell you this stuff for you to judge me or to feel sorry about it."

She reached for his arm and clasped him with her warm hand. "I do judge you and think about you, but not in the way you expect."

"Okay." It came out warier than he'd wanted.

"What I mean is, I think you're strong and respectful and you don't leave people in the lurch. And…you have no idea how important I think that is, do you?"

He reached out and cleared a strand of blond hair from her lips. She was wearing pink lip gloss. She'd been speaking so passionately she hadn't noticed the strands sticking. Her hair felt silky and her eyes were shining, and suddenly it was all he could do *not* to touch her.

"I like you," she whispered.

He brushed his thumb across her soft cheek. Sifted his fingers through her hair, near the delicate spot at the nape of her neck. He shifted in his chair, and was vaguely aware of Toby's weight shifting, then a set of claws digging into his thigh as Toby jumped to the floor.

John didn't care. He just wanted to touch Lyn. To lean closer and breathe in her aura. She smelled like warm chocolate and vanilla scent. He just knew she would taste like the sweetest woman he'd ever kissed.

Her tongue slowly licked her lips.

He leaned closer to her as she leaned closer to him, and they met halfway. He kissed Lyn Francis with gentleness, savoring the hunger she kissed him back with. Her hand lingered on his arm near the sleeve of his sweatshirt, then finally, tentatively, pressed against his bare chest, her small palm sending heat to his skin.

It felt right to him. She had a heart he could retreat to. A way about her that made him feel refreshed and regrouped.

AT WORK, LYNDSAY was Officer Fairfax. One of the members on the team. Asexual in her work uniform. Levelheaded on the gun range. Full of authority to the occasional motorist she had the duty of ticketing.

But John kissed her the way a man kissed a woman, in a way she hadn't been kissed in years.

She felt warm in her most intimate places. Damp between her legs. Tingling in her nipples.

She kissed him back, again and again. He tasted good, like her own baking, and he smelled good, like sandalwood soap, and he made her feel like she wanted to find a warm bed to climb into with him, get naked and curl up her toes...

She moaned, lacing her fingers through his fine, shower-damp hair. She moved to deepen their kiss, wanting to get closer to him. But their pace was sweet, leisurely and unhurried. Like a slowly building fire.

A sharp, piercing pain hit her in the bare ankle. "Ouch!"

Toby glared at her from under her kitchen

chair. If she wasn't mistaken, Justin's cat had just stabbed her with his claw.

"Bad Toby." Chuckling deeply from his chest, John reached to pick the tabby up. "Sorry, Lyn. I'll put him upstairs to bed."

She loved that John loved cats. It was a surprising, tender side of him that she hadn't expected. "Don't be too hard on him," she chided as John headed for the stairway. "He's jealous that I'm taking your attention."

"He's just going to have to get used to it," John called back.

"I didn't come here *planning* to kiss you," she said guiltily. She was thinking of her job. From a professional perspective, it had been an unwise move.

"No?" John came back and smiled at her from the doorjamb, Toby giving her a pouty-cat expression from the safety of John's arms. *Lucky cat.*

"I…just wanted your company," she said. It was the truth, she realized. Her old foe, loneliness, seemed to go away whenever she was with John. But now there was something more. She could get dangerously used to coming over here at night and kissing him.

"Tell you what," John said. "How about if I put Toby upstairs, then come back and open a bottle of wine? While I'm gone you can find an old movie on Netflix for us." He hitched a thumb toward a doorway that led to another room. "The television is in there. Bring the plate of cookies and we'll…"

We'll what? she thought, as his words trailed off. *We'll get comfortable together on the couch? We'll get along well, we'll crave and enjoy each other's company, build our rapport?*

She could just see them getting comfortably mellow with the wine, her feeling loved and excited by his company, then the two of them going upstairs. They would have a lovely, lovely night together. While Pete was at home watching on the camera, waiting for her to return, and wondering where she was—perhaps even calling her on his department phone to check up on what she was doing…

It could never happen. She had to stop this, now, because it was completely impossible with her job. She'd forgotten her work circumstances in the joy of getting closer to John. To bring up paintings, or art colonies now seemed silly. There was no place to gracefully slip that into their conversation, and honestly, she didn't want to. There was only…*this* she wanted. His company. The two of them talking. And kissing…

"Or not," John said slowly, his gaze on her face. He thought her hesitation had to do with *him*. It didn't; it had nothing to do with him. It had only to do with her ability to keep her two lives separate: work and personal. And yet, she was only one person, and they were both two sides of her, and all during this night, she had been showing him the true personal *her*.

She got up and went to him in the doorway, and this time she was the bold one. Stretching her arms around him and the furry, scowling Toby, she tilted her head and looked up to John. She gazed at his beautiful, masculine face, dark with stubble from not having shaved since morning, and gave him a quick but passionate goodbye kiss.

When he rested his hand on the curve of her back, she broke the kiss and whispered in his ear. "May we have a rain check for some other time?" Maybe once her assignment was over. "I have to be at the MacLaine house tonight because I—" she reached into her imagination and pulled out a perfectly plausible excuse "—I have to be present for a work call. I'm afraid I didn't plan this visit out very well, but I should head back now." She sighed. "I'm sorry I'm such a workaholic. It's just…"

"Yeah, I know how much your job means to you. That's good, actually." He nodded thoughtfully.

But before she could ponder over why she felt sad to hear him say that, he put Toby down, then sat on a kitchen chair as he reached for a pair of boots.

Wait, where was *he* going? Her heart leaped in alarm. "I can walk myself back," she said quickly.

He laughed. "Yes, I know you can. I know you have your weapon, too," he teased. "I can see it concealed at your hip. But, sorry, I can't let you walk back in the dark without company. It's just how I'm made."

He had to be such a protective gentleman, didn't he? She sighed, exasperated. Jason had been the same way. She knew better than to argue, because that was to criticize their definition of manly honor.

"In that case," she directed, "I'd rather you drive me than walk."

He shrugged without hesitation. "Okay."

There was a method to her madness. If they drove, then they could say goodbye in a darkened car, away from the cameras and Pete's watchful eye. If John kissed her goodbye in front of the MacLaines' door—and now it would be awkward if they *didn't* kiss—then Pete might get the wrong idea about her commitment to the case, and nothing could be further from the truth.

"Thank you, John," she said gently. With a light voice, she said, "You can keep the cookies."

He smiled in good humor, but he still looked

thoughtful as he stood and grabbed his truck keys from a nearby shelf. His gunmetal-blue eyes didn't meet hers now. His gaze seemed to skim away from hers, as if he was already withdrawing from her.

No! Something inside her stomped its foot and pouted. *Talk to him! Bring him back!*

This was very surprising to her.

Lyndsay pondered this new aspect to herself as she followed John to his truck. As he unlocked the driver's door, she headed over to the passenger side. Before she got there, though, he leaned over the seat and opened her door for her. Gentlemanly, but not *too* solicitous. She liked that.

As she climbed in his truck, the seats felt cold. It would be so much nicer in Wallis Point when the weather got warmer.

John started up the engine. Unfortunately, they were at the MacLaines' driveway in no time. She was still mulling over in her mind what to say to him by way of a goodbye.

"It's okay, you don't have to take me to the door," she murmured. The driveway was long and curved, and it was awkward to navigate into or out of. "Pull over here, on the street, and you can wait until I'm inside." Did she sound too bossy and meticulous to him?

But John did as she asked. As he put his hand

on the gearshift, she lightly placed hers on top of his. "I'm sorry if I'm confusing you, John. I really do like kissing you."

He turned to her. In the shadows, she couldn't see his expression. But he wasn't leaning toward her to kiss her goodbye.

"It's actually better for us," he said smoothly. They weren't connecting anymore. She could feel the shift in energy. "I have a lot of responsibilities right now, and I have to focus."

"Well, I'm willing to work with you," she said quickly. She just wasn't ready to stop being friends with him yet. There was a public, professional Lyndsay, and a private, lonely Lyndsay. It was true she'd crossed a line by kissing him, but maybe that would be okay if she didn't let it derail her from her work. She would always prioritize her investigation. In fact, keeping the lines open with him was the good choice, because then she could have that conversation with him about the paintings, later, and work it into dialog in a much more relaxed and naturally flowing way.

Maybe he'd heard the disappointment in her voice because he wasn't exactly tossing her out just yet. And she wasn't making a move for the door handle, either.

"Lyn," he said. "I have one failed marriage behind me. It happened because I couldn't make my relationship my priority. I let these family problems take over. It's still that way with me. It hasn't changed."

"I'm okay with your responsibilities," she said quickly. Heck, she had her own priorities—work priorities—even if she didn't voice them. He might even be—dare she think it—convenient for her with his family situation.

"I don't know," he said. "I think you should sleep on it."

"All right." That was fair. She reached for the door handle, and he didn't stop her.

As she exited his truck and walked down the driveway and up the front stairs, she thought of Pete. At least he wouldn't see her kiss a local man by the MacLaines' front door. She thought of giving Pete a small smile and a furtive wave, but the lights from John's truck remained on her until she'd safely entered the house.

Then his truck slowly pulled away. From the safety of the silent, empty home, Lyndsay watched John leave.

CHAPTER NINE

THE WATER STAIN in the MacLaines' foyer ceiling disappeared with each stroke from AJ's paintbrush, while upstairs in the master bath, Moon applied floor tile to the sounds of '80s music on XM radio.

Andy sipped coffee beside Lyndsay as he stared, appreciatively, at the artwork of Kitty over the fireplace. "Things are going pretty well here, I think," he remarked. "What time did you say they're delivering the new furniture?"

"After lunch," she murmured.

"Sounds good. Chet will be coming by then, and I'll send him and AJ to start installing the oak flooring in the den."

"Thank you." She should have been jumping for joy with the morning's developments. Her cover was immeasurably improved from the day before. Not even ten o'clock and her most pressing problems with maintaining her cover as an interior designer were disappearing, thanks to new contractors and internet shopping.

But her mind kept skipping to her kiss with

John Reilly, and to the abrupt way they'd parted. Restless, she put down her coffee mug and headed for the foyer.

"Where are you going?" Andy called.

"Upstairs." She needed to prepare for her phone call with Commander Harris at eleven o'clock. It was time to put Personal Lyndsay away, and bring out Work Lyndsay.

She checked in on Moon on her way past the master bath. The pungent odor of mortar smelled like progress to her. It was difficult to see how the tile pattern was progressing, given that Moon was on his hands and knees, working from the back corner toward the front. John had recommended that she should trust him, so trust him she would.

Sighing, she stuck the key in the lock to the master bedroom, then headed for the watercolors. She took them both down from the wall, setting them on the now-dry carpet in the center of the room. Kneeling, she flipped the frames over, unfastened the metal points that kept the matting in place, and removed the pictures from the glass.

It had occurred to her that Gary had never checked the backs of the paintings. Art snob that he apparently was, he'd turned his nose up at them, muttering that they were inconsequential to the investigation. She'd instinctively known otherwise.

But the underside of the stiff paper gave her no more clues.

She was on her knees, wondering what investigative step to take next, when Andy surprised her by poking his head in the door. "What are you doing, Lyn?"

Ouch. She should have turned the lock. "I need to reframe these pictures to match the new decor."

Andy sauntered inside, scratching his chin. Tilting his head, he gazed at the watercolors she'd turned over. He grunted. "That looks like the beach out front," he remarked.

She already knew that. "Yes, it does," she agreed. And since Andy was interested in them, it seemed like a good time to subtly grill him.

Smiling at him, she held up one of the pictures. "You've been a member of this community for a long time. Does the woman in this painting look like a former girlfriend or wife of the congressman?"

Andy took a swig of his coffee. "Sure does," he rasped. "Her name was Candace. I liked her a lot, but she passed away from cancer some years back."

Well, that solved the mystery as to why Kitty had disliked the paintings. Presumably, she disliked having the reminder of her husband's lost love in their bedroom. Lyndsay honestly didn't blame her.

"Do you know who painted this?" Lyndsay asked.

"Nope." Andy shook his head decisively.

"How about the dogs? Did the congressman and his lady love ever own golden retrievers like these?"

Andy peered closer, squinting. Then he shook his head. "I don't think they had dogs. They usually only spent summers here, once Congress was out of session, and I don't remember them having any pets at all."

"Well, then, do you ever remember seeing any artists setting up with easels on the beach? Or selling watercolors door to door, or at craft fairs?"

Andy narrowed his eyes. Shoot—she'd been too obvious. "No," he said. "But why are you asking all these questions?"

She sighed dramatically. "I'm trying to figure out if they're valuable and if they should be incorporated into the design or not. I'm inclined to think it's too controversial to keep them on display. But they are pretty, aren't they?"

"Um." Andy rocked on his heels. Then he squatted down and patted the carpet. "John did a good job drying this out."

There was no reason why the mention of John's name should cause her to stiffen, but it did. "Yes," she murmured.

"He got that broken pipe fixed up, too."

She nodded, not looking at Andy.

"Everything okay there, Lyn?"

No. Right now I'm Professional Lyndsay and you're mixing that up with Personal Lyndsay.

She got to her feet and carefully set the paintings and their framing materials in a corner. Then she took out the brass key from her pocket. "Let's go check on your team's work. Then I need to head out for a while. I have a conference call scheduled with my employer."

Andy straightened and wiped his hands. "I'll see if AJ is ready to get started on those floors."

"Thank you, Andy."

LYNDSAY WALKED DOWN the beach toward the busier, main section of boardwalk to meet Pete behind the market they'd been rendezvousing at. She'd never been here in full daylight and was surprised to see the foot traffic the store received. Though the vacation season was still about a month away, early-bird tourists wandered in and out, purchasing makeshift picnic items and extras like sunscreen and beach hats. Such an uncharacteristically warm, sunny day was surely good for business.

Pete sat on the bench wearing shorts, a T-shirt and sneakers, with a baseball cap and dark sunglasses covering his eyes. He silently scrolled through his phone. Beside him was a small paper bag with the top folded over.

She sat beside the bag and bent over to tie her laces. "How were my cookies?" she asked in a low voice. "Did you like them?" She'd brought a batch to him last night.

Even watching in her peripheral vision she could see his wide smile "They're gone already."

"Good. I hope it's a sufficient bribe," she murmured.

He chuckled softly. Still not looking at her, he said, "There's a throwaway phone inside that bag. Take it and head down the beach toward the boardwalk. When you're finished with it, bring it back to me."

"Will the congressman or his people be on the other end of the line?"

"No. Just members of our team." He checked his watch. "They'll be calling you in three minutes."

"Is anybody monitoring the cottage?"

"Yes. Wesley is watching the cameras."

"Good. I've left the local contractors there alone. They're laying floors." She stretched her arms and picked up the bag, then silently stood.

No one watched them. She walked about two

hundred yards into the wind. The weather was getting wilder, so she veered away from the surf where the waves seemed especially loud today.

Finally the phone rang and she answered, cupping her hand around her ear. "Hello."

"To whom am I speaking?" Commander Harris clearly asked.

"This is Lyn Francis."

"Officer Fairfax. Excellent. Tell us what you've found."

From the echo on the phone, plus the pronoun "us" that he'd used, she assumed she was on speakerphone. Likely Simon was there, but that didn't particularly matter to her.

"What I've found are two framed watercolor paintings, each about nine by twelve inches, of the same female subject against the backdrop of the beach here. I wouldn't have thought anything about them, but they were in the bedroom initially locked to me by the male homeowner, and when his wife let me into this room she made an offhand comment about them. I quote, 'I wouldn't mind if these were stolen in a break-in.'"

"Did you ascertain what she meant by this, Officer?"

"The woman in the paintings is a former love of his, but that's not what makes the paintings truly interesting."

"Go on."

Two people were walking past her. Lyndsay waited until they'd passed.

"Initially, I was suspicious of the wife's comment, so I showed the paintings to Pete. We believe paintings by this same artist are common to all our *clients*." Surely, they would understand she meant the burglaries. "Unfortunately, we haven't been able to locate the artist, because the other owners remember very little about where they acquired the art, likely because they're not valuable and seem to have been painted by an amateur. I'd like to ask our homeowner about them to figure out who the artist is. Then I could talk to the artist—maybe get more paintings or at least get some history about the ones we have." She was hoping that this information could break open the case.

There was a brief silence on the other end. "How is your cover?" Commander Harris asked.

"Intact."

"And work on the congressman's home?"

She gritted her teeth. "Coming along quite well."

"Excellent. I'll be the one to talk with Congressman MacLaine. You'll hear from Pete when I have news to pass to you. In the meantime, continue to keep your eyes and ears open."

She supposed that was the best she could hope for. Lyndsay let out her breath. "Very good."

"Let Pete know if you need any more assistance. And stay alert, Officer."

"I will."

Commander Harris ended the call. Lyndsay surreptitiously put the phone in the bag, then returned to the bench where Pete still sat. She took a seat, casually setting the bag between them.

"You good?" he asked her.

"Yes, we're good. He'll talk to the client, then get back to you with the results. Then I'm cleared to speak with the artist."

Pete nodded. He tilted his face to the warm sun. "I'd love to stay and chat, but I have an alarm company I need to visit."

"How I wish I could come," she said wistfully.

"Enjoy it here today. The beach is a lot nicer than an office park."

"When do you think he'll get back to us?"

Pete shrugged. "A day or two. Who knows when you're dealing with VIPs out of cell phone range."

A day or two. That gave her some time to breathe, for once.

She knew exactly how she wanted to spend that time.

"I'M GOING TO the Seaside for lunch today," Lyndsay said to Andy. They stood at the top of the staircase inside the MacLaine cottage.

The bathroom tile was halfway completed. The pattern of differing shades of blue looked even better than she'd imagined. Down the hall, AJ and Chet were opening the boxes of flooring, inspecting the gray-stained, oak-look planks. *Shouldn't take more than a day or two to finish*, Andy had promised.

She'd already inspected the painted ceilings downstairs. No trace of water stains. It was noon. She had an hour before the furniture shipment was expected.

"Great." Andy grinned at her. "Then my work here is done."

Lyndsay left and drove her black Audi with the sunroof open, breathing in the fresh air. The parking lot for the Seaside was almost full—just a spot near the front door was open. She pulled the car in.

Grabbing her purse off the passenger seat, she headed inside the restaurant. The smell of freshly baked bread was mouthwatering, and her stomach growled. There was already a line at the register to pay. Four people seemed to be waiting to pick up phone orders. Two parties sat at tables, digging into their sandwiches and soups. She glanced about, but didn't see John. Just Millie, the waitress with the graying brown hair, ringing up take-out orders as fast as she could.

Off to the waitress's side was the entrance

to the kitchen that Lyndsay had seen Andy use many times before. Taking a chance, Lyndsay headed through, unseen by the busy waitress.

She'd only made three steps inside the barrier before John stepped out, stopping in front of her.

She swallowed. He stood inches from her, wearing a gray, short-sleeve T-shirt that showed off his muscled arms and chest. He seemed to be radiating authority as he gazed at her with all of his formidable passion.

She met his eyes, so remarkably gray-blue that they seemed to match his shirt.

"Can I help you with something, Lyn?" His voice so deep, it gave her shivers.

She kept her eyes on his. She didn't step back, either. They stood so close to one another, anyone watching them would know they'd kissed before. The air between them seemed to crackle with energy.

"You asked me to sleep on it, John," she said in a low voice. "And I slept."

He ran his hand through his hair, slowly. Two lines appeared in the middle of his forehead. "And?" he asked in the same low voice.

She swallowed again. "I like our growing friendship. I appreciate that you told me about your family and your priorities. I want to keep seeing you."

He eyed her warily.

She took a breath and looked deeply into his eyes. He seemed to waver. That gave her the courage to continue. "A long time ago, somebody close to me also had a very busy life, with priorities that came before mine. All that came to me were crumbs from the table. Maybe that sounds bleak to you, but it's anything but bleak to me now. I wouldn't give up having those times for the world."

But that was then, and this is now. She'd grown and she'd learned since then. "I've seen that even crumbs from a table are better than starving." Her voice cracked. "I have six days left here, John. I want to make the most of them and spend as much time with you as possible. If you agree, then call me when you're off duty. I really hope you do." She took a breath and then turned away.

She'd been honest with him, too. Now it was up to him to decide.

She was in the parking lot halfway out to her car when he caught up with her.

He stepped in close, putting himself between her and her car door. "You deserve more than crumbs from a table," he said huskily.

"Maybe so. But that's for me to decide." She reached around him for the door handle, but he caught her wrist lightly.

She stilled, her body yearning for his touch.

Then his thumb dragged up her wrist, caressed the sensitive skin of her arm. She shivered, restraining herself from touching him like she wanted to.

He leaned his head close to hers. "You smell so good, Lyn. It's been driving me crazy, thinking of you."

"Well," she sighed, hoping that Pete wasn't anywhere near them at the moment. "Please, come see me when you get a chance. You know where I'm working."

"How about I come this afternoon?"

"Great, if you don't mind Andy and his crew being there. You can come and help us move furniture."

He grinned at her, undeterred. "Oh, you can bet I will."

She watched him head inside the Seaside, the door slapping shut behind him. She was still smiling when she got into her car and turned on the engine.

CHAPTER TEN

THREE HOURS LATER, Lyndsay gaped, amazed. After days of chaos, the MacLaine design seemed to be coming together.

Lyndsay let in the two men DesignSea had sent, who wheeled in a load of custom cabinets and bookcases for the upstairs sitting area. In the master bedroom that she had thought of as hopeless just a few days ago, all new furnishings, including bedding, pillows and accessories had been delivered. AJ and Chet installed the nice vinyl flooring, and Moon finished his tile job. Even outside, the patio landscaping had begun in earnest, and it looked great.

Her cover had held—thank goodness—and Kitty MacLaine would reap the benefit of a new, beautiful home. Lyndsay was up a ladder, installing a new set of blinds in the front window when she saw John's black truck pull into the driveway and park beside Andy's van.

She'd been waiting to see him. Stepping down from the ladder, she put her hand to her throat.

Tall, purposeful, head high. John was aiming for her. In a new way, it lifted her spirits.

She met him at the door, running her hands through her hair to smooth it.

"Hi," he said, gazing at her. His hands were stuffed inside his pockets. "I was able to get away for a while."

"Would you like to come in and see my design skills? The place is really coming together now."

"Yeah." He smiled at her. "I have to admit I'm curious."

She opened the door wide for him and led him inside. "It's the most important interior decorating job I've ever done." Feeling playful, she positioned her hands over his eyes. "Pretend that you're the homeowner and this is the big reveal. Well, what do you think?"

JOHN LIKED BEING part of Lyn's excitement. He liked the feel of her hands on his face. Liked that she was happy about having him there.

She'd done a great job. He walked around the house with her and looked at everything as she explained it all to him. Later, as the workmen hustled around them, he and Lyn flopped on a set of old couches in the still-unfinished living room that overlooked the ocean.

"I could get used to living the good life here,"

she said. "This place is much bigger than my tiny apartment."

"You live in an apartment?"

Her cheeks turned pink, but she nodded. "I'm hardly ever there. I'm always on assignment for my job, it seems."

"Do you travel a lot?" he couldn't help asking. He was genuinely curious.

She smiled wistfully at him. "Have you ever wondered what it would feel like to have a normal life sometimes? I mean, where you spend regular work hours in a place that fulfills you and then afterward in a personal life where you're not…?"

He understood what she was starting to say. And since her talk with him last night, he'd been thinking about how much he sacrificed for the family and the business, feeling responsible for all of them.

He checked his watch. "Speaking of, I hate to leave, but I have an appointment in ten minutes and then some errands I need to get done." He glanced at her. "You've been cooped up here all week. Would you like a change of scenery? I know you're an early bird. Do you want to see something special at sunrise tomorrow? Sort of like a private adventure."

"Where?" She sounded excited.

"It's a surprise. You'll see."

She grinned at him. "Yes, I think I would."

"Meet me at my house at a half hour before sunrise."

"Okay. Should I bring anything?"

"Just yourself."

LYNDSAY BARELY SLEPT, she felt so revved up about their clandestine meeting. As she got dressed the next morning, so early it was still dark outside, she debated bringing her Glock. She decided against it though, because this wasn't a work meeting.

She took just her flashlight and jogged over to John's house, across the street and through the wet grass, coarse because of the sandy soil it had to grow in.

John opened the door before she even knocked, as she'd expected. He had a motion detector in his driveway, after all.

She couldn't tell him, but he would make a great law enforcement officer. He had the right mind-set for it.

"I hope I'm not too early," she said, bending over to pet Toby.

"Nope." John picked up the big tabby and waved one of his paws at her. "Good morning, Lyn."

She laughed and headed inside with him and Toby. The kitchen smelled like brewing coffee.

"Have a seat," John said, directing her to the table in the breakfast nook. He sat, too, and quietly focused on what looked like medical supplies he'd assembled on the table. A plastic bag that looked like an IV bag was set up in front of a small table-top heating fan. It looked like he was warming the fluids up. Beside that was a plastic bag filled with plastic-covered needles.

"This will only take two minutes," he said, fiddling with one of the needles, "and then we'll be off."

"What do you have to do to Toby?" she asked nervously. He was settling the cat in his lap, petting him and talking in a low tone to him. Was he going to give the cat some kind of IV drip?

"My brother doted on his pets," John explained. "After he passed, well…" He smiled wistfully. "My mother is allergic to cats, so I had to take over caring for him. He had his yearly vet appointment last month, and come to find out, his kidneys are failing. The vet isn't sure how long he has, but it doesn't look good. Unless he gets his fluid, he's constantly dehydrated. So every morning before work, I give him his hundred milliliters. It seems to help him. He's happier and less cranky."

"I'm not sure I could give a cat a needle," she said nervously.

"It's not bad." John laughed softly, rubbing

Toby's furry head. "Six months ago if you'd told me I'd be doing this…" He shook his head. But he didn't seem embarrassed, just amused.

Watching him taking care of Justin's cat, a lump grew in her throat. It was clear to her that this was a way of keeping his brother's memory alive. Beneath his tough exterior, John hid a soft heart.

"What if you miss a session?" she asked. "Will it hurt Toby?"

"I don't know." His eyes gazed into hers. "I'm told the treatment won't reverse his condition, but it does improve his quality of life."

"Your family must get a measure of comfort from that."

A line appeared in his forehead. "I'm sure they do," he said. "I do, too."

She reached over and petted the tabby's head. He was purring. Even though he had, in effect, a plastic tube going into him subcutaneously between his shoulder blades he didn't appear to feel it. He seemed mostly happy for the attention and petting he got from John. She smiled to herself. She could relate to that.

She was getting insight into John's personality. There was a lot more to him than he showed on the surface.

"I should've asked if you were allergic to cats," he said.

"I'm not." She shook her head. "I had a cat as a girl. A big Maine coon." She smiled at the memory. But then she remembered how it ended, and that saddened her. Life was such a mixture of beginnings and endings. For once she wanted to build something and not see it disappear so quickly.

"What was your cat's name?"

"Milo. He crossed the Rainbow Bridge when I was in high school. I was so traumatized, I didn't ever want another cat. Love was too painful."

He made a faint smile. "Could explain your choice of profession—independent and traveling all the time."

"Could be. But I doubt it."

"Trust me." John stood. "I'll do what it takes to take care of Toby, for Justin's sake. It's what he would have wanted. But after Toby leaves this world, this is it for me."

"Why *not* get your own cat?" she asked. "You seem to take pleasure in it."

"I'd rather take pleasure in you." He reached out and touched her cheek. Then he deftly removed the IV before cleaning up the supplies. "Let's go. We'll leave Toby to his own devices."

"Where are we going?" she asked breathlessly, getting up with him and following him to the door.

He shot her a grin. "It's a surprise."

He locked the door behind them, then swept her up into his big black truck, along with a soft blanket that smelled of clean laundry soap and a heavy stainless steel thermos filled with hot coffee that smelled like heaven.

They drove through the small beach town she was beginning to think of as home. She really had no idea where he was taking her, which meant she felt a little nervous, too. Pete was monitoring the cameras at the cottage in real time. A hardship, he'd groaned, given that everyone but fishermen and lobstermen were in their beds.

Maybe that was why John pulled the pickup truck into the local marina. Boats of all sorts were moored at the line of docks, bobbing gently with the tide.

"We're going on a *boat*?" she asked.

He frowned. "Sorry. I should've asked that, too. Do you get seasick?"

"No. I love the ocean."

"Good." He grinned in relief. "Because my buddy is on his tenth-anniversary vacation, and I have the keys to his boats while he's gone."

She hopped out of the cab. "Boats, as in plural?"

"He's a lobsterman. His brother is watching his pots for him, but he's also got a powerboat that he entrusted to me. It's what we're going to take this morning."

"Oh." She carried the blanket and coffee and followed him, lingering behind only while he spoke with the harbormaster, retrieving the keys. Then John led her over to a speedboat docked at one of the outer berths.

"Your friend won't mind if we use it?" she asked.

"On the contrary. I'm just sorry you won't get a chance to meet him. He's not due back for two weeks."

"He asked you to watch his boats?" On top of everything else, how many responsibilities did John Reilly have?

"Yes, he did." John lifted his arms to help her, and she stepped inside.

The boat was beautiful. It even smelled new. John settled her into a snug leather seat beside the driver's wheel, then he set about untying rope and peeling back tarpaulin. It was still dark outside—the only light was from a lamp on the dock beside them—and cool, so she wrapped the woolen blanket around her shoulders.

John settled into the driver's seat. He turned on the ignition and kept the engine on low. She smelled the faint scent of fuel. John turned on the heater, and warm air began to blow at her feet.

They motored slowly away from the dock,

their pace almost a standstill so as not to raise a wake. She looked behind them and watched as the little harbor gradually receded into the distance, its lights twinkling in miniature.

She faced forward. The boat's headlights cut a glare across the dark ocean. Strangely, the water seemed calmer than she'd seen it. Almost like glass.

She held on to the dash in front of her and leaned over to speak into John's ear. With the noise of the engine, she had to raise her voice to be heard.

"It's beautiful out here!"

"It is. I haven't done this in quite a while."

And when they were far enough away, out in the middle of the vast ocean, not near any other boat, not where anyone could see them, John slowed the boat to a stop, then cut the engine.

They bobbed in place, in time with the swells.

He turned to smile at her. The sky on the horizon was brightening, bit by bit, the darkness lifting. She felt a tingle of anticipation.

John pointed to the skyline. "Another minute or so, and we'll see the sun."

Swallowing, she unwrapped herself from the blanket, then pressed it over his shoulders, too, so they were both cocooned. He gave her a short look of surprise, then understanding, then gratitude.

She supposed he was so used to taking care of everybody else that it surprised him when others did something to help him.

His arm slid around her waist. He leaned his mouth close to her lips.

"It would've been nice to jet you off to someplace warm," he said, "but we'll have to make do."

"I like that no one can see us," she murmured. "We're in our own world out here alone."

"I can't imagine not living near the ocean."

She drew in her breath. "There it is."

A faint ray of light appeared on the eastern horizon. And while she held her breath, it grew larger and larger. She could now see John clearly. He had a wide smile on his face, one she hadn't seen yet.

"This is the best time of the day."

It felt magical to her. "Is it always this calm?" she whispered.

"Never." His voice was low. "This is my first time, at least."

She turned her chin, and caught his gaze directly. For a moment they shared a look, then with a low groan, he leaned into her.

"I can't fight it anymore," he said, before catching her mouth with his. She drank deeply of his kiss. Tinged with coffee, and full of the desire that they'd both been fighting. She licked at his tongue when it pushed between her lips, and she wrapped her arms tighter around his neck. She needed him, too.

With a low groan, he shifted her so she was on his lap, tugging her closer to him. If the mood had been sweet earlier, it wasn't anymore. They might never have this opportunity again. But now she had him, alone, unwatched, on a bobbing boat in the middle of a calm sea, while the sun rose around them. It seemed to glow off the water in sparks of orange and gold.

His breath exhaled, and he paused to gaze at her. She had slid upward, over his lap. She blessed her foresight in wearing a long, flimsy skirt, because she easily hiked it up, nestling so close to him that she felt him against the soft juncture of her thighs, just where she needed him most. If she'd been a little afraid before, nervous about her first time with a man since her husband had passed, she didn't feel it now. She just wanted to be close to John. His hands cupped her bottom and he pulled her even closer. A feeling so sweet and achy that she could have cried aloud.

He took all his passion and poured it into loving her. Maybe because she'd seen him in his most private and vulnerable moments, unguarded, she could appreciate how different he was with her. Their kisses grew hotter, frantic, even. She was openly rubbing against him, grinding urgently, wanting more and more closeness with him. Wanting him to carry her away into a delicious feeling of ecstasy with him. She had so much built-up hunger, she knew she was being selfish, pleasing herself instead of heeding the responsibilities in her life, but it felt exhilarating. The smell of the sea, the vastness of the blue waves, the absolute aloneness they had—the only two people on earth—that made her feel safe with him.

She reached for the button on his pants. His hand rested on hers, and he helped by lowering the zipper. She closed her hand around him. His flesh was hot and hard. He sighed deeply.

The ocean. Such heat. No thoughts.

He kissed her, caressing her softly with his fingers, stroking her. She squirmed, feeling she could cry out with the pleasure of it. He pressed his mouth to her ear, whispering gently, "I have condoms. In the backpack behind you. If you could bring it over here…"

Fumbling, in a haze, she found the box, and took one out. Opened it. Sheathed him, kissing him as she did so.

She looked at John. Gazed into his blue-gray eyes. Sifted his hair through her fingers as they rocked up and down in the swells that the wind suddenly worked up. Making love with him was sweet, and glorious, and fun.

Afterward, she lay against him, his head against hers. Then he slowly nudged down her top. Kissed the tips of her breasts.

"I swear to you I didn't plan this when I woke up today," he murmured. "I only bought the condoms in case."

"I hoped it would happen for us." She smiled. "But I never imagined it like this."

"It can't be permanent, Lyn."

She reached over and gathered her flung-away skirt. "I know that."

He took her hand. "You don't like hearing that."

She pulled her hand away. "You could be kind about it. I know it's temporary, what we have. You don't need to *say* it again."

His mouth quirked. "You wish it wasn't."

She took a deep cleansing breath and thought about what he'd said. "You're right. In a lot of ways, I wish we could explore this as long as we want to," she said slowly. "But I also know that some things can't be changed. It's the way things are."

He stilled, looking up at her. "That's a depressing thought."

Her stomach sank. She wasn't going to let him have bad thoughts about what had just happened, because it had been wonderful for her. So she decided to let the bad thoughts slide. She leaned over and gently kissed him. Stroked her hand along his masculine cheek, smooth and freshly shaven. "I won't regret this, not for a minute."

He kissed her as gently as he ever had.

It was too bad she needed to be going. Pete would be waiting for her call. She sat back on her heels and sighed.

He leaned forward and pulled her closer. "Let's not go yet. I want to memorize you."

She let herself be caressed in a most loving way. He rested his palm on her belly and with his fingers, brought her to arousal again.

And just like that, she couldn't have enough of him again.

He grabbed the blanket and, with one hand, awkwardly spread it on the deck of the boat. Getting up from his chair, he pulled her down with him. Lowering her to her back, he drew up her legs and spread his hot tongue flat on her. She arched and gasped. He enclosed her with his lips and gently suckled, and she thought she would be driven mad.

"You're perfect to me." He rose, whispering into her ear, and she moaned. She clasped him closer until he was buried deep inside her. He filled her. She felt more deeply intimate with him.

They moved more slowly this time. It was less frenzied, and even nicer to her.

"Lyn." He said her name this time. "Lyn."

"It's Lyndsay," she whispered. She couldn't help it.

The sun glistening on his forehead, he gazed down at her.

"Lyndsay is my real name," she said quietly. "Lyn is a nickname."

"Lyndsay," he murmured.

"But nobody calls me that." It was true—here, at least.

"May I call you that?"

"Please do."

"I'm just John." His eyes seemed naked and vulnerable to her.

"I know," she whispered.

He closed his eyes, shading them from the sun, getting brighter by the moment.

"I came back to Wallis Point because I had to," he said finally. "My family was falling apart without me here, and I felt guilty. But if I could ever overcome it…"

She let him take his time forming his thoughts.

He sighed, and she knew he was speaking from his heart. "I'd like to drive away in this boat with you. I'd keep going, all the way south until it got warm. All the way to the Caribbean. And we'd stay there for a good long vacation together."

"That sounds lovely," she said dreamily.

"Yeah, it does. Until they call me home again," he said bitterly.

She knew who he meant. He thought all that came between them was his family. If only he knew the truth about her...

He shook his head. "Darling, I need to take you home now."

"Yes." Pete would be looking for her. She sat up. She was stark naked, out in the middle of the ocean with the sun shining on parts of her that had never been exposed before.

Funny, though, she was no longer cold. But her private interlude with John was...

"A memory I'll always have for myself," she heard herself muttering aloud.

"Lyndsay?"

"Nothing." She smiled at him. "Do you want me to pour you some coffee for the drive back?"

"Yeah. I'm covering for Millie this morning. She has an early doctor appointment."

"Okay. We'll see each other when we can."

He smiled sadly at her.

No matter what, she would enjoy what they had—these snatched moments alone—while they still had them.

CHAPTER ELEVEN

LYNDSAY NEVER WOULD have thought that John would make certain to see her every minute he could after that morning on his friend's boat. But he did. Their days together were some of the happiest times that she could remember.

On Sunday, she walked through the MacLaine cottage with her clipboard, noting what was yet to be finished with the renovation. She was still waiting for word from Commander Harris regarding his conversation with Congressman MacLaine. That was making her antsy, but there wasn't much she could do to speed him up.

A text message pinged on her phone, surprising her.

Frowning, she put down her clipboard. It definitely wasn't from John—he didn't have her phone number. The message could only be from a member of her task force. But they'd never sent a text before.

With a foreboding in her chest, she crossed the room and picked up the phone.

Report to headquarters in one hour.

She blinked, wanting to call Pete to verify that what she'd read was real, but it was a bad idea to use the emergency number for anything but an emergency.

Most likely the order to return to headquarters was due to the congressman. Maybe he'd been set up to Skype her on a secure line. If she left now, dressed as she was, then she just might make it to Concord in time.

She tucked away her clipboard and put on a professional-looking jacket from her bedroom upstairs. It occurred to Lyndsay that in just three weeks this cottage had become more home to her than her real home was. She hardly gave a thought, these days, to her apartment, her own clothing that didn't seem to suit her as well anymore, even her ancient SUV that she kept in an outdoor parking space. By now, its battery was probably dead.

So well had she assumed the persona of Lyn Francis, interior designer, that she dreaded going back to that lonely apartment when her assignment was over.

Sighing, she grabbed her purse and Glock. Outside in the beautifully landscaped front driveway, she climbed into her trendy car and faced the route that led to the state capital.

The Wallis Point peninsula receded in her rearview mirror. A wave of sadness overtook her. When the time came to leave for good, she would miss her newfound family in the beach-side cul-de-sac. John she would miss most of all.

"OFFICER FAIRFAX, PLEASE be seated."

Hitching in a breath, Lyndsay chose an empty seat at the oval conference table among the three men who'd been her support crew. Wesley, her shy young camera technician. Simon, of the sarcastic temperament and hard-core investigative beliefs. Pete, the seasoned detective who had ended up being her best ally.

She nodded to Commander Harris, then to each of the men. "Good morning, everyone."

"I like your purse," Simon remarked.

She nudged his knee out of her personal space. "I can get one for you, if you'd like."

He gave her a wide grin. Wesley snickered. Pete managed a smile.

"Congressman MacLaine wants to speak with you, Officer Fairfax." Commander Harris indicated a speakerphone in the center of the table. "He's currently in London."

"Great. But will Kitty be with him? I'd like to question him about the watercolor paintings, and that isn't a topic she appreciates."

"Good thinking. But no, the call will just include the congressman."

She nodded. To admit to Congressman Mac-Laine that she'd seen the watercolors in his bedroom would give his wife away for opening the room to Lyndsay, but Lyndsay was prepared to deal with any fallout.

Wesley made the telephone connection.

"Good morning," came Congressman Mac-Laine's distinctive, sharp voice from the speakerphone. "Am I speaking with the task force?"

"Good morning, Congressman." Commander Harris spoke for all of them. "I'm present with our detectives, including the officer whom your wife knows as Lyn Francis."

"Yes, good morning, Lyn," said Congressman MacLaine.

Commander Harris nodded to her. Lyndsay sat ramrod straight. "Good morning, Congressman."

"My wife is looking forward to seeing your work at the cottage."

"I'm looking forward to showing her, sir."

"Wonderful. We've decided to stay an extra week in London. I trust that gives you enough time to finish?"

She really only needed another day or two at most, but Commander Harris was signaling to her, nodding, so she said, "Yes, it does, sir."

"Would Mrs. MacLaine like to speak with Lyn today?" Commander Harris asked smoothly.

"No, she's not with me at the moment, but she's looking forward to the big reveal, as she's taken to calling it. Were there any difficulties we should be aware of?"

Commander Harris shook his head at her. In fact, all of the members of the task force collectively shot her a look. She couldn't help smiling.

"Everything has gone smoothly," she fibbed. She glanced at Commander Harris. *The watercolors?* she mouthed.

He made a gesture with his palm pushing downward, which she took to mean that he wanted her to wait. *All in good time.*

"That's what I like to hear." The congressman chuckled. "I'm looking forward to relaxing on the beach once we're home and the good weather starts."

It was a beautiful home, in quite a beautiful location, but she was getting tired of this chit-chat.

"Well, if you need me—" the congressman seemed to be wrapping up "—I'm reachable by phone. Commander Harris may give you my number."

"Thank you for your contact information. I appreciate that." Lyndsay passed her department phone to Commander Harris so that he could add the congressman's information to her contact list. She wasn't going to miss this opportunity to get the congressman's phone number directly so that she could call him if she needed to. She'd rather avoid the rigmarole of driving all the way to Concord to ask him a question in future.

Commander Harris raised an eyebrow, but he keyed the number into her phone, then slid it across the table.

"Congressman MacLaine," she said, only when she was sure that his number was safely stored inside her phone, "I have some questions about the watercolor paintings inside your master bedroom. Where did you get them, and what is the name of the artist who made them?"

"Whoa." The congressman chuckled. "I'm not sure what you're referring to. You might want to talk to Kitty about that."

"I did. She doesn't seem to know much, except that the paintings came from you."

There was a short silence. "I really don't know the answers to your questions, Officer." His tone had turned a bit cold. Lyndsay glanced at Commander Harris, and his arms were folded, but he nodded at her, so that meant he was backing her up.

"When did you acquire the paintings?" she asked calmly.

"Surely you don't think anybody cares about those cheap things?"

"We need to rule things out, sir. What can you tell me about them, please?"

He sighed. "My late wife bought them. I couldn't say where, I couldn't say how, I couldn't say from whom. In fact, you have my permission to throw the damn things out. It's been more tiring keeping them than letting them go."

She couldn't help smiling. Kitty would be happy to hear this. "I'm sorry to disturb you," she said, "but your answers are helpful to our investigation. Thank you." Then she remembered the golden retrievers. "Sir, one last question. Did the two golden retrievers in the watercolors belong to you?"

"What? No. I haven't had any pets since I was a boy."

"Thank you, sir."

The line clicked off. She glanced at her superior. "What's the status of the burglary investigation?" she asked.

"We have a suspect in custody."

"What?" She blinked. "How? When did this happen?"

Commander Harris leaned back in his chair. "Two nights ago, a maid was caught entering the home next door to where she worked." Commander Harris seemed to be focusing on her and Wesley when he spoke. It was likely that Pete and Simon already knew about this development. "We brought the maid in for questioning, and we have her confession that she's part of a burglary ring. She's being interviewed as we speak."

"That's great. Where was she caught?"

"Up the coast near Portland."

"In Maine? But that's—"

"Outside our jurisdiction. Yes, we know."

Lyndsay studied the looks on her colleagues' faces. Simon, in particular, seemed irritated, judging by his frown.

"Why didn't we tell the congressman this?" she asked.

"We don't report to him in the chain of command, Lyndsay," came the rebuke from Commander Harris.

"Yes, of course."

Simon leaned close to her ear and muttered, "His friend the governor probably already told him."

Politics. She understood.

"As of now, we're disbanding the task force," Commander Harris announced. "Each of you is responsible for writing a report. Lyndsay, include what you learned about the watercolor paintings during your investigation. Don't be discouraged—your input is valuable and may be used for further inquiries. Simon will be co-ordinating with the Maine group, arranging for our time to further interview the suspect, and this will be a necessary part of it."

That made her feel better somewhat, but she still wished she could take part in the interrogations and arrests.

"Lyndsay, you'll also be meeting with Mrs. MacLaine next week when she returns," the commander continued. "As far as she is to know, you're still Lyn Francis. For now, give Wesley access to the cottage to clear the site of our cameras. You may stay until you're finished. The design work is secondary to the investigation, of course, but it's still a necessary part of your cover. After you've finished the design work, close up the house."

She was reeling. This was it? The task force was finished? "Is there anything else to do, sir?"

"Yes. You'll meet with a department psychologist before you roll off."

"Why?"

"It's standard procedure. Everyone meets with the department psychologist after an undercover assignment. After that, I'd like you to take some time off. You've been working round the clock for weeks now."

Simon winked at her. "Lucky you. I could use time in the sun and sand about now."

She'd had all the sun and sand she wanted, right in Wallis Point. "I think I can finish in a few days. If I need to leave the house during this time, will I be required to call Pete?"

"No. At this point, I don't think your area is at further risk from break-ins. I know you're disappointed that the tip didn't pan out, but there will be other opportunities. Finish this undercover job for the MacLaines, see the psychologist and then take some time off. When you return, we'll discuss your next steps."

"I'd like to request a permanent position as a detective," she said.

Commander Harris inclined his head to her. "I'll put in a recommendation for your promotion."

"Thank you, sir."

LYNDSAY STILL HADN'T stopped smiling.

She, Simon, Wesley and Pete had met for a quick drink at a local pub near the headquarters building. It was after the meeting, and for the most part, they were off duty.

Wesley shot a game of pool with Pete. Lyndsay finished up her slice of pizza, then relaxed for a moment before she headed out for the drive to Wallis Point.

"You're looking happy." Simon took a long drink of beer.

"I am," she said. "Except for the part where we're not the ones making the arrests," she added hastily.

Simon laughed. "Don't count on it. The fat lady hasn't sung yet."

"With one of their own in custody, do you think the burglary ring will strike again?"

"It's the million-dollar question, isn't it?" Simon turned and walked off.

She put down her pizza slice.

"You okay with what he said?" Pete stood beside her, pool stick in hand.

"If what he says is true, then why is Commander Harris shutting down the task force?"

Pete shrugged. "Resources. That's what it always comes down to." He gave her a pointed look. "You okay with staying undercover?"

"I am." She smiled at him. She liked Lyn Francis, and she liked being in Wallis Point. "And your point is?"

Simon came back smirking. "I know where this is going," he said to Pete.

"What?" she asked.

Pete sighed. "Just keep your task-force phone with you at all times, all right? And call me if you need backup."

"He's such a softie." Simon laughed. "He's worried about you," he teased her in a sing-song voice.

"Thanks," she said to Pete, "I appreciate your concern, but really, I doubt I'll need backup this week."

She stood and wiped her hands, eager to get back and start the process of removing the cameras from the house. Then, she wanted to see John. She planned to spend as much time with him over the next week as they could manage. She didn't need to check in with anyone from her old life because she was still on undercover assignment. "Gentlemen, good luck with the interrogations. Maybe I'll get the chance to work with you all again someday."

Simon raised his beer mug to her. "Hear, hear."

"See you in about two hours, Lyndsay," Wesley called from behind the pool table.

Pete just sighed. "Be careful, Lyn," was all he said.

DING-DONG.

John saw Lyndsay's face through the side window. She stood on his front porch. The last he'd checked, Lyndsay's car hadn't been in the MacLaines' driveway. Wherever she'd gone, she was back now.

"Who is that, dear?" his mother asked. She sat at the table in his kitchen along with his uncle Frank. They were about to clear the dinner plates and bring in dessert. Uncle Frank often came on Sundays to see his sister, but they didn't usually meet at John's place.

"Ah…" John wasn't sure what to tell his mother. "It's a friend," he said. "Why don't you guys get dessert out, and I'll be back in five minutes."

"Don't take long," said Uncle Frank, rubbing his hands together. "I brought cannoli from that place in Portsmouth you like."

"Great," John murmured. The Italian half of him liked cannoli, too, but all of him craved Lyndsay.

He went out to the porch, careful to shut the door behind him.

"Hey." He caught Lyndsay up in a kiss. They always greeted each other this way now. He lingered longer this time, though. Maybe tomorrow would be the day she finally drove off for good. The end was coming—they both knew it—but he'd chosen to turn a blind eye to it, refusing to ask questions.

Releasing her lips, he leaned back to gaze at her in the sunlight.

She seemed happy. Wherever she'd been, it had been good for her. She worked way too much, in his opinion. He smoothed back her hair.

"I've got news," she said.

His heart skipped a beat. "What's going on?" He tried to keep his tone casual.

"The congressman's trip has been extended, so I can stay a bit longer and work at a more reasonable pace."

He exhaled. "No goodbyes just yet?"

She smiled shyly at him. Then she peered around him, gazing at the door. "Is somebody here?"

He had a choice. He could bring her in to introduce her to his mother and uncle, or not. It was a big step for him. His family, knowing them, would expect it to mean that he and Lyndsay were serious. Lyndsay might see it the same way, too.

Lyndsay put her hand to his forehead. Her hand felt cool on his hot skin.

She frowned at him. "Are you okay, John?"

"Yeah."

She shook her head. "No, you're not."

She knew him. She saw inside him more than anybody else did. She seemed to see past his duty and his baggage, to what he was really feeling.

"I'm trying to decide whether to invite you inside to meet my mother and my uncle Frank."

Her face lit up. "That would be lovely."

Not the reaction he'd been expecting. He rubbed the back of his neck. "She's probably going to ask you what your plans are beyond next week."

Her eyes met his. And held, like a line. The moment seemed to stand still for him.

I want her to stay, he thought. *Right here. I want her not to leave me.*

From the way she looked at him, he could tell she felt the same way. A calm settled over him. A feeling of *knowing*. He picked up both of her hands. She didn't wear rings or anything, and he found himself lifting her hands to his mouth and kissing her fingers where her rings would be.

She laid her head against his chest, pressed close within the circle of his arms.

"Shall we go inside?"

LYNDSAY WALKED INTO John's house with him close behind. Her high-heeled boots clicked on the tiled floor of the kitchen. His hand rested lightly on the small of her back, which felt nice.

The kitchen was sunny and warm, and it smelled of something savory that had been cooking on the stove. A huge pot of beef soup or stew was Lyndsay's guess.

A man and a woman sat at John's kitchen table, and a third place was set for him. The two were digging into a large box of cannoli.

Lyndsay smiled warmly at the couple. "Hello."

"This is Lyn." John introduced her. "She's

been working at the MacLaines' cottage for the past few weeks. Lyn, this is my mom."

"I'm Margie." John's mom smiled at her. She had short brown hair and a pleasant face. While patronizing the restaurant, Lyndsay had seen glimpses of Margie in the kitchen.

"Margie, hello."

"This is my uncle Frank, the plumber I told you about." John laughed. "Technically, I should have had him come over and inspect my work, remember?"

"Pleased to meet you." John's uncle was a handsome man, with a shock of white hair and clear blue eyes that were piercing. She would bet John would look similar when he was that age.

She took the chair John offered her. His mother and uncle were staring at her openly. She supposed she was a curiosity to them, but felt slightly awkward for being the center of attention.

"Would you like some coffee?" John asked.

A full pot already sat on the table. "Thank you. I would."

John poured her a cup, then sat opposite from her.

"Lyn is an interior designer," he said.

Margie gazed at Lyndsay. "Do you live in Wallis Point, Lyn?"

She took a sip to compose herself. She'd

known full well what she was getting herself into when she'd walked through that front door. "No. I'm here just while I finish this design project."

"Is your firm in town?" his uncle asked.

"No," she answered.

"Where are they?"

"Concord," she answered reluctantly, knowing how the locals felt about people from out of town being hired to do work.

"How did you end up here?"

She smiled politely. "Congressman MacLaine has a connection with my boss."

"He couldn't use a local firm?"

"Apparently not," she murmured, sipping at her coffee.

"Well," John said, scraping back his chair. "If you're ready to head out, I'll walk you back home."

Lyndsay put her cup down. "It was nice meeting you both."

When they were out the door, John whispered into her ear, "I'm sorry about the third degree. They're just anxious about me meeting someone new."

"I can understand that. My dad would be the same way."

"Yeah. A police officer. I can't wait." He chuckled and pulled her closer, his arm around her shoulder. Together they walked down his driveway toward the MacLaine cottage, but she felt uneasy.

She couldn't ever tell him who she really was.

She couldn't ever break her identity cover.

The sad thing was, she *wanted* to tell John who she really was. She didn't want to be Lyn Francis to him forever. She would love to be able to introduce him to her parents, too.

Her legs felt numb, as if she were going through the motions, walking toward the MacLaine cottage, and marching toward an eventual execution.

"Look." He abruptly stopped short. "Something's going on across the street."

She snapped her focus to the MacLaine residence. A police cruiser was parked in the driveway. Wallis Point Police Department, it said on the side.

She felt her jaw drop.

The driver's door opened, and a uniformed patrol officer stepped out. A young officer, bulked up, his head shaved. He wore a pair of Maui Jim sunglasses, and he strode up the walkway as if to take no prisoners.

She had to do something! But she couldn't run down there and announce herself as a member of the state police force. She was still undercover. Her old rules still applied.

The patrol officer knocked on the MacLaines' front door.

"Excuse me," Lyndsay said to John. "I'll be right back." She walked briskly toward the officer, wondering how she would handle this scenario when she got there.

Talk to him, just talk. A good police officer always knew how to defuse a difficult situation.

She took a deep breath and charged forward.

CHAPTER TWELVE

"HELLO, SIR. MY name is Lyn Francis. I'm staying here at the MacLaine house. Is there a problem?"

The police officer was unsmiling; he had on his duty face. The name tag on his uniform read P. Pierce.

"Do you have identification, ma'am?" he asked.

"Yes." Obviously a by-the-book guy, he was not the type to be charmed. She reached for her back pocket but came up empty. "My driver's license is inside the house, in my purse," she explained sheepishly.

"Ma'am, I'm going to ask you to please step off the stairs. Stay on the grass, please."

Her heart sinking, she did as she was told.

A small crowd was starting to gather at the end of the drive, drawn by the blue police lights. John was fast approaching, as well.

She couldn't tell the officer who she really was. If he decided to ask her to accompany him to the station, then she couldn't break cover there, either. To do so would no doubt get her fired. She couldn't even call Pete to bail her out. Her job was to sit and wait. To keep the undercover ruse going, at all cost.

"Officer," she said, trying again to reason with him, "what has happened? I'm responsible for this home. I have the congressman's phone number if we need to contact him and I—"

"Ma'am, I'm going to ask you again, please remain on the grass."

She stopped where she was. Went back to the grass. Officer P. Pierce was on his radio, perhaps even calling for backup.

Had someone tried to break in? Had an alarm gone off? She'd been told the system was a silent alarm; it went to the alarm company, who typically called the local police station if there was a problem.

"Officer," she called to him, "if it's the alarm that went off, then I—"

"Ma'am, I'm not going to tell you again. If you step off that grass once more, then I *will* cuff you."

She sucked in her breath. Now what? Her heart was pounding. If they cuffed her, if they processed her at the station, then her fingerprints might be on file—

Maybe if she called the congressman, then they

could straighten out this confusion. Her phone was in her pocket. She reached for it, and—

"Ma'am, please keep your hands where I can see them."

"I'm just reaching for my phone so we can call the congressman."

The officer strode up to her, his face red, and stepped into her personal zone, much too close.

Now she felt angry. This wasn't good. She struggled to bite her tongue, to control her temper.

"Whoa, Phil." Lyndsay heard a familiar voice and didn't know whether to laugh or cry. John stood beside her. And coming in the distance, down the hill, were Margie and Uncle Frank.

Great. Another few passersby were pausing to witness the commotion. *Pull up a chair and join the show*, she thought. If only Pete would mosey on by, they could make it a party.

"Phil, what's going on?" John asked. "Why've you got Lyn on the grass? She works here. I can vouch for her."

"You know her?"

"Yes, I do." John turned and smiled at her, giving her the buck-up sign.

Phil shook his head. "This is the congressman's house. I can't mess around with that. My butt will be in a sling."

"Don't worry, I can vouch for her, too," another familiar voice piped up. Lyndsay turned and saw Andy, hustling over as fast as he could jog. She smiled at him in relief.

A second patrol car pulled into the drive. Another officer stepped out. He was older. Less buff. He joined their little circle, moving with deliberation.

"Did an alarm go off?" he asked Phil, to the point.

"If so, it would be my fault," she interjected quickly. "Maybe I didn't enter the code in properly when I was locking up."

"I'm afraid I need to check on her story," Officer Phil said.

"Come on," Andy exclaimed. "This is Lyn Francis. She works for the DesignSea company, she's an interior designer. I can vouch for her. She's been out here with us for weeks. I'd swear to it. You can trust her."

Thank you, Andy, she thought silently.

"She is who she says she is," John added. "Ask any of us."

Moon was there, too. And AJ. All of them nodding at the police officers. John's family stepped forward, too.

Lyndsay swallowed. A realization hit her so hard, that she felt weak in the knees.

She had done her job. She'd done it so well that she'd fooled everybody.

And they trusted her.

Her throat felt raw. Somehow, though, she kept going with the charade she was supposed to keep going with. She used her phone to call Congressman MacLaine. She also spoke with the two police officers. It was decided that a mistake had been made, that Lyn Francis was fully trustworthy, and that they all would take a walk through the house—Lyn and Officer Pierce with Kitty MacLaine on the phone, which Lyndsay kept in her ear—to ascertain that everything inside was, indeed, where it was supposed to be.

Lyndsay felt as if all her blood had rushed to her cheeks. They didn't suspect what was really wrong with her, though—they seemed to assume it was just embarrassment that caused her to turn so red.

"Don't worry about it," Andy murmured to her, with John beside him. "We've all been there before—being embarrassed. But mistakes happen."

John nodded, too. "Yeah. Don't feel bad. We've got your back."

Swallowing, she punched the security code into the system, her palms sweaty, her conscience stabbing at her. In front of witnesses, they'd put their own reputations on the line and vouched for her false identity.

I'm undercover to protect them and their com-

munity. She needed to keep reminding herself that she was doing a service for them, something good. Otherwise, the guilt over lying to them would swamp her.

Honestly, once this incident was solved, she now saw how important it was to plan her exit. There would be a huge fallout if her real identity ever came to light—which she needed to make sure never happened.

A pang of regret stabbed her. It was true she wanted something longer term with John, but that was impossible. To tell him the truth would be to break her cover, which would no doubt get her fired.

Glumly, she entered the house, with all of them trooping after her, including Andy and John. Officer Pierce didn't move to exclude them, and at this point, Lyndsay was hard-pressed to think of a reason *not* to include them, given that she'd been letting them into the house all week.

In the living room, everything looked the same. The large portraits were over the fireplace. The gleaming kitchen was freshly cleaned. Even the sliding glass doors leading to the patio were intact. No signs of breaking or entering.

Upstairs, where she'd done the bulk of her work, everything seemed fine.

"Wow. This place looks really good," John

said in a low voice to her. "I hadn't seen the rest of what you've done."

She smiled sadly at him, her phone still pressed to her ear.

They all came to the locked master bedroom door. That's where the congressman's safe was. The two watercolors she'd been investigating were also inside, hanging on the wall in the alcove, though she supposed they were probably a moot point by now.

"Kitty? Hello?" Kitty hadn't been saying much to her on the phone. Officer Pierce's radio was squawking away.

"Yes," Kitty answered on the other side of the line. "I'm still here."

"Should I unlock the door to your bedroom suite and check inside?" Lyndsay asked.

"You'd better check it. Yes. There's a police officer with you, right?"

"Yes, there is."

"Okay, go ahead. You have my permission to let them in."

Lyndsay inserted the key. *Please, may nothing be missing.*

She unlocked the door and let the troupe of people inside. The new bed, the new bedding and window treatments and furniture greeted her. The new design looked great.

Inside the closet, the safe was still there, still

locked. She didn't need to ask Kitty for the combination. That it was there, locked and unmoved, was enough evidence to her that it was fine.

Officer Pierce paused by the alcove. His head cocked as he stared at the two watercolor portraits of the woman and the dogs frolicking outside on the cove.

"Those are two of Justin's paintings, aren't they?" he asked John.

John's arms were crossed. "Yeah," he murmured to Officer Pierce. "It appears so."

"Justin was a really talented kid," Officer Pierce said to John. "I was in his high school class. It's a shame what happened."

John nodded. He blinked once or twice. His eyes looked wet.

But she couldn't believe what she'd just heard. *Justin* had painted the watercolors? Openmouthed, she stared at John.

He winced slightly. "I'm sorry, Lyn, I wasn't sure when you asked me the first time about them. Then when I did know for sure they were Justin's work, I hadn't told you about him yet. It seemed awkward to explain it, so I just kept quiet."

You could have told me when you did *tell me about Justin!* she wanted to yell. But everyone was looking at her. And in the scheme of things, her lie to John was much worse than his small lie of omission to her.

Her lie was still in effect.

Andy cleared his throat. "John told me not to talk to you about him."

"So…you knew about the paintings, too?" she asked, covering the phone with her hand.

"Don't blame him." John reached over and pulled her close. "I told him to let me do the telling." He kissed her cheek, even in front of Andy and Officer Pierce.

John trusted her and believed they were getting closer with each day. Until this incident, she'd believed so, too. But after this incident with the Wallis Point police, she needed to focus on her exit plan, *now*.

If John found out about her, that would not only put the whole operation at risk, but also it would hurt him terribly. He would see it as a personal betrayal.

Everything was out of control.

"We'll talk later," John murmured to her.

"Yes," she mumbled. *I need to break it off with him.* There was no other choice.

She felt miserable inside. Rubbing her arms, she signed off on the call with Kitty, then followed the men from the room. She locked the door behind them. Out on the street, Officer

Pierce said to her, "Be careful with the alarm in future."

"Yes sir, I will."

"Welcome to Wallis Point, Ms. Francis."

"Thank you," she mumbled.

John stood beside her and watched as the two cruisers backed out of the driveway.

Her cover was safe. The crisis had been averted. And yet, inside, she was falling apart.

Andy came over and stood beside her. "You okay?" he asked Lyndsay.

She couldn't even tell him the truth about how she felt. At least until now, she'd been honest with her feelings.

"I'm embarrassed," she muttered by way of an excuse. "I probably put in the wrong alarm code."

"Don't be," Andy said. "Like I said, it's happened to all of us."

"Yeah," John agreed.

They were being kind, and she felt like weeping for that reason only. They were really good to her. Actually, they were just good people.

Then, within the crowd around her, she saw Pete, her backup. What was he doing here?

I'm okay, she signaled him. *You can please go away now.* Making sure to carefully look away from him, she raised her right hand and deliberately scratched her head.

From her peripheral vision, she saw Pete nod. Still, he hung around.

"I, um, should go fill up my car before the station closes at six," she said to John.

"Want me to come with you?" John asked.

The crux of it was, she didn't want to break off with him, but she had to. She shook her head. "No. That's okay. You can go back to visit with your mom and uncle."

He frowned. "You really don't have to be embarrassed about it, Lyn."

"I'll be right back," was all she said.

"Good, then come and have dessert with me." He gave her a sly wink. Andy had turned away—by now, he knew what they were up to. Or maybe not. John didn't speak to people about his private business; she was sure of that.

"Okay," she said. But she wasn't looking forward to it.

He leaned over and kissed her cheek again. In front of Andy. In front of his mother and uncle, watching them from across the street.

And in front of Pete.

"Lyndsay," he murmured. "I'm glad you're staying for a while longer."

Her heart seemed to crack in two. This was so difficult for her. In different circumstances, she could so easily love him.

LYNDSAY GOT IN her car and drove directly to the convenience store on the beach, the regular rendezvous place. She parked in the small lot in front, then went inside directly to the frozen food aisle. Pete was standing by the waffles, his phone to his ear.

She mentally squared her shoulders, then walked up beside him. She didn't even make a pretense of shopping. She was tired of always having to pretend.

He raised an eye at her then hung up his phone. "Is everything okay, Lyn?"

"I've kept my cover, if that's what you mean." She was so tired of pretending she couldn't even speak in code.

"What happened out there?"

"I don't know." She sighed. "I assume I made a mistake keying in the alarm code. I might have been arrested if not for the locals knowing the police officer."

"The important thing is that you were professional." Pete said it as a statement.

She nodded, still feeling troubled.

Pete tilted his head to her, concerned. "Lyn, I'll ask again. What's wrong?"

How could she say to Pete, *I'm a lousy undercover cop because I'm falling for one of my informants*? Impossible, unless she wanted to guarantee a black mark next to her name. Realistically, who could she talk to about it?

Not her dad. *No way.* For one thing, he would be disappointed in her for hurting her opportunity to advance, and for another, she was his daughter.

The only person she *wanted* to talk to was John. She actually would like to come clean with him and tell him the truth, but she couldn't deliberately blow her cover or she'd jeopardize everyone on her task force, and quite possibly the case itself. Simon was still interrogating witnesses.

Pete was staring at her, waiting for an answer, so she said, "Nothing's wrong. I'm just realizing how serious it is being undercover."

Pete pursed his lips, nodding. He glanced at the mirror overhead. Nobody was in the market, nobody was watching them from the front. "I'm going to keep backing you up, Lyn. In fact, I called to cancel the order with Wesley to remove the cameras so I can keep a closer eye on them. How long do you think it will take to finish the MacLaines' cottage, realistically?"

"Tomorrow there's a final delivery of accessories for the living room at ten o'clock. I can finish up tomorrow afternoon, if I rush, which I'm planning to do. I really need an exit plan, Pete."

"Good thinking. Meet me here, packed and ready, tomorrow night at seven. We'll officially pull you out then. I'll talk to Commander Harris, maybe work on getting you assigned to the interrogation team. Just don't say goodbye to any of the locals, all right?"

She swallowed. Could she do that? "I have to say goodbye to one person," she said softly.

Pete pursed his lips again. He'd seen John kiss her. He must know what was going on there. "You need to tread carefully," he said. "You're good at this job precisely because nobody suspects you. You need to keep that advantage, Lyn."

Yes, she'd even fooled John. Her cynical John.

Pete gave her a careful look. "I didn't just insult you, did I?"

"No." She smiled gently at him. "And thanks for understanding. I'll think carefully about how I handle this. I can't stay here anymore."

CHAPTER THIRTEEN

JOHN WAITED AT his house for Lyndsay, but over an hour had passed, and she hadn't returned. So he postponed his plans for TV with Patrick and instead headed to the MacLaine cottage.

First, he stopped by the local supermarket and picked up a bouquet of flowers, just because. Small things like that seemed to cheer her, and she'd just had an upsetting experience.

He knocked on her door, and she answered, arms crossed. She wore a pink windbreaker, and her blond hair was drawn back and up to expose the delicate skin on her neck and collarbone.

He held up the flowers and smiled, but he didn't get a reaction beyond a robotic "Thanks."

This wasn't like her. She seemed preoccupied. The late afternoon sun framed her face, and she blinked at him as if in a daze. The purse she wore around her shoulder slipped and was going to fall, but he stepped forward and caught it.

"Sorry," she muttered.

"Why are you sorry?"

She blinked at him. "Um, did your mother and your uncle leave yet?"

"Yes. They headed home an hour ago." He walked past her and into the kitchen, intending to help her by putting the flowers in water. Maybe find a pitcher or a vase in a cabinet somewhere. He turned to find her standing behind him, staring numbly at him.

She was more shaken by what she'd gone through than he'd expected. He drew her over to sit on a stool at the kitchen island beside him. "Hey. It's okay, Lyndsay. Nothing was taken from the house. Phil was just being a hard-ass, trying to do his job the way he thinks he's supposed to. I know you're a conscientious worker, but it's not your fault."

She put her elbows on the counter and rested her head in her hands. "That's not an excuse." She looked so miserable, his heart went out to her. She *hated* screwing up. She seemed to be a perfectionist in her work habits, but not in a bad way.

"Aw. Come here." He dragged her stool closer to him. The hot tub was visible through the sliding glass door on the patio. "Maybe we can think of something fun to do tonight. That will help you get over it."

She stiffened in his arms, then slightly backed

away. "I've been…reconsidering, John." Her voice was strained, and her eyes didn't meet his.

"Reconsidering what?"

She stood and stepped away. Pacing, she seemed to be searching for words, but hadn't found the right ones, or maybe the courage to voice them.

She's ending this…

A slight panic filled him. He wondered if this had something to do with Phil mentioning that Justin had painted the watercolors? He'd been thinking about that incident and her small, shocked reaction to it, ever since the awkward way Phil had brought it up during the walk-through.

John hadn't mentioned it to her after he'd told her about Justin, because he hadn't realized it was such a big deal to her. If he'd known, he'd definitely would have told her.

"John, I made a mistake," she said softly, her gaze fixed on the countertop. "Our relationship was always doomed. I never should have let it get this far to begin with."

"Please don't say that. You're just upset about the police being here."

She shook her head, miserable. Her eyes were glistening, which made him want to fix everything for her.

"Why don't we talk about it, Lyndsay?"

"No. I'm sorry," she said in a whisper. "I'd hoped to make a clean break." She wiped her damp eyes with her hand.

His breath expelled as if he'd been punched. "It doesn't have to be this way."

Her big blue eyes gazed up at him. "Yes. It does. We have no future."

"I was thinking the opposite—" *Great.* He hadn't expected it, but his heart had softened, more and more, just by being with her, and now...

I'm in love with her.

He hadn't wanted it to be true, and yet, here it was.

Raking his hands through his hair, he tried to figure out what to say that might change her mind. This feeling of *being left* was too uncomfortably close. He'd been through it before, and for a long time afterward, he'd regretted that he hadn't spoken the truth or even tried to stop it from happening.

"Can I just tell you a few things before you make your decision?" He grasped at straws. Anything to convince her to give them a second chance. "Justin's drawings in the bedroom upstairs...do you want to know about them? Can I tell you why I didn't explain about him and the paintings earlier?"

Her lip quivered. But she wasn't pushing

back on him any longer, so he spoke before she stopped him.

"I never used to open up enough, Lyndsay. I know." Hadn't he heard this time and again? It was why he'd initially been reluctant to start a relationship with her. "But since I've met you, I've learned to risk more. I'm better with Patrick than I used to be. In fact, he was the one who told me how Justin had turned into an artist after I left home. He's even got one of Justin's paintings in his bedroom. Once I saw it and I knew, the only reason I didn't tell you Justin painted those watercolors was because I hadn't told you yet who Justin was. It's painful to talk about him. I didn't see the point in bringing him up again. But now there is a point, because you're hurt by it, and I don't want you to be hurt."

He paused because she was paying attention, really listening to him. And suddenly, letting her into his inner world, all of it, was less dangerous to his well-being than keeping her out. "This is how I really feel about my brother Justin. He was…one of a kind. I wish you could have met him, Lyndsay—he would have loved you. He used to talk to people, especially people on the beach and he—"

"Justin was an artist on the beach?"

"Yes. I think he developed into one after I left. I mean, he was always creative, so I'm not surprised. I'd like to talk to Patrick more about that, because I want to know what happened to him. His drowning never made sense to me. Maybe you could go with me when I talk to him?" He was grasping at straws again, but she seemed to be wavering.

"I *would* like to meet Patrick," she said softly.

"Then we can do that." He nodded, relieved. "If I can help Patrick past his problems, then that will help a lot of people. Justin was really the one who was suited to running the business. I never felt the same way he did. But after he drowned… I always felt guilty that I wasn't here for him. I felt like I'd left him behind, and guilty that I hadn't tried harder to stay in Wallis Point and make a life here."

"You *shouldn't* feel guilty," she said, leaning forward and touching his arm. "You're not guilty of *anything*."

"No, but I'm responsible for my brother." Literally. He'd sworn in a court of law to be responsible for employing him, for watching over him while he wore the monitoring bracelet. For keeping him off drugs and out of trouble.

"Why is that on you? If anyone, shouldn't your mom be taking care of it, not you?"

"Maybe, but at the time she was too distraught to make any promises to the court, and since I'm the Marine veteran, I stepped forward. But,

Lyndsay, I'm not willing to sacrifice my life any longer." He searched her face. "Am I swaying your decision at all? Because I can't accept the thought of you leaving just yet. It's killing me."

Suddenly, her face crumpled as if she was going to cry. "It's killing me, too." She leaned her head into his shoulder. "You have no idea," she whispered.

"Shh. It's okay," he said gruffly, his voice muffled by her hair. But he pulled her as close to him as he could without hurting her. Her soft body melded against his. Her arms squeezed him tight.

"There's so much we don't tell each other," she whispered, her breath warm against his neck. "There's so much you don't know about me, either."

He tried to lighten the mood. "I don't need to know about your hero husband, if that's all right with you."

She chuckled softly. "I wasn't thinking about him, John."

"Okay, that's good." He took a breath. "Here's a proposal for you. Let's go slowly. One small noncommittal step at a time."

"How does *that* work? Honestly? Because I don't see it happening, no matter how much I try."

"Let's just start with one night. Now. For the

next few hours, we'll put aside your job and my family. There will be nothing but you and me. A mini-vacation. We won't talk about anything beyond these next few hours."

She pressed her forehead against his chest. "That is so tempting. You have no idea, John. None."

He was glad to have something to tempt her with, because she always tempted him. He angled his head beside hers. Caught her lips and kissed her. Feeling her kissing him back was an immediate turn-on.

She closed the space between them, and he felt how much she cared about him too. They had an attraction that just wouldn't die, no matter how futile a longer-term relationship might feel to her.

She broke their kiss. "I want to, John," she murmured. "I *so* want to. But I have to leave soon, you know that."

"How many days until your next job?"

She hesitated.

Maybe he wasn't being fair, but he wasn't going to let her concentrate, because to concentrate was to come up with a reason why this wouldn't work. Why *they* wouldn't work. He kissed her with as much feeling as he had in him. He didn't stop kissing her.

"I…can't think…" She ran her hands over his

chest. Down his shoulders and then his arms. She groaned.

"Just think about one night at a time," he murmured. "I have another idea." He stopped kissing her long enough to reach for his phone. "I'll make a reservation at a hotel for tonight. We'll get away from all this."

"I'm sure I'm going to regret it," she said, "but…okay. Just…for this one night."

"You won't regret it, Lyndsay." He kissed her one last time. "Let's get out of here."

BREAKING IT OFF with John was turning out to be the hardest thing she'd ever done.

Even as she stepped into his truck with him, she knew she was only prolonging the pain.

She justified it by telling herself that tonight was their goodbye. As Personal Lyndsay, she spent one last night with John in a romantic, moon-soaked room at the Grand Beachfront Hotel, a beautiful old rambling structure in the center of the beach district at Wallis Point. They ordered room service and stayed in bed. She didn't want the dawn to come, but of course, it did.

The next morning, not having really slept, she pulled the tousled sheets around her shoulders and nestled in John's arms while he slumbered beside her. His hand rested on her hip, his breathing light and regular against her hair. She watched helplessly as the sun's rays snuck in through the slats in the blinds of the balcony window.

A phone would ring soon—probably John's first, followed by hers. The restaurant business started early. Toby needed his fluids, then the MacLaines' last delivery would be arriving. By nightfall, she would be gone from Wallis Point. Pete would help pull her out.

Moisture prickled her eyelids.

A sharp knock sounded on the door. She started while John groaned and stretched. When he saw her lying beside him, he smiled. "Good morning, darling."

"Who's at the door?" she whispered.

"Probably room service. I put in an order last night while I was ordering dinner."

She relaxed. That was so like John. "Good thinking," she murmured. She watched him as he got up, naked, and put on a terry cloth robe.

He opened the door, then stepped out, and she heard voices, followed by the rattle of a cart being wheeled past. She smelled the fresh aroma of breakfast. She'd pulled the covers up to her chin, just in case the hotel employee caught a glimpse inside the bedroom area. Little chance of that, though, because John stood in the doorway like a wall, blocking her from view. He signed a receipt, then made sure the heavy door shut behind him.

She sat up as he placed the tray on the bed. It would be hard to eat when her heart was breaking.

I'm leaving today and he can't know it.

In the face of that, what could she say to him? How could she make idle chitchat?

"I'm hoping you like this treatment," he said shyly.

Her fingers clutched the sheets. "I've loved every minute of it," she whispered. Her voice cracked. She meant it, she had loved every moment of her time with him.

"You deserve a good life." He passed her a glass, taking care of her, and it was so bittersweet a feeling. Nobody ever took care of her.

He raised his glass to her. "Someday soon we'll go on a real vacation."

Somehow managing to hold her glass without spilling it, she drank the freshly squeezed orange juice. The vision of flying away with him was too much to bear.

I'm in love with him.

But she couldn't be. There was zero chance of a happy ending for them.

Biting her lip, she glanced at the clock. "Toby will be needing his fluids."

"Yes, Toby." John nodded. "You can stay here and sleep in if you'd like."

"Maybe I'll do that." If she did, then she wouldn't have to say goodbye to him twice. "I have a delivery truck to meet at ten o'clock."

He put his arm around her waist and pulled her closer. A lump was forming in her throat, and if she wasn't careful, she was going to cry.

JOHN COULD FEEL his heart opening to her even as he accepted her embrace. She was the one for him. He loved being with her. Loved the progression of closeness that they were experiencing. Yes, she had to leave this week, but he was confident that would be temporary. They would work something out. A long-distance relationship wasn't so great an obstacle that they couldn't overcome it.

His phone rang. He would have liked to ignore it, but given his family, that wasn't an option. He reached for his phone on the bedside table and accepted the call.

"John? This is Mom." Her voice sounded anxious.

His heart sped up. "Is everything okay?"

"I'm a bit swamped. And I'm worried because you're usually here by now."

"Where's Patrick?"

"He's still sleeping. I tried to wake him, but I think he was up most of the night."

"This has got to stop, Mom."

"I know, but I'm beyond knowing how to handle it anymore."

John glanced at Lyndsay. She was alert, head cocked, listening. He'd told her about his desire to reorder his priorities, and yet, here he was being sucked into them again.

"I'll be right there." He hung up, tasting the regret in his mouth.

"Was that your mom?" she asked quietly.

"I need to go to the restaurant. I'm sorry about that."

"Patrick is giving her trouble." She said it as a statement.

"Yes," he said in a low voice.

She nibbled her lip, and appeared to be thinking. He sincerely hoped his family problems didn't sway her against him.

"I'd like to come with you, too," she finally said.

He exhaled. "Okay. Yeah, we'll do that."

She nodded at him. Her mood was somber and tentative, but he *had* promised last night to let her meet Patrick.

He couldn't help feeling that this would be a test. What would Lyndsay think of his brother?

SHE WAS STILL leaving tonight. There was no confusion about that on her part. The problem was that Work Lyndsay needed to see the watercolor painting in Patrick's bedroom. It was a loose end that the professional side of her couldn't leave hanging. Yes, prolonging her time with John was painful, but it needed to be done. The reason she'd come to Wallis Point in the first place had been to complete her investigative work.

She packed and tried to focus on each moment as it came. When they arrived at the Seaside, Lyndsay noted that the lot was busy even at this early hour. Andy hadn't made his appearance yet, but he was surely on his way. John parked on the side lane up the hill, beside his mom's small white Cape-style house.

John stepped up to the side porch, then unlocked the door with a key he took from his pocket. He held the screen door open for her as he led her inside directly into the kitchen. Tiny, really.

Yet, the home was small and scrubbed immaculately clean. While she was busy glancing around, noting the pretty windows overlooking a grassy side yard hemmed in by a tall fence, John said, "I'll wake Patrick up."

She watched him walk down a short hallway with two doors, one of which she could see was a bathroom. The second must have been Patrick's bedroom, because the door was open and he peered inside.

"He's not here," John called.

She noticed a staircase. "Is he on the second floor, maybe?"

"No. My mom sleeps up there. He's probably in the restaurant kitchen. I'll go check."

"All right. I'll wait here for you." She reached over and pulled out a kitchen chair. She had no intention of sitting, though.

He nodded at her, distracted with his thoughts.

Before he could head out the door that led through the sheltered entryway to the restaurant, his mom came through it. "John, I'm glad you're here." She turned and noticed Lyndsay. "Oh." She glanced from Lyndsay to John.

"Good morning, Margie," Lyndsay said. "I'm sorry you've been having trouble."

"I'll go down and talk to Patrick," John said to Margie.

Margie wrung her hands. "I was mistaken when I called you. He wasn't actually sleeping. His door was locked, so I just assumed…"

"Where was he?" John demanded.

"In the business office." She sighed. "He was…using your laptop."

"I lock that door." John spoke tightly, through

his teeth. He seemed to be holding in his anger for his mom's sake.

"I know. He must have figured out a way in. He's upset, and he asked me not to tell you. He knew you'd be angry."

John tore his hand through his hair. He paced from one end of the kitchen to the next.

Lyndsay put her hand on John's shoulder. "It will be okay," she murmured, even though she instinctively knew that it wouldn't. She felt for him, personally, but she was also starting to get a sickening hunch about Patrick.

If he could sneak into a locked room, could he also sneak out of the bracelet that tracked him?

She would give anything to search the house for evidence. There was a legal limit to how much she could snoop while undercover, though. If she made a mistake and overstepped her boundaries, then any evidence she found could be ruled inadmissible in the event of a prosecution. She had to be invited in, for one thing—she couldn't just barge or sneak her way past.

She eyed the hallway that led to Patrick's room. It was true that her initial motivation for coming here this morning had been to see the painting that John had said hung in Patrick's room. Somehow, she needed to wrangle an invitation in there.

She squeezed John's arm. "Maybe Patrick would like to talk with someone outside the family."

"It couldn't hurt," Margie agreed.

John closed his eyes and shook his head. "We're so close to his court date," he muttered.

"*Why* is using the laptop forbidden?" she asked, curious. "Was that a stipulation from the court?"

"No. It's my rule, because that's how he used to buy his drugs, and he fooled me once already," John said curtly.

"That was before he finished rehab," Margie insisted. "He's clean now."

"He'd better be," John muttered under his breath.

Margie cringed. Lyndsay could see how upsetting this was for the family. She rubbed her hand on John's back, wishing she could help them.

She couldn't. She was trained to take criminals off the street, and she considered that hugely important. But she'd honestly never thought about it much from the point of view of the criminals' families.

You're jumping to conclusions, she chastened herself. Something strange might be going on with Patrick's behavior, but she hadn't investigated him enough to determine just what that was. It might be completely innocent.

"Wait for me here, Lyndsay," John said abruptly. "I'm going to talk to him." A muscle ticked in his jaw. He headed for the door, his mother on his heels.

"May I use the restroom?" Lyndsay called.

"Of course. First door on the right, down the hall."

"Thank you." She waited until the door shut behind them, then headed into the bathroom. She turned on the faucet and washed her hands, considering her reflection in the mirror. She looked drawn and haggard. That was loss of sleep and anxiety over the way that she was leaving John.

She didn't *want* to leave him. But she did need to solve this case.

Cocking an ear and hearing nothing, she headed into the hallway and stopped before Patrick's small bedroom. The door was open. An unmade bed, clothes on the floor. No watercolor on the wall.

She stepped inside and looked again... There it was.

The same size as the MacLaines', on the same type of paper, but with a different frame.

"What are you doing?" said a cold voice.

She took a calming breath and plastered a smile on her face before she turned.

A young man wearing a gray sweatshirt and black track pants glowered at her. He looked like John—handsome face—but he was a thinner, slighter version of him. John *looked* like a soldier. Patrick didn't. She caught a flash of defiance in his dark blue eyes.

He isn't like John at all. The cop in her whispered a warning. If she'd come up on Patrick's vehicle for a routine traffic stop, she would have taken extra care. The fact that he wore an ankle bracelet made the warning sound louder.

She smiled even more cheerfully. "You must be Patrick. I'm Lyn. Hi."

"You're John's girlfriend, aren't you?"

"Yes. Yes, I am." She turned toward his room and continued in a chatty voice. "John told me about Justin. I recognized his watercolor in your room."

Patrick didn't say anything, but he didn't close the door to the room, either.

"I'm an interior decorator at the MacLaine cottage. You know—the congressman's house down in the cul-de-sac near where John lives? I'm pretty much finished with the job—I'm leaving this afternoon and headed up to Maine next—and then tomorrow the MacLaines are coming back to live there full-time."

Patrick remained silent.

"Anyway..." She shrugged nonchalantly.

"There are two of these watercolors in the master bedroom upstairs in the MacLaines' house. A lady and two golden retrievers frolicking on the beach."

"Jack and Annabelle," he murmured, excited. "Justin's dogs."

"How did *that* painting end up with the MacLaines?"

"Justin painted people on the beach. Later he bought some of the pictures back, but not everybody would sell them."

"Why did he want them back?"

"Because he wanted to have a showing." Patrick crossed his arms. "That's why."

"I'd love to see more of his work. Do you have any more I can look at?"

Patrick eyed at her suspiciously. She gave him her most guileless look. He glanced toward his room. "Some," he said softly.

She breathed slowly, careful not to give away her excitement. *May I see them?* she was just about to ask.

"There you are." John's voice. She turned.

"I was just talking with Patrick." She turned to Patrick. "It's nice to finally meet you. John's told me a lot about you and Justin."

There was a silence while Patrick reached down to scratch his ankle. Overall, she had a hinky feeling where Patrick was concerned. People wore ankle bracelets in law enforcement for a few reasons. Patrick's was presentencing in extenuating circumstances. That was the explanation that Pete had given her when he'd done the background check on Patrick.

The extenuating circumstances appeared to be that Patrick was help in the kitchen. The way bracelets worked was that if Patrick left the perimeter, then a phone call would be generated. If drugs were involved, some bracelets were armed with sensors that could detect the drugs and transmit the information to law enforcement. Not every jurisdiction had access to those bracelets, but she was pretty certain this one did.

She doubted Patrick was on drugs any longer. He didn't have the telltale dark hollows and blank look to his eyes. She would bet that he was clean.

It was the anger that rolled off him in waves that alarmed her. Patrick was obviously troubled.

"Lyn?" John touched her arm. "I need to give Toby his fluids now. I'll give you a lift to the MacLaines' if you'd like."

"Yes," she said with reluctance.

Patrick needed more investigating. The part of her that wanted to solve the case was in tune with that fact. But the part of her that loved John was in turmoil.

CHAPTER FOURTEEN

IN THE TRUCK, headed toward the cottage, she listened to John as the wind rushed through this hair. The window was open, and the air smelled and felt on her skin like a day at the beach, except that it wasn't.

"We don't usually let people into our confidence where Patrick is concerned," John was saying. "But I'm glad that we did. He seemed to be opening up to you."

She swallowed. The statement was eerily ironic.

He glanced at her. "What did you think of Patrick? Honestly?"

She wet her lips. This was a fine line between her work and her love, and she'd more than realized that it couldn't be separated anymore. She struggled with one big, messy problem of illusions, mistakes and honest emotions.

She opted for honest emotions. "I think that Patrick is emotionally troubled about something. Maybe Justin's death." She pressed her lips together, aware that John watched every nuance on her face. Despite believing her lies about not being undercover, he perceived her emotions quite well. "If Patrick were my brother, I'd try to convince him to talk with a trained counselor. I don't have any expertise there, I'm afraid."

John nodded. He ran a hand through his hair again. "You and I agree about that. The problem is, our hands are somewhat tied until he makes it through his hearing with the judge on June fifth." He gave her a wry smile. "My biggest goal is to keep him out of prison so that he can get that help, and the judge is the one who will decide his sentencing fate. As part of the terms of the bracelet, we're actually limited on who we can bring him in contact with. I made a judgment call with you."

Her breath sucked in. John was completely unaware that he'd let a cobra into his den. And yet, if Patrick was part of the burglary ring, then he needed to be stopped, as soon as possible. If what she feared was true, he *needed* to be arrested. Whether incarceration was to be involved or not was the judge's call. "No one else has been to see him?" she asked.

"Other than my mother, Millie's family, Andy and you—no." He smiled at her. "You were good with him. I mean, don't get me wrong, I expect it of you. You're different. That's why I trust you."

She swallowed.

"I won't lie to you," he continued. "Patrick stole to support his drug habit." He was silent for a moment, lightly drumming his hand on the steering wheel. "You're right, though. There was probably an underlying reason why Patrick turned to drugs in the first place. I'm not sure that rehab dug deeply enough into figuring out what the reasons were."

"It *is* a long road—" She added quickly, "I've heard." She glanced at John. "Patrick wasn't like this until Justin and your dad died?"

"Not from what my mother has said, but I'm not sure I believe her, either. Justin wrote me once that he was working with Patrick. I never got to hear from him exactly what that meant."

"It's not uncommon for young teens to fall into the drug life, unfortunately. I hope you don't think it's a stigma on your family."

He tilted his head. "I do, a little," he said softly.

She knew more about this than she was outwardly letting on. When she'd earned her criminal justice degree in the fog after her husband had been killed, she'd gravitated toward taking psychology electives, just because the classes had helped her personally. Obviously, drug addiction had been touched upon in those courses, and as a police officer, the knowledge had been helpful to her.

"I'm sorry your family has had to go through this."

He reached over and clasped her hand. "Thank you."

She squeezed his hand tight, hating that she had to ask this question, but…

"Who do you think he's communicating with on the laptop, if it's not his dealer?"

John pursed his lips, thinking, as he flicked on the directional signal. They were heading into the cul-de-sac. She didn't have much time left in the truck with him.

"He could," John said slowly, "be hacking something."

"Hacking?"

"He's good with computers. I always thought that maybe he was a little different from most kids his age, because he's lousy with emotions and good with tasks that require focus and technical problem-solving." John sighed. "Right before I left home for the Marines, I remember him being all excited about pulling apart his home computer and then putting it back together again with new and improved parts. He read books to figure everything out, and he played around with all the different operating systems. He was just a kid then."

"Did he ever get in trouble with his hacking?"

"Once. When I first got home and he was mad at me for something, he got into our restaurant website and screwed it up royally. He did it without even knowing the password—and I know, because it was in my head only, and it wasn't something he'd ever guess. It was then that I realized my brother was scary smart with computers. And it's such a waste, because if directed well, that talent could really help people, and Patrick could make a good life for himself." He shook his head bitterly and stepped on the brake.

They were stopped now in the MacLaines' driveway, the engine idling. She was reluctant to open the door and leave John, for two reasons. One was to continue questioning him about Patrick for her investigation. The second...

Her eyes teared up. She suddenly looked over at John, not able to keep it inside any longer.

"I love you," she said. "Please don't ever forget that. I honestly love you, John."

JOHN TURNED IN his seat, one hand on the steering wheel, one hand wrapped up in Lyndsay's. He was fast getting to a place where he couldn't imagine not having her in his life. She made it easier to press on, to slog along with Patrick's problems. She was smart. Whip smart. And she loved *him*.

It was all he could do to believe it. But tears were streaming down her cheeks.

"Hey," he said softly, wiping a tear away with his thumb. "We'll make this work, have no doubt about that. You've got a huge talent, and I want you to take it where it goes, use it and not worry about me. Things will get easier on the Patrick front in a few weeks. I'll be able to drive to see you wherever you end up."

She nodded, swallowing. "I really hope so. It would be so perfect if this could work."

Her phone made the chiming sound of an incoming text message. She pulled it out of her jacket pocket and glanced at it, then smiled tightly at him.

"My dad. He wants me to call him back. He's worried that I didn't call him last night like I said I would."

"Are you going to talk to him about us?"

Her cheeks reddened, but she nodded. "He'll be happy for me," she said softly. "He wants me to be happy."

"Then I like him already."

The phone rang this time, and she turned off the sound. "He's getting insistent," she said as an apology. "I really need to go call him."

"Yeah. Toby's waiting for me, too."

She held on to his hand tighter, as if by letting it go, she would be letting go of the relationship.

"Don't worry, Lyndsay. You can count on me. I've got your back."

Her eyes flooded with tears again. "Me too, John," she sniffed. "And... I promise I'll help you with Patrick however I can."

He exhaled, his eyes closed. Then he drew her closer. In relief and in love. She leaned over and kissed him on the cheek.

"I have to go," she whispered. "You do, too."

LYNDSAY STOOD IN the driveway, waving limply, until John's truck disappeared from the cul-de-sac. She was in so much trouble. She wanted nothing more than to climb into bed and cry her eyes out.

But she couldn't, because Pete had texted her.

Meet me now.

His subsequent phone call had been part of their signal. In ten minutes, if she didn't show up at the prearranged meeting place, then Pete would come look for her.

Even if Pete hadn't called her first, she would have had to call him anyway. He was her partner. He needed to be told what she was working on. That was Detective School 101.

As soon as John's truck was out of sight, she sucked it up and put on her work mind-set. She dropped her purse inside the entryway of the MacLaine home, then ran out the back slider and onto the beach. Vaguely, she registered that it was sunny today, and warmer. She jogged in the direction of the convenience store, mentally running through everything she'd learned this morning and directing her brain to avoid any personal thoughts of John.

Inside the frozen food section, she found Pete. "Why did you text?" she asked him, wasting no time.

"Because the suspect we brought in has been released," Pete said in a low tone behind her. "We're back to square one."

She crossed her arms and leaned against the freezer case. She hadn't expected that bit of news in the least. "What happened?"

"The maid didn't have anything real behind her confession. We got a connection through her—her cousin—but that didn't pan out either, and we didn't have enough evidence to continue holding them."

"But we were so sure we had them."

"Believe me, no one is happy about this turn of events."

She put her hand to her chest. "What happens now? I'm still leaving Wallis Point, right?"

Pete nodded. "Tonight."

She took a breath. "I have news, too. Justin

Reilly—deceased brother of Patrick and John—painted the watercolors."

Pete stared hard at her. "Really?"

He knows about John and me. She bit her lip and nodded. "I had a chance to talk with Patrick this morning. He's got watercolor paintings of Justin's, he says, a collection of them. They're in his bedroom, but I didn't get to see them because our conversation was interrupted."

"So you don't know if they're stolen property or if they're just more paintings of Justin's?"

"Exactly right." Lyndsay shivered. It was cold in this section of the store. "Do you mind if we move to the canned goods aisle?"

Pete nodded, and they walked slowly. She picked up a deserted red basket and plucked items off the shelf and put them in her basket as they walked. "Evidently," she murmured as she pretended to shop, stopping to peruse a can of pineapple slices, "Justin was trying to buy back his paintings right before he died. Patrick is sullen and full of anger. He's trouble for his family. It could be that he's been participating in the burglaries. He's also quite a hacker. The family has been locking away the business laptop, but they caught him using it this morning. I highly doubt this was the first time he's used it."

"Do you think he could have been hacking his ankle bracelet and sneaking out?"

"Possibly. But I'm more intrigued that he could have been hacking the alarm systems. I want to go up the coast today and interview the company that the MacLaines use."

"That's a good idea. I'll watch Wesley's cameras while you're gone."

She reddened, thinking of Pete watching them last night and seeing John knock on her door. Then, watching her leave with John.

But he said nothing about it, and that relieved her.

"There is one other thing, Pete. I told Patrick about Justin's two watercolors that hang in the MacLaines' upstairs master bedroom. I also told him that I was leaving this evening and that no one would be home tonight. To tee it up, I told a fib that the MacLaines were returning tomorrow morning to live full-time."

Pete chuckled. "Not real subtle, but it works."

"Yes, he was interested. I could see him practically drooling for it."

Pete rubbed his chin. "He might show tonight or he might not. Or, he could be passing along alarm codes to his friends on the outside." He glanced at her. "I was going to pull you out of Wallis Point, but I think it's best for you to stay one more night."

She swallowed. She hadn't been thinking too far ahead this morning as she'd been taking her investigative steps. She'd been living moment by moment, just to survive the conflict she was having between her personal and professional sides.

But Pete was right. Who else should be in the MacLaine house for a stakeout and a potential robbery but her?

"Keep alert tonight, Lyndsay. So far, the burglary ring has always hit at night, either two or three burglars, judging by the evidence. Don't mess with them. The physical threat is real."

She nodded. She wasn't worried about that part.

"I'd like to get warrants for the Reilly home and restaurant," he said. "I want the laptop and I want the painting collection. I also want to question Patrick at the station."

"What? No!" She felt panicked. John would freak out about that. "We don't have enough evidence to do that yet. This hunch might not even pan out, Pete."

He gave her a hard look. But he backed down, shaking his head. "We'll wait and see what happens tonight."

"Thank you," she said with relief.

He gave her another hard look. "Lyndsay, you've got to be prepared for the possibility that you'll be arresting Patrick Reilly this evening."

"As Lyn Francis," she said.

"No, as Officer Fairfax. Because when you make an arrest, you break your cover."

Right, she knew this. She rubbed her forehead. "Please don't apply for the warrants until we find out what happens tonight," she begged.

He looked closely at her. "*Are* you prepared to arrest Patrick? You've gotten close to his brother."

"I'll do my job. You know I always do my job."

"I don't know." He crossed his arms. "You've gotten real close to him."

"Will you tell anyone?"

He stared at her for a moment. Then he glanced down the empty aisle. Turning back, he asked, "Do you want to take a drive with me?"

"No, it would risk my cover. I've come too far to do that." She glanced at him. "*Are* you going to tell Commander Harris?"

He sighed. "No."

"Thank you."

"I've been in your shoes, if that helps."

Her mouth dropped open. "*You* have?" She never would have expected that of seasoned, steady Pete.

He nodded grimly. "All I can say is, be careful there."

"From a personal perspective or a professional perspective?"

He snorted. "Both."

"You're speaking from experience?"

"I am," he conceded.

"Would you mind telling me if you were able to make it work? Both ways, I mean?" She held her breath. She wanted so much to believe in the dream that she could both solve the case no matter where it led her, and that she could continue to see John, that he would forgive her for her mixed loyalties and her undercover deceit, no matter what happened with the case in the end.

Pete glanced quickly around before speaking, careful that no one could overhear them. "All I can say," he said in a low tone, "is that I was once an undercover drug dealer. Now I'm married to the sister of a perp I put in jail. But it's a very long road, and I'm an outlier. In the vast majority of cases, mixing a personal life with undercover work never works."

"So...it is possible to recover from this?" she asked with hope.

He shook his head. "You've got to remember that from his point of view, you've been lying to him romantically *and* you're hurting his family in the process. It's among the most personal wounds you can ever inflict upon anyone."

Pete was right. It was going to break his heart if he ever found out.

"Lyn," Pete said gently, "you have to believe this is important work we do, or you can never look yourself in a mirror afterwards. We *help* people. You have to trust in that."

She wanted to. But that remained to be seen.

She checked the time on her phone, then swallowed. "Thank you for talking honestly with me, Pete. I need to get going if I'm going to meet my delivery at the MacLaine cottage."

"Take a moment to run me through your day ahead so I know how to best cover you. Keep in mind that I'll be your backup, but I won't be on-site with you tonight."

"Okay." She nodded. "First, I'm meeting with the last furniture delivery van at ten o'clock. Then I'll take a couple of hours to finish up the cottage. Next, I stop by the Seaside to let John know I'll be up the coast tonight, working on billing or some such with my design employer. Then, over to interview the alarm company, and finally, back to the MacLaine home just after dark."

"You have your service weapon with you?"

"I do."

He shook his head. "I don't know. I could pull you out of here with one phone call and put Simon in your place."

"*Please* don't. If I leave now, that will look suspicious, and it could endanger future operations. Let me handle the situation as best I can."

Pete wiped his hand over his face. "Fine. I'll

support you as long as possible. Tonight, we'll do it this way. Two rings, we meet. Three rings, you pick up your phone. And if you need me to come in and assist with an arrest, just say, 'Not now.' That's it, 'Not now.'"

"Okay."

"Lyn, I'm not sure about this."

"*You* were undercover before. You know that when you're undercover, sometimes you need leeway. Please trust me enough to give me that leeway."

LYNDSAY HURRIED TO the MacLaine cottage in time to meet the delivery guys bringing in the new living room furniture. She spent an hour or so putting out all the accessories and staging it to look sophisticated and appealing. *There.* The house was good enough to show Kitty. There were other extras Lyndsay would have liked to do, including adding fresh flowers and new lighting, but there wasn't time for that. She had police work to do.

Rushing upstairs, she took a quick shower and changed into jeans, running shoes and a turtleneck. The rest of her clothes and personal items she gathered together and removed so that there was no trace of her anywhere. Then she locked the doors and turned on the alarm. Pocketing her keys, she flipped up the hood on her nylon jacket. Outside, rain softly pelted the sidewalk, turning the dry asphalt into a polka-dot canvas of wet raindrops.

She jogged the quarter mile to John's house, but he wasn't in the kitchen to greet her. Peeking through the window before she knocked, just to make sure, she saw no one inside.

His jacket was missing from the hook beside the door. Only sleepy Toby gazed up at her from his spot on the chair, atop one of John's T-shirts.

For a minute, she almost lost her nerve. But she swallowed and said a silent goodbye to the cat she was glad John had with him.

She would need to talk with John at the Seaside. She jogged back to the MacLaines' driveway and hopped into her car, then headed for the restaurant. It was well past the lunch rush. Her fingers curling into a fist, she rapped on Margie's residence window.

When Margie saw her, she broke into a smile. "John is in the business office," she said, poking her head out of the doorway. "Come in out of the rain."

"Thank you."

Margie led her down the covered walkway and into the large industrial kitchen. Tucked into a far corner was a closed door. Margie rapped on it. "Lyndsay is here to see you."

The door opened, and Lyndsay saw him sitting at a desk. Papers surrounded him, and a laptop sat open, displaying a spreadsheet.

"Hey." He greeted her with a yawn, then leaned back, rubbing his eyes. "Sorry. Didn't get much sleep last night." He grinned wickedly at her.

How could she not smile back at him? He was handsome and fun, and for the moment at least, he was hers. She spent a guilty second taking in the laptop that might very likely be confiscated later, and she fought the urge to shout to him, "Back up all your work to the cloud! Trust me!" The police who eventually searched the office would even take the memory sticks and CDs.

"Lyndsay?" He waved his hand in front of her eyes.

"I guess I'm a zombie today, too."

"Yeah. Our mini-vacation was good while it lasted. I'm thinking we need another one tonight."

She swallowed, removing some papers from the spare chair and sitting to face him. John reached over and swung the door closed again.

"Privacy," he explained. "These walls have ears."

She expelled a long breath. "I just came to tell you that I got called to go to the office tonight. I received the last delivery of furniture, so my boss wants to send out the billing. Which means..." She gestured to his laptop. "I need to do paperwork, too." She made a face indicating her distaste for that part of her job, which was real. There was nothing she disliked more than writing up reports. "My boss wants to have a late dinner afterward. I figure I'll just stay there in my apartment rather than drive back here in the rain."

John nodded, fingers steepled together. Before he could ask her where her apartment was—she wasn't prepared to tell him that—she tore off a blank slip of paper from a notepad on his desk.

"Would you mind giving me your mobile number, John?" She laughed softly. "It's sort of embarrassing that we haven't exchanged numbers yet."

He grinned at her. "I was spoiled, being able to look out my bedroom window and see your car in the drive. I liked that."

"Me, too. But I'm afraid I might be reassigned tonight after all," she said carefully. "I think that's partly why Karen wants to take me out to dinner—to talk about my next assignment."

His grin faded. "Yeah. We knew this day was coming."

But he took the pen from her and scribbled down his number. She stuck that in her pocket. When this was all over, however it turned out, she longed to call him and explain herself.

Then he handed her his phone for her to program her contact information.

She hesitated for just a split second. She couldn't give him her task force number—if he phoned, it would show up in investigative and possibly court records.

She gave him her real, personal mobile number. She owed him that. If she had to disappear without explanation tomorrow, then he would be sick with worry if he didn't know that she was okay. That was the kind of man he was. Her hand shook as she typed in her number.

Handing the phone to him, it was hard to meet his knowing eyes, but she did. Her lip was quivering, though, giving her away, so she made the motions of fanning herself. "Whew. If I'm not careful, I'm going to cry again."

"Don't." He stood, enveloping her in a gentle bear hug. She wished she could stay with him for longer.

"Well." She stepped back. "I'm going to be late if I don't get going. I've got to dig out my laptop and start on a spreadsheet, too."

"Drive safely," he said softly.

As she left him, alone in that small room in his family's restaurant, she wondered if this was the last time she would ever see him again as Lyn Francis, interior designer.

AN HOUR LATER, Lyndsay pulled into the parking lot of her real-life apartment complex. Squat redbrick buildings. Fenced-off trash containers. Lined parking spaces dotted with oil spills.

Contrasted to the lovely ocean view, fresh air and presence of John Reilly that Wallis Point afforded her, she honestly wasn't thrilled to be home.

She realized she didn't want to go back to it at all.

When she unlocked her door, her apartment smelled stale and unused. It also seemed small and closed compared to the MacLaine cottage. A lot of interior touches needed changing, which was surprising to her, because she'd never paid much notice to her own decor before.

Closing her eyes to the shabby surroundings, she dropped off her bags, then opened her bedroom dresser drawer and grabbed her identification—wallet and badge. She also took her personal phone, which she'd left on the bedside table, still plugged in and fully charged.

That was the main reason she'd come—to program John's number into her phone and to keep it close beside her, tonight and in the coming days. She wouldn't let go of the shred of hope that a miracle would happen and John would someday be able to forgive her.

Then she locked up her home, hustled to the car, and roared off to meet with the manager at the MacLaines' home security-alarm company.

The aptly named Mr. Key received her cordially. He acknowledged her law enforcement credentials as part of the team investigating several burglaries. She recited the names and addresses of the three homes she knew of that had had watercolor paintings stolen from them. "I'd like to verify again that all three homes are customers of yours, please."

She waited while Mr. Key checked his files. He finally returned from a back office. "Yes. Would you like to know about the others?"

"That's not necessary. I would like to review the files. In all three cases, has it been verified that the correct security code was input to the homes?"

"Yes, it was."

"Are there employees who would have access to those codes?"

Mr. Key gave her a wary look. "We've all been interviewed. The company was investigated thoroughly."

Of course, her team would have done their jobs. She understood that.

"I'm just double-checking," she assured him.

"One last question. Could the computer files with the passwords have been hacked?"

"They're encrypted," he said with clipped syllables.

But the files *existed*. They were online. Anything online could be hacked.

She smiled faintly. "Thank you, Mr. Key. I appreciate your time."

As she left the premises, rather than feeling pleased with her efforts, she felt sad. Yes, she desperately wanted to solve this case, but she'd had more than enough of the undercover life. In the future, she wanted to be honest and have honest relationships.

When this was over, she owed it to John to tell him the whole truth about herself, once and for all.

She had a lot to tell him.

CHAPTER FIFTEEN

LYNDSAY STOOD IN the entry to the MacLaine cottage, trying to keep her mind clear. She'd parked her car farther down the beach so that the MacLaine driveway would be empty and the house appear unoccupied. She wasn't sure what time the perp—or, heaven forbid, perps—intended to strike, but if they did indeed strike, she was ready. Her pockets were filled with the essentials—small flashlight, flexible plastic handcuffs, badge, ammunition.

She armed herself. Once again, she took out her Glock, loaded it and holstered it at her waist. She wore a hip-length tunic that covered it loosely, but she was fully prepared to draw and use her weapon if needed. She was so familiar with the heft and shape of her firearm that she could operate it blind if she had to.

She planned to sit upstairs at the guest-room window overlooking the street. If the burglars did arrive, then she expected them to enter by the front door. The rear sliding doors were unlikely—to enter, a burglar would have to break heavy glass, and so far, their past methods didn't support that action. And just to be safe, she also checked and rechecked the locks on every window.

The front door was locked both electronically with the commercial burglar-alarm system, and mechanically. But the lock could be picked, the alarm code hacked. Whatever happened, she was prepared.

She went into the kitchen and found the last of the premade chicken salads she'd bought and stacked in the refrigerator. She brought it upstairs to her sentry position and ate quickly, barely tasting her meal because of the adrenaline coursing through her. But she needed to stay awake and alert, possibly all night, and so she needed fuel for her stamina. Finishing off a bottle of iced tea, she shifted her weight to find a more comfortable position.

The doorbell rang.

She froze. One hand on the windowsill, her heart pounded. Could this be the perpetrators? It was a common tactic for gangs to ring the doorbell before they attempted to break into a home.

She decided to remain quiet and wait.

"Lyndsay, I know you're in there!"

John's voice—it was John!

Jumbled, panicked thoughts ran through her head. *What is he doing here? How does he know I'm home?* She ran downstairs and gazed through the side window first, just to use caution. John's back was to her. He'd put on well-worn jeans and a beat-up leather jacket.

What was her story? *Think of a cover story for why you're here and not at a meeting with your boss*, she chided herself.

Opening the door, she made an exaggerated yawn, as if she'd been sleeping. "Sorry, I fell asleep." That explained why the lights were off. "My meeting was canceled at the last minute. I meant to call you, but I couldn't keep my eyes open."

"Your phone must have been turned off. I left a message."

"Sorry." She patted her pocket, blinking, as if still waking up. "I guess last night's lack of sleep has finally caught up with me," she said sheepishly.

He nodded. There was a small outdoor light which turned on automatically at the same time every night, so she could clearly see his expression. He looked tired, too. And grim.

She had to get him off the stoop in case anyone was watching them. At least he hadn't arrived in his truck—the driveway was thankfully empty.

She smiled at him and opened the door wider. "Come in. I'll see if I can scrounge up something to eat if you're hungry." Maybe in the kitchen she could think of an excuse to get him to leave.

"All right." He followed her inside, and she closed the door behind him, then locked it and reset the alarm.

"I don't want anything to eat," he said. "I just need to check on you."

Her heart pounded. *Something* was going on. She gave him her best innocent grin, to let him know she was okay with it. Where to go?

Not upstairs. She had to keep him away from her lair. Thinking fast, she led him to the living room in back.

No, that didn't work, either. They would be seen from the beach. She didn't want to spook the bad guys if they were watching the house.

She needed a place with no windows so she could turn on the light.

Upstairs. In the new part of the house.

Taking his hand, she headed for the stairs again.

He gave her a look of concern. His whole being was concerned. Or was she misinterpreting his stiffness?

An excuse popped into her head, a reason she could give to get him to leave. She stopped at the top of the stairs. "You know, John, I have an early morning tomorrow. The MacLaines are calling me, and—"

"Lyn, can I just ask you something?"

"Okay," she murmured.

He leaned against the railing, crossing his arms. She could see his dim outline from the porch light that shone in the window. With his leather jacket, he appeared like a tough guy. Not somebody to mess with.

"Why did you park your car down the street?" he asked. "Moon saw you walking back. He was going to offer you a ride, but he said you looked serious, and he figured something was up. When he told me, I came over to investigate, and here I find you in a dark house, wearing your pistol in a holster at your waist." He pointed. "I could see the outline clearly, by the way."

She'd been busted.

"Well, I strapped on my gun before I answered the door because it's nerve-racking being home alone. And Moon should have stopped and offered me a ride," she finished lamely.

John stared at her.

She needed to make up another lie to fool him. One lie after another—it seemed to never end. She put her palms against her flaming cheeks. *This work is important*, she reminded herself.

She took a deep breath. "I walked home because something is screwy with my car engine. It stalled out, so I just left it there. John, I'm so tired..."

His shoulders relaxed. "Yeah, that's partly my fault. Let me put you to bed. I'll let you sleep. We'll figure out something with the car in the morning." He reached for the light switch.

"No! Please don't turn on the light. My eyes hurt. Honestly."

Incredibly, a low beam of light shone on the stair tread.

"You brought a flashlight?" she asked.

"I'm always prepared." He took her arm and led her upstairs. "You know how you told me you love me today?" he said.

"Yes."

"Well, I wanted you to know that I do, too."

She blinked at the wonder of it. His declaration was unexpected. It made her feel happy to the core of her heart.

But she shook herself. Though it was great for her personal life, it was horrible timing for a professional stakeout. "Thanks, John," she said quickly. "Can we meet up in the morning?"

"Yeah. Can I lie down with you for a while? We'll just sleep. I'm tired, too."

No! No, we can't sleep!

They were at the door to her bedroom lair, over the front porch. She didn't know how to handle John's request. Nothing in her training explained how to back out from her own cover story.

A loud noise like a chain dropping sounded outside on the driveway.

She leaped forward, beelining to the window. From here she had the perfect view to the porch below.

The person standing before the door was a shadow. A slight shadow.

As slight as Patrick Reilly.

"Are you expecting anyone?" John stood beside her, peering out the window.

"No. Are you?"

"No."

The shadow moved. It appeared he'd entered the house, though she couldn't hear anything so she wasn't sure.

She needed to get John out of this guest room. There was only one exit to it and no lock on the door. She took her own penlight from her pocket—she was prepared, too—and lit the way. "Let's move to the master bedroom," she said in John's ear. "Now."

"No. It's better that I go downstairs and see what—"

Another loud noise sounded—a loud thump—and this from inside the house. It sounded like it was coming from the hallway just below them.

"Do as I say, John," she hissed, "I know this house better than you." She literally pulled his arm and jerked him across the hall to the master bathroom they'd fixed together, during what seemed like ages ago. To his credit, he dropped to a crouch and moved like a man who'd had military training, holding up the rear as in stealth platoon formation.

Good. She was glad he was listening to her. Deftly, they entered by the bathroom entrance, and she reached for the key to the locked master bedroom by feel, as she'd practiced this afternoon.

The door opened noiselessly. *Thank you, John, for fixing the sticking door*, she silently praised him. Together, they crept inside the bedroom and stood on the plush carpet he'd dried out for her. He silently closed the door to the hallway behind them and locked it.

His phone screen lit up the darkness. She took his phone from him and turned it off. "No, I'll call the police," she instructed in a low tone. "On my phone. This is *my* job at the MacLaine house, and I want it protected."

The muscles on his arms were tight. She knew he wasn't happy with her brusque actions—she wouldn't be, either, in his shoes—but it couldn't be helped.

He went over to crouch at the entrance by the hallway. She retreated into a closet and pulled out her task force phone and called Pete's number. "Don't come," she whispered when he picked up. Their prearranged signal that meant, *yes, do come.*

"I'm on my way," Pete replied. "I'm watching the cameras, and I saw the perps. There are two of them, one small, one large. No weapons that I could see."

"I'll stay on with you until you're here," she said. "I'll leave the phone on, on the floor in the upstairs bedroom, so you can hear what's going on."

John came back and nudged her. She could see him by her cell phone light. "Is there something valuable in this room?" he whispered. "Because it sounded like they drilled out a safe or something downstairs, and now they've come up the stairs and are right outside the door."

"Yes. There's a safe in here, too, in the other closet." They were crouching together in Kitty's closet, and she pointed to Congressman Mac-Laine's closet with the safe.

He nodded and took up his position again behind the other locked door, the one that led directly to the hallway. If anyone entered they would encounter him first.

Of course she couldn't let that happen. Marine veteran or not, he was still a civilian, and she was the police officer. She had protocol to follow.

As she considered the situation, it might be

safer to go downstairs and arrest the two perps immediately. She had them on breaking-and-entering charges. However, she'd wanted to catch them red-handed before she declared herself. If she was going to end her cover identity in Wallis Point with an arrest, then she wanted a *good* arrest, one that bore fruit.

Swallowing, she went over and crouched beside John. He spoke close to her ear. "I know this is your design job, but let me take the lead." He said it as a command. "I've fought in urban warfare. You haven't."

"And here I thought you were a nice, steady bartender," she quipped.

He made a low, faint chuckle in the heavy silence.

"Sorry, John, but I'm overruling you. I have the gun. When they attempt to enter this room, I'll draw on them and you stand out of the way."

He chuckled again. "In your dreams, darling."

Was she going to have to out herself to John before she made the arrests?

It was looking that way.

John's chuckling stopped. In the hallway on the other side of the door, there was a louder murmuring of voices. Men, she guessed. Two of them, as Pete had said.

John nudged her. He appeared to be holding up two fingers. It was hard to see him—it was just so dark. The phone was flat on the floor beside her, still on, but the light suddenly dimmed. Her Glock grew slippery in her sweaty hands. She wasn't planning on shooting anybody tonight, but she'd been through enough drills and police academy training simulations to know that crazy things started happening when adrenaline and firearms and criminal behavior were mixed together.

The door handle was moving. She heard the faint rattle of metal in the lock. Whoever was out there, they were attempting to break inside. A flashlight turned on—she could see the sliver of light along the cracks that outlined the door. Strangely, she felt calm.

"I'll take the first one," he whispered into her ear. "I'll hammer him fast. You use your weapon to train it on him while I handle the second man next."

"No," she whispered back. Unfortunately, to do her job correctly she was going to have to overrule a trained combat veteran. She took a deep breath to deliver the most difficult words she'd ever spoken to John Reilly:

"I am Officer Lyndsay Fairfax of the New Hampshire State Police, Seacoast Burglary Task Force. I order you to follow my lead."

He didn't respond. Whether he was stunned or simply ignoring her, she couldn't tell in the darkness. "Don't test me on this," she whispered. "You stay back, stay safe, stay out of this operation. That is a direct order."

He gave absolutely no reaction that she could perceive in the pitch-black and sweaty bedroom.

All of a sudden, two headlights coursed across the hallway outside the bedroom. She recognized the movement and color of the light even under the doorway. It meant that a vehicle had pulled into the driveway outside.

Was it Pete? Her heart pounded. Her thighs were aching from being in a crouching position. Her muscles cramping. And she honestly didn't know what John was going to do.

There was absolute silence in the hallway. The flashlight switched off. She and John waited again in inky darkness.

And then the doorbell rang.

"Expecting someone?" John hissed in her ear.

"It's not my backup partner ringing the doorbell," she murmured. "That's not how he rolls."

"Well, it isn't the Girl Scouts," John muttered sarcastically. Obviously, he was angry with her. But she couldn't do anything about that right now.

"It's Andy," she decided aloud. "Or Moon. If he noticed me walking back from my car, then maybe he's investigating."

Just then, the house alarm went off. A loud,

piercing shriek sounded. What was happening? It had been a silent alarm before. Maybe Kitty had called the alarm company to change the security settings.

At the same time, a light in the hallway started flashing. Over and over again. It was chaos. She also knew that in the background, the Wallis Point Police Station would be alerted. Soon, a cruiser would arrive. Lyndsay had noticed that the congressman's property seemed to receive widespread attention in his hometown.

But that wasn't the worst of it. A loud shout came from the front door area, followed by a male scream.

She and John leaped up together as one. John tore the door open and was halfway down the stairs, damn him, while she was still running across the balcony landing.

"Police! Freeze!" she boomed in her most authoritative voice. "Get down on the floor! Put your hands on your heads! All of you!"

But John was already midflight, tackling the beefier of the two assailants. They rolled on the floor, trading punches.

The second, skinny assailant kept running, looking back at them, which made him smack directly into the armoire she'd moved to block the sliding glass door. He hit the wood hard, then collapsed into a heap on the floor.

Lyndsay ran over to him, checked his pulse, and then took a pair of plastic handcuffs from her back pocket and slapped them on him. Clearly now, she could see that he wasn't Patrick. He looked to be about Patrick's age—nineteen or twenty—with dark hair and a sparse beard.

Sighing, she stepped over him and approached John and the beefy perp. The two were on the floor, grappling and throwing punches at each other. Shining her flashlight in their faces, she boomed, "Police! Hands on your heads, both of you! Now!"

John, on top of the perp, reluctantly rolled off him and did as she'd ordered. Groaning, the perp followed suit.

She knelt beside the perp and slapped the cuffs on him. Then she proceeded to read him his rights. Huge, stocky, his head shaved bald, the perpetrator looked like a mean character. However, he moaned and closed his eyes, rolled over, and groaned again. It appeared he needed medical attention, as did the second perp, still passed out on Kitty's living room floor.

The wail of a police siren sounded, adding to the cacophony, and blue lights bounced across the living room, now brightly lit and flashing, the home burglar alarm still wailing. Lyndsay took out her police badge and clipped it at her waist, waiting for them.

"Freeze, police! Put your guns down!" Officer Phil Pierce, the big, ripped, Wallis Point cop stood in the doorway, feet planted in shooting position, both his hands on his service revolver.

"I am Officer Fairfax of the New Hampshire State Police, Seacoast Burglary Task Force," she boomed back at him. "I've handcuffed two perps and arrested one. Call for three ambulances."

He lowered his revolver. "Will do, Officer Fairfax."

A second Wallis Point officer joined them, one she didn't recognize, a detective in plain clothes. He wore his badge pinned to his belt as she did.

"I'm Officer Fairfax," she shouted to him over the cacophony.

The alarm suddenly stopped and the lights stopped flashing. In the blessed silence, she spoke in a lower tone. Pete, striding in through the front door, joined them, as well. He, too, had his badge displayed at his waist and wore his holster visible at his hip.

"About time you joined us," she said jovially, feeling better now that the perps were in custody and the chaos controlled. She'd made a good arrest, and she was pleased.

"He's my partner," she explained to Officer Pierce and the unnamed detective.

Clearly, her investigative work had paid off. The two paintings of Kitty MacLaine had been taken down and were stacked against the wall. A knife lay beside them, but the burglars hadn't yet used it to cut naked Kitty from the frames. Instead, the safe behind the upper painting was drilled open and empty. And upstairs, the two men had been attempting to gain entry to the master bedroom with the other safe and Justin's watercolors. They had clearly committed theft and attempted theft.

Once the burglars were deemed medically fit, the task force would have these two perps to interrogate about the details of the larger burglary ring.

Pete glanced around, taking it all in. The two handcuffed perps, one knocked out, one dazed. The evidence of the thefts in process. "Good job," he said to Lyndsay. But then he glanced at John, sitting on the floor, face marred with blood and cold, hard anger, and Pete cocked an eyebrow at her.

"A civilian was present?" he murmured in her ear.

She saw how it would look to Commander Harris. "It couldn't be helped," she murmured back.

John wiped the blood from his mouth. Gazing at her, he didn't bother to hide his disdain.

The uniformed officer was radioing in, repeating her name over the air. Pete gave him the cut sign. "Don't mention her name," he said. "She was undercover."

The plainclothes detective approached her. "I'm Detective Michael Donovan," he introduced himself. He glanced at John. "What's with John Reilly? Is he part of the task force, too?"

"You two know each other?" she asked, surprised, even though she shouldn't be. Wallis Point wasn't a big city.

"I know his brother's court officer," Detective Donovan answered.

John just scowled and turned away.

Personal Lyndsay had a very big problem here, and Professional Lyndsay had a slightly smaller one. In both cases, she realized that the less said in John's presence for now, the better.

She pulled Detective Donovan aside. "John is a civilian who happened to be caught in the action," she murmured in a low tone.

"An informant?" he asked.

In a strict sense, that was how Commander Harris would interpret John's role. And from the standpoint of the investigation to follow, she wanted John dealt with as an innocent party, not as a suspect.

"He's involved in the arrest," she murmured. "Yes."

John sat facing away from her. He didn't give

any indication that he wanted anything to do with her, now that he knew who she really was.

She couldn't help John's hurt and anger toward her, not now. Her main concern was to process the perps, and her other concern was to get all three men medical attention. Blood marred John's face, and she was sure that he was hurting. Hopefully, he wasn't seriously injured, but they couldn't know until he saw a doctor.

From the front windows, Lyndsay saw an ambulance with lights flashing rounding the corner of the drive and pulling past the police line at the street. A second ambulance followed close behind.

"We need an ambulance for John Reilly, as well," she told Detective Donovan.

"I'm fine," John said gruffly. He stood, back against the wall, but even in the dim light she could see the blood on his cheek.

"You should be checked out at the hospital," she said to him. "You could have a concussion."

"I said I'm fine." He spoke with clenched teeth and could barely look at her.

"Are you refusing transport, John?" Detective Donovan asked him.

"I am," John replied stubbornly.

"You'll have to come to the station with us," Pete informed him. "We need to interview you and take a statement."

Inside, Lyndsay bristled. She hadn't wanted John to be involved in this way, but Pete was right—he'd been at the scene. Still, she wished that Pete would let her handle it.

Pete got on his phone to call in Simon and Wesley. The scene needed to be secured; a team needed to accompany the two perps to the hospital. As soon as the doctors cleared them, the arrests needed to be processed and interrogations would begin. Her mind whirred again, and she saw meetings with state's attorneys, the eventual plea bargains, trials, sentencing.

She thought of that fiery spark plug, Kitty MacLaine. Lyndsay glanced around. Despite the fighting, her interior decorating job had held up. Somewhat. She would leave it to Kitty's husband to explain to her what had happened with Lyn Francis. She sincerely doubted that a final meeting with Kitty would be authorized now.

Pete pulled her aside. "Commander Harris wants to meet you at the Wallis Point police station," he informed her, tucking his phone into his pocket. "You're to stay there and wait for him before you go anywhere else. He said he wants to keep your name and contribution to the case under wraps as much as possible. I'm ordered to take the lead here now."

She sighed. "Understood."

"It was good detective work and a good arrest,

Lyndsay. Don't fall into the trap of discourage-
ment just because you're ordered to take a back
seat now."

"Does Commander Harris have a problem
with John being present?"

"He may punish you a bit. Don't be surprised
if he takes his sweet time getting down here to
see you."

In other words, she might be spending the
night in the local police station.

Detective Donovan stepped in. "I'll give you
a ride to the station," he offered. Wesley had already arrived, Lyndsay noted, with a team of
evidence processors. The gears of police activity moved quickly.

"Thank you," she told Detective Donovan.

"Don't know how much we can hide you,
though, Officer Fairfax. The locals are pretty
curious."

She saw what he meant. Outside on the street
a crowd was gathering, even at this late hour.
People just couldn't stay away from police lights
and activity. Two emergency medical attendants
were loading the slightly built burglar, now acting groggy as he held his head and moaned, into
one ambulance, and the beefy assailant—also
alert, sullen and angry—into the other.

"Okay, I'm ready," she said to Detective Donovan as she unclipped the badge at her waist and

tucked it into a pocket. "We'll do the best we can to get out of here unmolested."

His squad car was across the grass and parked on the street. The MacLaines' beautiful land-scaping had been marred by all the vehicles squeezed in to the small area, some of them parked not on the driveway, but on the lawn. Lyndsay would be glad not to be present to see Kitty's reaction to that. They walked by Officer Phil Pierce, standing beside John and a medical attendant who carried a clipboard. John didn't even look at her as she passed.

Andy lifted the police tape as if he belonged there and strode right over. "Lyn! What's going on?"

"Step back behind the barrier, Andy," Detective Donovan reprimanded him.

"Yeah, sorry, Michael." Andy made a limp movement toward the tape. But he kept his eyes pinned to her.

She needed to take care of the rumors as quickly and quietly as possible. "Excuse me," she said to Detective Donovan, and stepped over to Andy, putting her arm around him and speaking close to his ear. "We interrupted a burglary," she said calmly. "But everyone is okay. Where's Moon?"

"He ran down the street and called me after he saw the burglars and accidentally tripped the alarm. He's over there." Andy pointed. Indeed, Moon was gesturing wildly, dictating his story to a female, uniformed police officer.

"So he wasn't hurt?" Lyndsay qualified.

"No. Just freaked out." Andy shifted. "I can't believe our cul-de-sac got hit by burglars."

"It's over now."

"Officer Fairfax, could I speak to you a moment?" Officer Pierce stood by her elbow. She shook her head at him. He blanched, realizing his mistake. "Sorry. I'll see you at the station," he said, stepping away from them and heading back to John.

"Officer Fairfax?" Andy repeated.

Just a moment, she signaled to Detective Donovan, patiently waiting by his squad car for her. Taking a breath, she turned to Andy. She was aware that she had eyes on her. From the corner of her vision she noticed John was signing the EMT disclaimer, refusing transport to the hospital. Stubborn man.

"I'm an undercover state police officer," she said in a low tone to Andy, and looked him straight in the eyes. "That is on a need-to-know basis only. The case may be damaged if that news gets spread."

He looked hurt, and she was well aware of the betrayal he must feel. Andy had trusted her, introduced her, let her into their community. She briefly considered leaving it at that—the less said, the better to protect the upcoming prosecutions—but she also weighed that he deserved to hear her story from her own lips, or as much as she could divulge, anyway.

"You know I won't say anything, Lyn," Andy said. She perceived then that he was hurt not that she was undercover, but that she'd implied he had a big mouth.

John stared over at her. Wordlessly, he moved on with Officer Pierce toward his squad car.

She felt her heart sink. The adrenaline of the bust was wearing off; the reality of what had just happened with John was sinking in.

"Andy," Lyndsay said, turning to her contractor friend. "I was investigating a series of burglaries, and those burglaries are still under investigation. I'm sorry I had to deceive people to do so, but it was for a good purpose, the best outcome for the community and for all of us, and that's why I did it."

Andy softly whistled. "You could knock me over with a feather," he said in his gruff, teddy-bear voice. "You know, I had no freaking idea."

"Nobody did," she said softly, thinking of John.

Andy patted her on the arm. But for once, he couldn't seem to find another word to say.

"You helped me," she said. "I'll never forget that."

"So...you're not an interior decorator?" he asked, scratching his head.

"I went to design school, *and* I'm a police officer," she clarified. "How's that?"

"Well, if you ever need a job, come see me. You're good."

She made a small laugh. "Honestly, even though I would love to work with you again, we're best off where I am." But she needed to wrap this up and get back to her job, so she gave Andy a quick hug. "Goodbye," she whispered. "Take care of John, please."

Then she climbed into the police cruiser with Detective Donovan, headed to the station to face Commander Harris and whatever he had to say.

CHAPTER SIXTEEN

JOHN SAT IN the back of Phil Pierce's cruiser nursing his wounds. Physically, he would live. Emotionally, he felt worse than he'd ever felt, even after a firefight from his Marine days.

His vision swam before him. Honestly, he wasn't sure if he was in a dream or if he understood reality correctly.

Lyndsay had been playing him for a dupe, lying to him all along.

How the hell was he supposed to deal with that fact?

He remembered the first time he'd talked with her in the Seaside parking lot, back when he'd been wary of her lurking around the place. She'd talked him out of his doubts with such charm and sweetness, and he'd been fooled. She'd countered every argument he had, grinding his defenses to dust.

He gritted his teeth. Come to find out, his suspicions had been correct. She'd manipulated him from the beginning.

As the cruiser pulled into the back lot of the

Wallis Point Police Department, a slow boil built in his blood, especially when Phil opened the door for him and led him inside the station as if John was one step from being a common criminal.

"John?" Phil said. "We're going to need you to step inside an interview room."

"What for?" he snapped at Phil, even though Phil was just following orders and had nothing to do with Lyndsay's perfidy. What did she say her real name was? *Fairfax*. She'd even lied to Phil Pierce about that just this past Sunday afternoon.

Phil closed the door behind them. "Why don't you write down what happened tonight. You're going to want to fill this out." He plunked down a clipboard with a form on it and a pen. "I'll need you to explain what you were doing at the MacLaine place to begin with."

John just stared at the paper. *Why* had he been there? For Lyndsay. Because he'd cared about her and loved her and he'd been worried for her safety, even as she'd lied to him, even as he'd poured out his guts to her.

He stared at the pen, no idea what to write. He should have known she was too good to be true.

THREE HOURS. THAT was how long Lyndsay waited for Commander Harris at the Wallis Point police station. Detective Donovan found her a

comfortable interview room and kept her sup-
plied with stale, police-house coffee, but no one
from the task force called, or even stopped by to
keep her informed.

She was missing out on all the action.

Despite the fact that it was past two o'clock in
the morning, she kept her posture straight and
tried not to let herself despair, as Pete had suggested. She reminded herself that her actions
had helped break the case. At some point, Commander Harris would recognize that. Professionally, she had nothing to worry about.

She closed her eyes. Where was John? How
was he doing?

Thoughts of him kept creeping in, no matter
how she tried not to think about him. She worried about him. He'd looked horrible, and she
wished he had gone to the hospital to be examined. If she could have ordered him to do so,
she would have.

Once again, she debated whether to disobey
orders, get up and track him down. He probably
sat in another interview room somewhere in the
station. So close to her, and yet so far removed.

The door opened, and Detective Donovan
poked his head in. "Sorry, Officer Fairfax. I still
haven't heard word from your task force commander."

"All right. Thanks for letting me know." It was

apparent that Commander Harris *was* taking his sweet time. The drive from Concord to Wallis Point took one hour, not three. "Is John Reilly being questioned?" she asked the detective.

"Phil just finished taking his statement."

"Is he still here?"

"No. Andy Hannaman gave him a ride home."

She could only hope that Andy would take care of John, and that John would be okay. "So… did someone from the task force also interview him?"

"Not yet," Detective Donovan replied. "They're tied up at the hospital. Your partner asked us to get John's statement about what happened tonight. He said they'll send someone out to interview him later."

She nodded. Hopefully it would be Pete and not Simon who did the interviewing. Pete would be the better person to feel empathy for his situation, given what he'd shared with her this afternoon.

What a long day. She couldn't help stifling a yawn. The adrenaline had worn off, and she could barely keep her eyes open. At this point, she was simply exhausted.

"We have a room in the back with a cot," Detective Donovan offered. "If you'd like, rest up until your commander shows."

"Thank you, I appreciate the offer." Lyndsay

smiled at him. She would accept the hospitality and figure out what she was going to do about John later.

THE NEXT THING Lyndsay knew, she was being shaken awake by a female uniformed officer. "A detective is here to see you, Officer Fairfax."

Groggy, Lyndsay took a few minutes to use the facilities and splash cold water on her face, then followed the officer down a corridor. Faint light glowed from a skylight window—Lyndsay guessed that it was nearly sunrise. She'd managed to catch a few hours of sleep, at least, but she was still worried about John. Hopefully, Andy had talked him into going to the hospital.

She remained silent as the officer led her to the interview room where she had waited for a good part of the night. Inside, she was relieved to see Pete, pacing and glancing at his watch.

"Finally," she replied, seating herself in the uncomfortable bucket chair. The officer discreetly left her and Pete alone.

"Sorry." Pete grimaced after the door shut. "I honestly didn't think that Commander Harris would leave you here all night, Lyn."

"I'm not surprised. We both know that he's not happy with me for having a civilian present at the stakeout."

He sighed. "Yes." His suit was rumpled, and his eyes had a red glaze to them.

"Have you been up all night, too?" she asked.

"Yeah, mostly. There's a lot going on. I couldn't sleep if I wanted to."

She knew that feeling. Envious that he'd been dealing with the questioning she'd hoped to have a part in, she asked, "What's happened with the two perps at the hospital? Tell me everything."

Pete laughed dryly, shaking his head. "The big guy with the bald head? We'd had him in custody before. Remember the maid up in Maine? He was the cousin they interrogated."

"What does that mean?"

"It means he's *still* not talking to us. Not then, and not now. We had to let him go the first time we suspected him because we didn't have evidence to keep him in custody. Now we have evidence, but not enough to break open the rest of the burglary ring." Pete lifted his arms and stretched. "Sorry. I'm exhausted. We've been questioning him, but he's shut up tight as a drum. If there is a conspiracy, he won't say."

"What's the other perp saying?"

"Nothing yet. The doctors haven't cleared him to talk to us. I'm on standby, waiting. One of the nurses assured me that she didn't think it would be long."

"Well…at least we've got enough to take him

and his cohort off the street. They *were* caught in the act."

"Yes, they were." He grinned at her. "You've made a good undercover cop, Lyndsay."

She wished she could say she'd enjoyed it more, but lately it felt like she'd paid too high a personal price. "I don't like that I had to deceive someone I cared about," she said softly.

"Yeah." He nodded. "Though if I didn't understand where you're coming from, I would throttle you. Why *did* you involve a civilian in the arrest?"

"Because I had to—he simply showed up at a bad time because he was worried about me. And it's worse than that, Pete." She took a deep breath. "I'm so worried about him. Could you *please* see that he's physically okay? *Please?* I keep seeing him rolling around with that big perp, all the hard punches thrown, and I feel sick with worry that he's lying at home maybe passed out with a concussion, or something worse..."

"Lyn," he said softly, "you've got it bad."

Yes, she did.

His phone chimed. He glanced at the text message. "It's Commander Harris. We have clearance to interrogate the second perp. Hang tight, Lyndsay. I'll be back."

Hang tight? It felt impossible to just sit still and wait, twiddling her thumbs.

She ached to call John. And yet, it wasn't appropriate for her to seek him out. She simply had to wait until Commander Harris arrived and the investigation was wrapped up. Somewhere, in an evidence bag, would be her personal phone with John's number in it. No matter what, there would be an eventual time and place when she could call him. She desperately wanted to apologize to him and to explain why she'd done it. She needed him to know that with him, in the most important ways, she'd never lied. She did love him. She did respect him. She did want a longer-term relationship with him, if he could find it in his heart to forgive her deception.

All she could do now was to keep her faith and remember patience. *Wait.* At some point, the time would be right for them. The best thing she could do was to keep her mind clear and alert because sooner or later there would be an opening, and when that happened, she would need all her wits and energy to convince him.

In need of breakfast, she headed down a corridor, looking for a break room. The officers on duty knew who she was and while they showed a mild curiosity about her, they were busy, too. No one paid much attention while she headed past the security barrier and walked the section of the police station that was open to the public.

It was bustling with activity. For all these

weeks, she'd been tied down to the small beach neighborhood where the congressman lived. But Wallis Point was a much larger town than the small lake village she'd grown up in.

A stream of families—small children and adults—headed into a room at the end of a corridor. Food, there must be food there. Lyndsay fell into line beside a woman who appeared to be in a rush, pushing a baby carriage with one hand, clutching a young girl in the other, and balancing a leather briefcase strapped around her shoulder.

"Oh!" The woman bumped into Lyndsay with the soft edge of the carriage. "I'm so sorry! Are you all right?"

"It's no problem," Lyndsay assured her. "I'm fine."

The infant in the carriage smiled a cute, gummy smile at her, and Lyndsay felt her heart melting. "Your baby is adorable." The baby was dressed in a blue onesie, so she guessed he was a boy.

"This is Jamie." The woman gave her an apologetic look. "I need to get Hannah seated with her class inside the conference room. The patrolmen are giving a tour to the first graders today. She's so excited."

The little girl, who was presumably Hannah,

smiled at Lyndsay. "I want to see the jails where the bad guys go."

Lyndsay chuckled. Some departments hosted community programs like this so that kids wouldn't be frightened of police officers. She was pretty sure little Hannah wouldn't be seeing a jail cell, but Lyndsay wasn't about to burst her bubble. "It sounds like fun," she said to Hannah. "I'm a police officer, too, in another agency, but I'm not in my uniform right now."

Hannah looked at her with awe.

She swallowed, a lump in her throat. She had to admit, she needed this validation today. It was good to feel that she was doing something positive for the community and that not everybody was angry with her. She did place bad guys in jail.

"We need to get going," the woman remarked. She looked curiously at Lyndsay. "Can I help you find something? I'm familiar with the station."

"I'm just looking for a break room," Lyndsay said. "Or someplace with a juice or water machine. The coffee here isn't my favorite."

The woman laughed. "I know how you feel." She pointed down the corridor. "Second door on the left. Though if you're looking for a real breakfast place, let me know. I'll join you in a minute or two, after I get Hannah settled."

"Thanks," Lyndsay said. "I appreciate it."

She followed the directions and found a large room with rows of vending machines, a microwave oven, a coffee station and two large round tables.

Another woman who looked like she worked there was busy pouring coffee from a pot into a large plastic mug. She glanced up when Lyndsay came in. "Can I help you with something?"

"I'm Officer Fairfax. I'm waiting for my team members to rejoin me. In the meantime, I heard a rumor that there's a juice machine available?"

"I'm Zena Baines, Wallis Point PD dispatcher." Zena pointed toward the end of a row of machines. "It's right over there, though there's just apple juice right now, I'm afraid."

"At this point, that sounds like heaven." Lyndsay fished two crumpled bills from her pocket and smoothed them out as best she could. Then she fed them to the machine, retrieved her beverage and sat at one of the communal tables.

"This is a nice station," Lyndsay remarked, glancing around at the freshly painted walls and new furniture. "It's bigger than I realized."

Zena took her breakfast from the microwave—a large muffin that she'd heated up—and joined Lyndsay at the table. "Yes. It's home to me."

"I noticed the community room in the back. And the training room."

Zena cocked her head. "Are you new here?

I haven't been in the job long myself, but I've never noticed you before."

"I'm a state police officer."

"Oh." Zena nodded. She looked a bit intimidated, but open to talking.

Lyndsay gave her a wide smile. "You can call me Lyndsay."

"Okay. Hi, Lyndsay."

The woman Lyndsay had met earlier in the hallway entered, pushing baby Jamie in his carriage. "Hi, again," she called to Lyndsay. Lyndsay waved back.

The woman turned to Zena. "Is Officer Pierce in this morning? I have a document I need to file with him."

"No," Zena answered. "He was on shift last night." She smiled at Lyndsay. "Natalie is my former employer. She's an attorney in town." She turned to Natalie. "This is Officer Fairfax—Lyndsay. She's a state police officer."

"Pleased to meet you." Natalie shifted her folder to her left hand and extended her right hand to Lyndsay. "I'm Natalie Kimball. I own the Kimball Law office in town."

"Oh. Do you work in criminal cases?" Lyndsay asked.

"I specialize in wills, probates, estates and minor criminal cases, yes."

Natalie was someone John might call if he

needed legal help. Lyndsay would need to watch what she said. Still, she shook Natalie's hand. "Why don't you sit down with us? I was going to have breakfast."

"Okay." Natalie glanced at her watch. "While I wait for Hannah, I have a free hour. A very rare thing for me these days."

"I can imagine the little ones keep you busy." Lyndsay smiled at little Jamie with his dimpled cheeks and wispy tuft of brown baby hair.

"Yes," Natalie said softly. "But I wouldn't change it for the world."

It dared to cross Lyndsay's mind then. *Wouldn't I love to have a little one like this with John someday?* The unexpected longing went so deep that she needed to blink away the moisture in her eyes.

Wallis Point was a place she had grown to love, too. She could see herself here. Given her present difficulties, though, it was a near impossibility.

"Would you like half of my blueberry muffin, Lyndsay?" Zena asked. "It's huge, and I wasn't going to eat it all, anyway."

"Well…if you're sure you don't mind?"

But Zena was already cutting it with her plastic knife. "You'll love it. Trust me on this."

Lyndsay felt teary with gratitude. *Imagine that*, she thought. She was trained to be outwardly tough, but now it seemed she was softening on the inside.

Maybe John could eventually soften, too, enough to find it in his heart to forgive her.

She hoped so, fervently.

Please, Pete, hurry up. She needed to find out if he'd been able to check on John. She needed to know how he was, good or bad.

CHAPTER SEVENTEEN

JOHN FOUGHT THE urge to lean against the wall of his shower stall and stay there, zoning out as the hot water sluiced over his aching back.

He had no idea what time it was.

He was fuzzy on last night's details.

But he remembered everything that had happened with Lyndsay—the worry about her safety, the fight with the combatant, the shock to learn that Lyndsay was a police officer, then the raw, cold fury over the way she had duped him.

After that, though, he wasn't real clear on what had happened or how he'd gotten home. He just had the memory of the shock of her betrayal wearing off him, followed by a raging headache from the fight he'd had with the thief. He remembered sitting on his couch for two seconds to pop down some ibuprofen tablets, and the next thing he knew, he'd felt an overpowering urge to close his eyes and rest for just a moment.

Evidently, he'd faded. Hours had passed while he'd either slept or been passed out—he still wasn't sure which—and the remnants of that monster headache remained even now in the sunlight.

Wincing with pain, he straightened. He didn't have the luxury to waste minutes babying himself in a hot shower. He had to get to his mother before somebody else in this too-small town scared her with the details of last night's incident. She would be a wreck once she heard. He needed to check on Patrick, too.

He still didn't know what, if anything, he would tell his family about Lyndsay. The pain in his heart hurt worse than the pain in his head. He twisted the knob to cut the flow of water, then grabbed a dry towel, stepping onto the mat.

Immediately, he was confronted with his reflection in the mirror over the sink. He saw how he looked through other people's eyes. Like a monster.

He had a black eye, facial bruises and a deep cut that was red and raw. He should put a bandage on it if he didn't want to scare the public.

Averting his head, he dried himself—gingerly—with the towel. He hurt all over, from head to toe. It even hurt to breathe, which probably meant he had a cracked rib or two. He'd been through worse. He could take it for now—he would deal with any medical issues later. He'd most wanted to wash off the blood because he didn't want his mother to be upset when she saw him.

Go. Get dressed. Get to work. Get on with your life.

It was what he knew best. He screwed his eyes shut. He hadn't known Lyndsay long, but she'd shredded him. The force of her betrayal had hit him worse than the work over he'd gotten from that goon. He would rather fight a thousand goons than think about Lyndsay again, talking to Patrick, having coffee with his mom.

In bed with me.

Ding. The motion-detector alarm in his driveway went off. John blinked. It had to be Lyndsay. Who else would it be?

Ding-dong.

That was his doorbell. If he didn't go face her, she would force herself inside anyway. The woman could handle herself defensively, he would give her that. Still, she could wait.

With a groan, he bandaged his cut. Put on a long-sleeved, button-up shirt, then winced again as he pulled on his jeans. Pocketed his wallet and keys and phone. He found a clean pair of socks and laced on his work boots.

Strangely, he felt naked. And foolish. Outwitted by a woman he'd put his trust in. Last night he hadn't fully dealt with his anger—the fight with the intruder and the presence of the police had confused him more. Now that the action was behind him, John didn't want to talk to her or revisit her betrayal.

Ding-dong.

"I'm coming!" he called out peevishly. *But you're gonna wish I hadn't.*

His brother's cat curled around his ankle. He took the time to gingerly bend over and pat his furry head. "Hang tight, Toby," he murmured. "I promise I won't forget you this morning."

He took the stairs slowly. It was the best he could do.

But the face in John's front window wasn't Lyndsay's. It was the guy from last night. Forty-ish, with a haircut that screamed *authority figure.* Lyndsay's partner.

A law enforcement badge slapped against the window. "Pete West. Police. Open up."

John opened the door a crack. "I already made my statement."

"You look like crap," Pete said in a matter-of-fact tone.

No kidding, John thought.

Pete shifted his stance. "I want to talk to you."

"Fine. We'll talk outside."

Pete shrugged. "Suit yourself."

John stepped out on the porch and shut the door behind him. Pete was dressed like John, except he wore a Glock pistol on a holster at his waist, right out in the open.

Pete gave him the up and down. "Did you go to the hospital yet?"

"Why? Is this a welfare check?"

"Actually, it is. Don't get defensive with me. I'm here to help you."

"Does *she* know you're here?" John couldn't help asking.

Pete sighed. "I got your address from your interview sheet, if that's what you mean."

John had given little to no information in his incident statement. Name, rank and serial number. The very bare minimum he could get away with, anyway.

But this guy had him at a disadvantage. As Lyndsay's partner, he likely knew everything that John had told Lyndsay. Just knowing that was like salt on his wound.

"Are you undercover, too?" John asked sarcastically.

A tick went off in the guy's cheek, but he controlled himself. "Lyn covered for you. You might not realize this, but she's in trouble for letting you interfere in a police response. You're lucky you weren't charged for your actions last night."

John drew in his breath. "She's in trouble?" He crossed his arms. It was cool in the early morning wind.

"Yes. And it's going to get worse for her, and you, because your brother is involved, and that's just a bad thing all around."

"*My* brother?" Alarm screamed through him. "Why are you bringing him into this?"

Pete slowly exhaled. He stared John square in the eye, and John saw pity. He instinctively braced himself for bad news.

"I just got back from a hospital-bed interrogation," Pete said. "The perp had a lot to tell us about the burglary ring that's been hitting the seacoast region. Does that strike a chord with you?"

"No." But John's heart quickened. Could Patrick be involved in something criminal that John didn't know about?

"The perp told us how the burglaries happened. He told us about Patrick's involvement. Are you ready to hear this, John?"

All John could do was give him a short nod.

"Patrick hacked into the alarm company's password files. In exchange for deliveries of mostly worthless paintings, he colluded with a criminal gang."

John reached for the porch railing. His head felt dizzy again. "My God."

Right under his nose. Right under his freaking nose.

"I'm telling you this before Lyndsay even

knows. She's still in an interview room at Wallis Point Police Department, waiting for her boss to reprimand her. Tell me, John, what do *you* know about the burglaries?"

"Nothing." *Patrick is going to jail.* He couldn't think. For once in his life, he didn't know exactly what to do.

The ringing of his phone brought him to life again. He checked his screen.

His mother.

Adrenaline pumped through him. John knew what he had to do—what he'd always had to do. *Protect his family.*

"Before you answer that call," Pete said, checking his watch, "you should know that the search warrant has already been delivered to the Seaside Bar and Grill. If you are involved in the burglaries at all, then you'll be hearing from me again."

With that, while John swallowed his shock, Pete headed to a black SUV that blocked John's truck in his own driveway.

John answered the still-ringing phone. "Mom?"

"The police are here! There are four cruisers in the parking lot with their lights flashing. John, please, you have to come!"

"I'm on my way. When they knock on the door, check their warrant before you let them into the house. If the warrant is for the Seaside, don't let them in. They can only search the restaurant."

"I haven't talked to them yet. They haven't approached the house—"

"Whatever happens, don't let Patrick say anything without his lawyer present. I'll call his office now."

John ended the call and shoved the phone in his pocket even as he ran toward his truck.

The cop's SUV went roaring out of the driveway, and John followed behind. But the cop didn't know Wallis Point like John did, so he took the main road—the long way—while John cut across a side street that was more direct. It was a back-alley shortcut and it would buy John a few minutes. If the cop hit the traffic light on a red instead of a green, it would be even more time to gain.

When John got to his mother's house a few moments later, he saw the ring of police cruisers surrounding the Seaside. The grounds of the two properties were swarming with police officers. John parked beside one of the SUVs, cut the engine, then jumped out.

As he ran up the hill toward his mother's house, he put in a call to Patrick's lawyer.

WITH MOUNTING HORROR, Lyndsay sat outside the Reilly residence in a black SUV with Commander Harris and his personal driver. She sat in relative comfort—dark windows, leather seats, VIP access. As she watched the search unfolding before her, it was dawning on her that she was also watching her hopes for a life with John being ripped to shreds.

He would be devastated. Lyndsay had seen Margie's stricken face in the window. That Lyndsay had been the mole who'd used her relationship with John to get inside their home, to connect the pieces she'd pried from John—and which John had unselfishly, unknowingly given her—and to instigate Patrick into striking the congressman's home, would certainly feel like the worst possible personal betrayal.

The outcome that John had most dreaded for Patrick was happening now, and solely because of her influence. How could he possibly forgive her?

Commander Harris watched the arrest preparations with satisfaction. He turned to smile at her in the back seat. "I talked with both the governor and the congressman an hour ago, and they're pleased with the work the task force has performed, especially you. Despite a last-minute glitch or two, I have to agree with that assessment. Overall, Lyndsay, you've done good undercover police work in Wallis Point."

From a professional perspective, she supposed

he was right. She'd helped solve the case, done everything asked of her and met her goals.

Still, it had devastated her personal relationship. Or maybe her work life simply prevented her from having the satisfying personal relationship she'd desired. It appeared she'd been fooling herself thinking she could keep the two lives separated.

Now that she saw the pain John's family was going through because of her work, a big part of her regretted her role in deceiving them and taking advantage of their relationship with her.

She'd learned a lot of things during this job, that was for sure. About herself, mainly. And she didn't want to ever again do anything that wasn't right for her values. She'd thought she'd been doing what she was supposed to, but she hadn't examined the situation closely enough. All her life, it seemed, she'd been influenced by other people and what they wanted for her. Maybe, in a sense, she'd been undercover from her true desires, acting a part.

Ironic that being undercover, acting contrary to her normal personality, had caused her to see herself more clearly. She wasn't just a lonely widow, a loyal policeman's daughter, an all-around good employee, busying herself with work. Those were parts she played. She was none of those things at heart. She was…herself. Messy, complicated, passionate, alive.

"We have another undercover assignment for you," Commander Harris said. "After you debrief and roll off this assignment, we have a bigger job this time, more important, with higher-profile criminals to take down."

"No," she said softly.

"But you haven't heard what the job is—"

"No," she repeated.

She couldn't go back to deceiving people, especially good people, who were only trying to live their lives honestly.

Commander Harris twisted in the spot, expressing his surprise at her reaction. His pressed uniform squeaked against the leather seats. "Lyndsay, why don't you take time off and think about it?"

She said nothing, because just as the commander spoke, John's truck pulled up beside them. Her heart broke to see him. His handsome face was a marred, bruised-and-bandaged pulp, and she ached for the physical pain he was feeling. But his mental anguish would be far worse, she knew.

She placed her hand on the window, wishing she could reach out to him. The SUV was so close to his truck that if she had access to the electric window, then she could touch his face with her fingertips.

He didn't notice her. He was so focused on the house, Margie and Patrick, so desperate to protect them from the arrest that would rip his remaining family apart.

John had loved her so much, he had tried to change for her. He'd left his comfort zone and confided in her—but it had come back to bite him, hadn't it? She wondered how a person could recover from such a betrayal.

"WHAT ARE YOU telling me?" Margie gazed at John, her shocked face not appearing to see his bruises and cuts. John needn't have gone through the trouble to clean up—it hadn't mattered. "Patrick couldn't have been involved with any burglaries," she protested. "How could he? He's wearing a tracking bracelet."

"The police are saying that he managed it anyway." And the more John thought about it, the more he realized it was probably true.

Hacking into passwords. Yeah, that was classic Patrick. He'd also been staying up late and sneaking into the business office to use John's laptop. More disappointed than anything, John shook his head. "Wait here, Mom. I'm going to talk to the police."

John headed outside and buttonholed the detective in charge of the group. "I understand you have a search warrant," John said to him after he'd introduced himself. "May I see it, please?"

The detective held it forward.

John scanned it quickly. He passed it back. "This is for the restaurant. You don't have a search warrant for the house."

The detective seemed irritated, but he nodded. "We're waiting for that one. Until then, we'll start on the restaurant. Please unlock the door for us."

The restaurant *should* have been open already. In a panic, his mother must have locked up the place once the police cruisers had shown up in the parking lot. "I'll get the key," he said.

John signaled his mother, watching them through the curtains.

When she came outside, wrapping herself in her thin sweater, her face pale and drained, John went up and took her arm and squeezed it in support. "Please walk the officers to the restaurant. Unlock the door and let them in."

She nodded, wiping her eyes with a tissue.

He stood on the doorstep and watched, his heart breaking in half as she stumbled, hugging herself tight, down the slight hill to the restaurant, then opened the doors. The whole circus followed her. Four plainclothes officers with their shields clipped to their belts moved inside.

Pete, Lyndsay's partner, pulled up in his black SUV and parked behind John's truck, blocking one lane in the street but also effectively boxing John in again. Pete joined the crowd going into the restaurant, too.

John rubbed his eyes. He was no lawyer, but the search warrant he'd skimmed appeared to be open-ended. It wouldn't surprise him if they went directly to his business laptop in the office where he'd been working on the books, and confiscated it. They would probably also tear apart and search the closets, the drawers and the kitchen, just for good measure. The information leading them to the laptop surely came from Lyndsay. John thought of the long, candid conversation he'd had with her, admitting his fears, sharing his innermost thoughts, all because he'd loved her and had wanted a relationship with her. He'd gone from being too closed in the past, to too trusting with Lyndsay. And it hurt.

Shaking it off, he pulled his house key from his pocket. All he could control right now was what was in front of him.

His mother hurried up the hill, looking bewildered. "They're tearing into everything!" she cried. "Even your Nonna's recipe cards."

That was their job—to tear into everything. "Call Cynthia," he instructed her, just to give her something concrete to do. Andy's wife went to the same church as his mom—she'd be a comfort of sorts. "Wait outside until she arrives."

His mother nodded, reaching for her phone.

While she was busy, he let himself into the house, then locked the door behind him. The blinds were already closed.

He strode through the house and into Patrick's room. Patrick's bedsheets and pillows were messed up, but Patrick wasn't there. John opened the first drawer he found, and there sat a pile of Justin's watercolors, stacked in a mishmash of frames. Patrick hadn't even attempted to hide his contraband.

It made John feel sick to his stomach to see it all.

Looking at the paintings this way, he could easily believe they were stolen from the various homes up the coast where Justin had originally sold them. If Patrick possessed them, then that meant he'd been involved like the skinny burglar had said.

John sat on the bed. He'd meant to find his brother and shake him, to make him tell him the truth, but he found that he just couldn't do it anymore.

Justin's death had hit them all hard. Everyone in John's family had handled it in their own way—the only way that they knew how. His father had died of a broken heart. His mom clung more tightly to her religion and her faith that all would be well, as long as her family stayed together. She'd summoned John home for good, and like a dutiful son, John had returned, even though he hadn't really wanted to.

And Patrick...he'd turned inward. At first, he'd given himself over to drugs. John was still pretty sure he was off drugs now—he got tested too often to be able to cheat that system—but wherever John's kid brother had gone, he'd never come back. Not really. Patrick was a stranger to him, and John had failed to reach him.

John stood and shuffled through the drawings again. Carefree drawings. So much talent. Such a good heart. Justin would never have wanted them all to suffer the way that they had. He certainly wouldn't have wanted to see Patrick in jail, especially for something so foolish and futile.

"Patrick, where are you?" he called.

There was no answer. John cocked his ear and listened. There appeared to be someone coming down the stairs.

Patrick shuffled into the bedroom, his hair wild, his eyes bloodshot. *He's tired from being up all night*, John realized.

John pointed at Justin's paintings. "Where did these come from?"

"Nowhere," Patrick said sullenly.

"You know the police are here."

Patrick pushed past him. "I didn't do anything." He climbed into bed again, as if that would solve anything for him.

"Are these stolen?" John asked.

"No. They're Justin's."

"Justin sold them."

"He wanted them back."

"Why, Patrick? I don't get it. I really don't." He watched Patrick's face for a reaction, but it was as if Patrick was deadened inside, because all he could do was slowly blink at him.

"Your cohorts already talked to the police," John said softly, "so I called your lawyer. Beyond that, I can't help you anymore. I wish I could. I really wanted to, but I can't."

John just felt broken inside. He couldn't even make himself talk. His voice was catching. He just didn't see a light out of this darkness anymore.

Patrick slumped down, his arms crossed over his stomach. "I don't care if I go to jail."

"I know," John answered. "You're already in jail."

Patrick just looked at him.

John swallowed and stood. His hands were shaking. He'd never felt so powerless or crushed down in his life.

His slight, frail, depressed and sullen younger

brother didn't stand a chance in a prison. John could fight for himself, could give it back to anyone who dished it out to him. But his sensitive younger brother? No way.

At least John could console himself that their dad wasn't alive to see it.

John wished he could tell his brother that he loved him. He could, but Patrick never seemed to hear.

So he said nothing more.

There was a sharp rap on the front door. To John, it felt as if a boom had lowered. *This is it. They're coming to take Patrick away in handcuffs for good.*

John looked out the side window and on to the porch. A man he didn't recognize—another law enforcement official—slapped a piece of paper to the window.

Another search warrant. This one with the correct street address.

John went into Patrick's room and shut the drawer he'd opened. Lyndsay probably already knew the paintings were there anyway. Then he returned and opened the front door. He said nothing, just stepped aside and let them sweep past him.

This was a different group of law enforcement from the officers who were currently tearing apart the restaurant. Pete was with them. Behind

him came Patrick's original lawyer—Natalie
Kimball—the town lawyer who'd helped John
find the expensive, high-power criminal attorney he now used.

"I talked with Stephen," Natalie said, referring to Patrick's lawyer. "He's out of town today,
so I'm sitting with Patrick until Stephen's substitute gets to the station. They'll be interrogating Patrick, possibly charging him. You need to
prepare your mother for that."

John nodded. *His mother.* That was his job
now, to comfort her as best he could. He stepped
outside, and the cool wind hit his messed-up face
and made him hurt all over again.

Andy ran up the hill from the restaurant toward him. "I came as soon as Margie called. I
brought Cynthia, too, so she can sit with Margie."

John nodded. "Thank you," he said gruffly.

Over Andy's shoulder, John saw Cynthia giving his mother a comforting hug. His mother had
tears streaming down her face.

"They're going to take Patrick out in handcuffs," John told Andy. "I'd rather my mother
not see that."

"Don't worry," Andy said. "We'll all handle it together." He paused, then said, "I know
you didn't want to tell me about Patrick's prob-

lems, but it's good that I know. It's good for your mother to have Cynthia with her now."

All John could do was nod.

Still, he went into the house to assess what was happening with Patrick. Inside his brother's room, a group of officers were taking out Justin's watercolors, one by one, photographing them. Wrapping them up. Putting them into evidence kits. Plastic bags and boxes.

Sickened anew, he moved into the kitchen, where Patrick was being handcuffed and read his rights. It tore a hole through John's heart. Like nothing that had happened before, this was visual, photographic evidence of the truth that John had failed.

One job. He'd had one job: keep his brother safe. Keep his brother out of trouble. John had tried so hard, yet the worst that he could imagine for Patrick had happened anyway. It was like cold water being thrown on his face. He'd sacrificed himself—his life, what he wanted—and it hadn't helped anyone.

Natalie, the lawyer, approached him. "John, they're taking Patrick to Concord now. I'll go to sit with him in the interrogation room, at least until Stephen's associate arrives."

"Thank you, Natalie," he said quietly.

"I met Officer Fairfax purely by chance this

morning, and I have a feeling it might turn out to be positive for Patrick's case."

"Excuse me?" he asked.

"Officer Fairfax—Lyndsay. She's a police officer on the case. I passed her outside just now."

"She's here?"

"Inside the black SUV with the tinted windows. She's in the back seat."

He nodded tersely. Was he supposed to feel gratitude toward Lyndsay that she'd covered for him, as her partner had said? He didn't even know if theirs had been a real relationship anymore, or just an undercover ruse.

"Are you all right?" Natalie asked him. "That's a nasty bruise on your cheek. It's bleeding through the bandage. Maybe you should go to the hospital and—"

"I'm fine," he said abruptly. He stood aside as two cops perp-walked his brother outside. The crowd would be there still. For a moment, he felt dizzy.

Patrick said nothing as they passed. To John, it was just zombie-ville. As if Patrick wanted to die, too, along with Justin and Dad. John stepped off the porch and stood by himself. An officer held Patrick's head while they helped him into the back of an unmarked police vehicle. Natalie hurried to her Volvo, probably to follow them.

He knew he should go, too. But something and everything had changed inside him.

They're responsible for themselves.

No one listened to him, or seemed to care what he thought. Maybe the only person he was responsible for was himself.

His life, and he needed to find something to do with it that made him happy and fulfilled. Because he didn't want to be here, watching something like this that he had no control over.

He headed out. Down the hill toward his boxed-in truck. The cruiser with his brother inside and Natalie's Volvo had both started up, and Cynthia was taking care of his mother.

John climbed into his truck, intending to claw his way out of here and just go home. Toby needed his fluids. That was what it came down to. The only thing that John had the ability to help was a sixteen-year-old tabby cat who couldn't even talk back to him.

Come to think of it, that was exactly what he wanted right now.

For nobody to talk back to him.

But still, he couldn't look away as the police car drove off with his younger brother looking at him through the rear window.

Then he heard the cry. His mother rushed down the hill, wailing. Cynthia was doing her best to comfort her, and Andy stood with a hurt frown on his face, but no one could contain his mother's pain. John had never seen her like this. Never.

"He's my baby," she called to the retreating police car.

He felt filled with horror. It didn't matter that silent strangers gaped. He couldn't move. It was unlike him. He wasn't taking charge. Instead, he felt as if he was outside it all. As if it was a play, and instead of participating, for the first time, he was just observing.

He was suddenly thinking very clearly. Maybe it was the realization that this wasn't his place. That cleared up the fog he was in, more than anything.

"I'm not responsible for him," he said aloud.

He'd sacrificed everything. His own life. His relationships. His career. He'd tried, as hard as he could, as best as he knew how, and it hadn't been what Patrick needed. It was past time the professionals took over, because John obviously couldn't give what Patrick needed.

Outside, it was a cool and sunny morning; a hint of late spring in the air. The sun hurt his eyes, it was so bright.

He turned his head suddenly, realizing there were people in the black SUV parked beside him. It was an official-looking vehicle with tinted windows, a professional driver, a member of the police brass of some sort, and...

Lyndsay. In the back seat, her window facing his, but slightly behind him. He turned his head to meet her gaze. She was a pale, still face through the shadowy glass.

She was crying. The men in the front didn't seem to see. But John could see. Tears spilled down her cheeks, one after another. He thought she looked like she was sorry for what had happened. He thought he saw pain and regret in her eyes.

She placed her palm to the glass as if to touch him. What she was communicating was private to John alone.

And that was the first he realized that things maybe hadn't turned out the way she'd wanted, either. That he wasn't the only one who hadn't gotten what he'd thought he'd signed on for.

THE HOLE IN Lyndsay's heart grew larger as she watched John drive away from her. She hoped that he'd received her silent apology to him, but she couldn't be sure. Commander Harris had made it crystal clear that she wasn't allowed to speak with him or his family until after Patrick's case was finished being processed, and no one knew exactly how long that would take.

She could only hope that someday John's pain would recede and that she could make her redemption.

CHAPTER EIGHTEEN

Two months later

PATRICK'S SENTENCING HEARING took place on a hot July morning. John took a few hours off from his classes to head to the courthouse to sit in on the proceedings. It was easier this time. John was no longer his brother's keeper. He didn't feel responsible for anybody but himself, with the exception of a sixteen-year-old cat who was still hanging in with John and taking his fluids daily.

John made his way through the metal detectors at the entrance to the courthouse and found directions to the hearing room upstairs. But he was surprised when the elevator door opened, and out walked not only his mother, but also Cynthia Hannaman and Natalie Kimball. Natalie had taken over his brother's case, on his mother's preference. She thought the local attorney provided better care than the high-powered specialist. John hadn't intervened. He also hadn't expected them to be leaving the courthouse so early.

"John!" His mother bracketed his cheeks and gave him a kiss. She smiled from ear to ear, with a look of relief on her tired face.

"Hi, Mom. What happened?"

"We met with the judge earlier than planned." Natalie shifted both her briefcase and a shopping bag to her left hand, then shook John's hand. "The principals in the case were all present, and this judge is a stickler for keeping things moving, so he processed us right away."

A second elevator door opened and more people streamed out. Natalie paused to take his mom's elbow and lead her and Cynthia away from the traffic in front of the elevator banks. "Why don't we all find a seating area in the lower courthouse where we can talk?"

"Yes," he replied. Whatever had happened to Patrick, he gave them his support. Cynthia now worked in the Seaside with his mom, having taken John's old place behind the counter and in the kitchen. Andy had purchased John's share of the business, and that was a relief to John. He could pursue his own interests now and do what he thought was best for himself.

They found a sunny spot in a far corner of the lobby. The women sat on a bench before a glass table, but John preferred to remain standing.

"Where is Patrick now?" he asked.

Natalie curled a lock of short blond hair behind her ear. "He's being transported to an in-patient facility to help with his emotional issues. Later, he'll be transferred for a year's sentence to be served at a halfway house."

John was surprised and pleased that the sentence didn't involve prison. "Did he cooperate with the prosecutors?"

"Yes," Natalie replied. "He cooperated fully with the authorities."

"That's good news."

She nodded. "I have to give credit to Officer Fairfax. She sent a letter to the judge on Patrick's behalf. I believe her support helped in obtaining these favorable results."

John hadn't heard anyone speak Lyndsay's name to him since the morning Patrick had been arrested. He took a long breath. He still wasn't sure what was real with her and what wasn't. He still hadn't *processed* everything, as they said in the psychology elective course he was taking this semester.

"I hear you've embarked on some new endeavors," Natalie remarked to him.

"I have." He had enrolled in a college degree program in criminal justice using his military benefit. He'd also found part-time work counseling transitioning military veterans, but in the future, he planned to enter law enforcement. For the first time in a long time, he felt like he was doing meaningful work that suited him and made him happy.

But that wasn't what he wanted to talk about now. "When are the trials scheduled for the others in the burglary ring?"

"I don't expect any trials—I expect that the defendants will plead out," she replied. "As far as I know, the respective parties are working out agreements now."

His mom touched his arm. "Did you know that the congressman gave us two of Justin's paintings?"

No, he hadn't. A feeling of sadness passed through him, but his mother seemed happy, so he smiled for her.

"Lyndsay arranged that," Cynthia piped in. "She phoned the congressman and asked him if he would give the paintings to Margie."

"And you're okay with that?" he asked his mother.

"Yes. Patrick explained to me why he did what he did. I understand and I'm coming to grips with it better." His mom paused and looked at Natalie. "I've asked to speak with Lyndsay personally. I'm still working through all of this, and I think it will do me good to see her."

"She…agreed to see you?"

"Yes. We've been communicating through

Natalie. Lyndsay isn't allowed to contact us directly until the case is finished."

"Which reminds me…" Natalie glanced at him. "John, may I speak privately with you before I leave?"

He stiffened. Had Lyndsay asked her to communicate with him, too? Many times he'd considered that he had a contact number for Lyndsay in his phone. In his more cynical moments, he'd wondered if it was even really her number, or as fake as the rest of their relationship.

"John, why don't you stay here with Natalie?" Cynthia suggested, rising. "Margie and I will head out now. We need to get back to the Seaside."

He kissed his mother goodbye and gave Cynthia a hug of thanks.

He and the attorney were alone in the quiet, sunny alcove. This time John sat on the bench with her. A bank of windows showed a small courtyard with green leaves and bright annual flowers.

Natalie cleared her throat and rooted in her briefcase. "Officer Fairfax asked me to give you this." She took out a letter-size envelope.

Pale yellow stationery, the color of Lyndsay's hair. His name written on the sealed envelope in blue fountain pen.

He accepted the envelope, not knowing what

to expect. He hadn't seen Lyndsay's handwriting before, but it was bold and appealing, like her.

"She asked me to give you something else." Natalie put the small shopping bag down on the glass table. "It's, ah, rather unorthodox. I hesitated to bring it along, but…"

"What is this?" he asked, eying the bag.

"Baked goods." Natalie looked flummoxed.

He snorted with laughter. It just seemed funny, like something Lyndsay would do. "Chocolate-chip cookies, by any chance?"

Natalie seemed relieved. "You expected it."

"No, actually, it's the last thing I expected." He shook his head in wonder. Did this mean she missed him, too? He opened the bag and breathed deeply.

Yes, these were Lyndsay's chocolate-chip cookies, presented on a fancy plate, wrapped in cellophane and tied with ribbon as an interior decorator might do. The gift had to be designed to make him think of that night in his kitchen when they'd first kissed.

He remembered it clearly. She'd walked over to his house, in the dark, and she'd been wearing pink lip gloss and her hair down. They hadn't talked about anything regarding the investigation that night. She hadn't *had* to kiss him in order to gain any relevant information. At that point, she wouldn't have even suspected that Patrick was involved in the burglary ring.

In fact, kissing John then would have been more of a complication to her investigation than a benefit.

Maybe her feelings for him *had* been real. Maybe she'd tried to keep their relationship separate from her work, but ultimately couldn't.

He turned the envelope over in his hands.

"Well, I'll leave you now." Natalie stood with her briefcase.

"Thank you," he said quietly to the kind attorney, standing, too, as she took her leave.

He sat again, holding the envelope for a long time, just rubbing the edges with his thumb and letting himself remember other things about Lyndsay.

The way she'd cried the last time he'd seen her when she'd been faced with the fruits of her investigation. The way she'd pressed her hand against the window.

All those times they'd made love. He honestly doubted she'd faked that.

He felt the pain in his heart. He most wanted to know if she'd ever planned to tell him.

And if she really loved him.

And…

He opened the envelope. Two sheets of folded stationery paper, written in neat rows of cur-

sive script. Not a blot on the page, not a cross
out or a scribble. She'd written drafts, and she'd
practiced to make it just so, perfectionist that
she was. He smiled. He also liked that it wasn't
written in the formal block letters he now knew
that police officers were trained to use in their
reports. So many reports they generated. Lyndsay had gone out of her way to make this letter
to him personal.

Dear John,
I've written and rewritten this letter a dozen
times, wanting to let you know why I did
what I did. I'm not proud of the way I de-
ceived you. My only explanation is that I
behaved in a way that I thought a good undercover officer should. The first time we
spoke in the parking lot and you accused
me of being a cop, I was scared of losing
my cover. But it didn't end up the way I expected, because the only way to continue
with my cover was to tell you the truth
about my background. Everything I told
you about my parents, my childhood, my
husband, my (one year) at interior design
school—it was all true. More important to
me, the hopes and fears I disclosed to you
were true. And when I told you I love you,
that was the truest thing of all.

Nothing about the undercover assignment worked out the way I expected. When I got to know you, and started having feelings for you, I thought that I could keep our relationship separate from the investigation. I was assigned to investigate the paintings, but I had no idea that it would lead back to your family, to Patrick. I always had a foolish plan that I could finish the assignment, then come back to you afterward and beg your forgiveness. I learned it isn't that simple. I never examined closely enough what I was doing, or why. I discovered that I can't live with myself being dishonest, especially with good people like you. I only have respect and love for you.

What happened later, the day that I made a mistake with setting the alarm, and subsequently figuring out that Patrick was possibly involved in the burglary ring, made me realize that I can't keep my work and personal lives separate. They're entwined. They're always entwined. I wanted so desperately to keep our relationship, but I was trapped at that point. If I let my job down, then many other people besides you and I would have been hurt. I suppose in my mind I sacrificed us for them. Those next twenty-four hours were so painful personally, even though something positive happened for the community with the burglary ring being caught.

It's devastating to me that you and Margie were swept up in this. I promised you that day that I would do what I could for Patrick, and I honored that promise. I sincerely hope he's able to get the help he needs. I wish only the best for him and for you and your family.

I'm sorry.

If you ever want to call and talk, you have my (real) phone number.

Sincerely,

Lyndsay

John read and reread the letter. Then he got out his phone and sent her a text message.

LYNDSAY ARRIVED EARLY at their meeting place. She chose to sit at a corner table with views to the entrance and parking lot as well as to the side door. It was noon, and her overnight detective shift had ended hours earlier. She'd been able to take her time bathing, putting on a short summer dress, doing her hair and makeup…

She was nervous to see him. Other than their two-line text messages arranging the meeting today, she had no idea what was running through

John's mind. Did he believe her letter? Did he forgive her? Did he still care?

And what about the significance of the location he'd chosen, a beautiful ski resort restaurant overlooking a clear blue lake? They weren't far from the village she'd grown up in. They were about an hour and a half from Wallis Point.

Wallis Point. She'd only been back once, to stop at Natalie Kimball's office. She hadn't visited the Seaside, or Andy, or Kitty MacLaine in her newly decorated beach cottage. Lyndsay was welcome any time in their home, the congressman had assured her. But visiting the cul-de-sac was too uncomfortable to think about.

A new SUV pulled into the lot, and John got out. She straightened, craning her neck to study him. He wore khakis and a button-down shirt that matched his eyes. His hair was shorter. The cuts and bruises that had marred his face the last time she'd seen him were healed now.

She sighed in relief, smiled and waved to him as he walked into the restaurant, but she needn't have bothered; he zoned in on her with his typical laser focus. As he approached her table she leaned forward, hoping he would kiss her in greeting, and he did.

He smelled like that soap she'd liked. His touch lit a spark in her, and she was lost, gazing into his eyes again.

He sat not opposite her, but at the corner seat beside her. *The co-power spot*, she thought. Now they both had the view of the street. His hand bumped hers, and suddenly it was old times and they were holding hands like they used to.

"Lyndsay," he breathed.

"You look good, John."

"You always looked good." He laced his fingers in hers, and her heart seemed to swell in her chest. There were so many things they needed to talk about, but at the moment she just wanted to *be* in his presence.

The waitress arrived and handed them menus, launching into her introductory greeting. A busboy set about filling water glasses.

She and John smiled at each other.

"We'll take a few minutes to decide," John told the waitress.

After they'd finished and left, Lyndsay said to John, "I've missed you."

"I missed you, too." His clear gray-blue eyes drank her in. "I wasn't myself for a long time. But I forgive you, Lyndsay."

She sighed. She hadn't realized she'd been holding her breath, hoping for these words from him. She knew that trust, once shattered, wasn't easily regained. She'd been in detective training lately, partnered with Pete as an observer. Just being in the presence of him and his wife had shown her a path that, with enough love, she'd hoped she and John might follow, as well.

"Are you okay?" he murmured, peering at her. "You're crying."

"They're happy tears." They were forehead to forehead now. "You read my letter and forgave me. What's not to be happy about?"

"You're worth it. And Lyndsay," he said softly, "I hope you can forgive me, too."

"You! Why?"

"I never stopped to hear your point of view. I promise I'll never do that again."

This was why she loved this man. He was honorable, and he paid attention.

"I was wondering." His lips quirked.

"What?"

"I want to know about your real life. Where you live and places you like to go. I was wondering if you could show me some of that some-day soon." He glanced around the restaurant. "I actually chose this place because I know it's near where you grew up. It's nice up here in the mountains."

"Do you think I can ever go back to Wallis Point?" she asked wistfully.

"Of course. You're a legend there. A real bad-ass with a gun." He grinned at her.

She laughed genuinely. Coming from a Marine veteran, that was pretty funny.

Then she sobered. "Seriously, John. Integrating all of this is what I'm working toward. Redemption. A real personal life and an honest professional life. And…" She lowered her voice, her cheeks feeling warm. "I'd like children."

"Would you?" He seemed surprised.

"Yes," she said softly, and she took a deep breath. "When I first met Natalie Kimball at the police station, she had her baby with her, Jamie. He gave me this big, gummy smile, and it just took the breath out of me. I lost my heart to him, and it made me realize…" She could feel herself blushing. He probably knew where this was going, and it warmed her to think so, but he let her speak her feelings without interruption. "Well, that's the kind of life I would like to have, too. I thought of having a little one, and that maybe someday it could be you and I together…" She glanced at him, and his head was still tilted, listening. "Well, I wanted to tell you now, and hope that you do, too—"

"Yes," he said.

"Yes?"

"Yes." He nodded firmly.

She didn't see how she could be happier.

EPILOGUE

Five months later
Christmas Day

"COME HERE, MRS. REILLY."

Lyndsay glanced around, looking for her mother-in-law, but then realized that John was speaking to her. *Her husband.* She could only laugh with happiness.

"You know I'm keeping my maiden name," she teased.

"Sure. But you're not Mrs. Fairfax, you're Mrs. Reilly. See, look at the sign." A smile playing on his lips, John pointed toward the limo stand, and it was all she could do not to sigh and gaze at him all day in starstruck, newlywed love.

But she reluctantly looked over to the island transportation stand he'd pointed toward, just outside the small sandy airport. Sure enough, their prearranged driver held up a handwritten sign:

Mr. and Mrs. Reilly.

"Well, I guess that settles it," she said. "This

week, I must be Mrs. Reilly." They headed to the car, John pulling their suitcases, but before they made it off the curb, she hooked a finger in the back pocket of his cargo shorts, and reeled him in for a kiss.

They'd barely been able to keep their hands off one another. The evening before, they'd had a Christmas Eve wedding ceremony in Wallis Point at the Grand Beachfront Hotel. She'd found that going back to Wallis Point hadn't been as difficult as she'd feared, not with John's ironclad support. Plus, the friends she'd made—Andy and his crew, the MacLaines, John's mom and Natalie— had made her transition to moving there easier. John's cove house had transformed into a snug, comfortable home for the two of them.

John caught her hand, and they headed toward their transportation for their Caribbean beach honeymoon. John was excited about his dream vacation finally coming to fruition.

But there was a bit of news she'd been waiting to tell him, too. She'd found out for certain only this morning. In all the rush over their wedding plans, she'd missed some telltale signs. She'd confirmed it with a quick test before their early morning flight out of Boston.

"John?" she said.

"Hmm?"

"I have to confess—I've been keeping a secret from you."

He turned and quirked an eye at her. "You'd better tell me about it *right now*," he said in his lighthearted tone.

"All right." She shrugged nonchalantly. "If all goes well, we'll be welcoming a little one by late summer."

"Well, yeah." He smirked at her. "We're on our honeymoon." *We've talked about this*, he implied. Their honeymoon was when they'd decided to start trying to have a baby.

"Um. I think we may have accidentally jumped the gun."

"You mean?" His eyebrows rose in question.

"Yes. A little boy or girl." She paused. "There's always the possibility we might have twins, I suppose." She smiled at him. "Is that all right with you?"

He didn't hesitate. "Yes."

"Yes?"

"Yes." An emphatic nod.

This was another reason she loved John Reilly. They made an excellent team.

* * * * *

Get 2 Free Books,
__Plus__ 2 Free Gifts—
just for trying the Reader Service!

Get 2 Free Books,
Plus 2 Free Gifts—

just for trying the
Reader Service!

Get 2 Free Books,
Plus 2 Free Gifts—
just for trying the
Reader Service!

READERSERVICE.COM

Manage your account online!

- Review your order history
- Manage your payments
- Update your address

**We've designed the
Reader Service website
just for you.**

Enjoy all the features!

- Discover new series available to you,
  and read excerpts from any series.
- Respond to mailings and special
  monthly offers.
- Browse the Bonus Bucks catalog and
  online-only exculsives.
- Share your feedback.

Visit us at:
ReaderService.com

RS16R